Columbus
Slaughters Braves

Columbus
Slaughters Braves

Mark Friedman

HOUGHTON MIFFLIN COMPANY

BOSTON • NEW YORK

2001

For information about permission to reproduce selections
from this book, write to Permissions, Houghton Mifflin Company,
215 Park Avenue South, New York, New York 10003.

Visit our Web site: www.houghtonmifflinbooks.com

Library of Congress Cataloging-in-Publication Data
Friedman, Mark.
Columbus slaughters Braves / Mark Friedman.
p.   cm.
ISBN 0-618-02520-0
1. Baseball players — Fiction. I. Title.
PS3556.R5276 C65 2001
813'.6 — dc21   00-033432

Printed in the United States of America

QUM 10 9 8 7 6 5 4 3 2 1

Part One

1

ow did it start? they always asked. *When did you know?* And I always told them that it started when we were very young.

I was seven and my brother was four. We grew up in Southern California, my brother and me. It was late August, and I remember how his blond hair was almost white, and as summer ended, our little arms and legs, soft like rising dough, were showing some wear and tear — scratches, scabs, and mosquito bites. On that day I was shirtless, wearing a dark green bathing suit instead of shorts. My brother wore navy Bermudas and a white T-shirt with a brown stain on the collar that was probably Fudgsicle. I carried him on my shoulders so the two of us could see the same world.

We lived two blocks from South Pasadena High School, massive and daunting at our young age, with its endless squares of one-story buildings and green courtyards. The playing fields were in the back, and empty when we got there. I dragged a baseball bat along the ground as I moved toward the plate; my brother held the glove we shared out in front of him with both hands, like the steering wheel of a bumper car, as he careened beyond the pitcher's mound, which rose, uneven, like a muffin top.

He looked back at me. I stood in the batter's box and waved

him farther. He moved deeper into the no man's land of tamped grass between the mound and second, still looking at me, wondering if he had gone far enough.

"Keep going," I said, full of confidence. He took a few more reluctant steps, as if the outfield were the deeps of the ocean and he was afraid of getting sucked in. The breeze picked up, raking my face with bracing desert heat. A real hitter would have noticed that the wind was blowing in. But I was just a kid.

My brother finally stopped behind second base, in the shallow of center field. I held the bat in my left hand and tossed the baseball to myself with my right. The contact I made was crisp, but the swing was clumsy, and the ball went nowhere. I tried again, starting my swing at virtually the same instant that I tossed the ball, but the head start made no difference. The ball kicked down, thumping the ground and rolling slightly forward, not even out of my reach.

It is difficult to foul off pitches to yourself, but I managed to do it. Repeatedly. It was close to 100 degrees that day, and the field seemed empty and enormous with only the two of us. All the elements that were missing from a real game — crowds, players, and their overlapping chatter — were suddenly apparent. I fouled off another. Sweat beaded on my forehead. I was starting to get angry, which never helped my game. I didn't understand how to convert frustration into usable energy. All I knew was that I should swing harder and keep trying to put the ball in play.

At some point I looked up. My brother wasn't in center field anymore. For some reason, he'd begun to shuffle toward left.

"What are you doing?" I asked.

He didn't answer. He just squinted at me, the sun blinding him. He pounded his tiny fist into his glove — he must have seen someone do this and decided to mimic the gesture. And he continued to shuffle, still facing me but now angling back toward the infield.

"Stop moving around!"

He stopped at third base and looked at me again. Taking a

few tentative steps in front of where the bag would have been, he popped the glove with his fist one more time — a sound at once more ordinary and convincing than any I'd been able to produce between the ball and the bat. Then he sat down.

"Get up!" I yelled.

"It's hot. I'm tired," he said.

"I'm gonna hit it far," I said.

He didn't answer. He looked happy.

"You're going to have to run," I said.

He smiled, his legs straight in front of him, and clicked the tips of his sneakers together. Dried mud from some other day popped loose, tumbling out like tiny bricks. I watched as he began picking blades of grass and lining them up in a row on his thigh.

In retrospect, his grin is delightful and beatific. At the time, it was the vicious, toothy taunt of a punk toddler entirely disrespectful of his older brother's athletic prowess. So I ignored him, the little fucker. I was going to hit it *hard*. The bat would crack and the world would snap to attention, in a brief reverent moment, and then complete its bow before me. I would scorch the blood-red seams of the ball and send a slingshot of fire high in the air, where it would kiss the sun. Or something like that.

I tossed the ball in the air, perfectly. It was on a string that slowed it down yet somehow made it big — the ball ballooned and hovered, beckoning for me to smack it. I closed my eyes, grabbed the bat with both hands, felt my weight shift forward, and swung.

I made obscenely full contact, absolutely authoritative. The sound was deep, different, beautiful. It was not a dribbler, but it wasn't a long drive, either. It was my first screamer, a low-lining rocket, a foot off the ground. And it was ticketed directly for my brother's head.

Things do not often happen quickly in baseball; the game has an endearing lassitude that can make you feel like you own it. But speed is speed in any game, and baseball has its fractional moments, more powerful because they surprise you —

that savory shock and then the swift resolution. My brother was ready, though. In one fluid and relaxed gesture, he raised his glove in front of his face and caught the ball.

I dropped the bat and looked at him. His head was still hidden behind the glove, which remained frozen and clamped around the baseball. Then he peeked around it and smiled, rolled the ball back to me, and the game went on.

Only years later did I realize why my brother had moved from the outfield and shuffled toward third and raised his glove so fearlessly. He was only four years old, but he had watched me swing, seen the way my tosses leaned, the nature of the contact I was trying to make. And he knew that after all my straining and my dramatic posture of power, down the left-field line was exactly where I would end up hitting the ball.

That was the day my brother moved to third base, and he never left.

I told that story well. No one ever doubted the simple truth it delivered, because it wasn't outlandish enough to be fabricated. It was uneven and natural; it triggered a smile and celebrated foible. It painted him as human in a way that only an intimate could do. It was a story people liked to hear.

At first I told it haltingly, but after my brother made the majors and his career began to soar, I grew more familiar with living in his reflected glow. Without even noticing what I was doing, I tightened the story and made it better. I hit the ball harder and harder, shaving split seconds off the amount of time I gave him to react. I added that brief beat of aging-sportswriter wisdom — the bit of "endearing lassitude" pablum — which made me seem smart about the poetry of the game. And I added it immediately after mentioning that I'd hit the ball right at his head but *before* revealing that he'd caught it — taking a step back from the play-by-play narrative, simultaneously philosophizing and adding suspense.

I also must confess that the last part — about him keeping the glove in front of his face and then peering around it — was a fabrication. I don't remember if that really happened, though it seems like something that might have, like something CJ would have done. Who the hell can remember all the details of a summer day twenty years ago?

Also, I usually didn't refer to him as "the little fucker" when I told it.

I told the story to a national magazine that didn't cover sports. They ran a short profile of my brother, together with a photo where he stood, shirtless, to flaunt his physique. ("Ever since that August afternoon when he was four . . ." the snippet began.) I told it to the female network sports reporter who, fifteen years earlier, had wanted to be the first female player in the majors and later sued her minor-league hitting instructor for sexual harassment. I told it to my brother's unofficial biographer, a man not much older than me, a law school graduate who had decided to become a ghostwriter and wore the wobbly smile of a boy not sure he'd get away with it.

And of course I told it to my dentist, strangers at the car wash and the dry cleaner, students in my first-period honors physics class, and the woman who became my wife.

And now I'm telling it once more, a final time. But I'm doing that to reclaim it, to view it in a different light, and to use it to answer different questions, ones that no one has ever asked. Because only after everything happened did I realize that it wasn't a story about him. It was a story about me.

CJ Columbus — it was a great ballplayer name. The initials made it work. They suggested boyish familiarity, a kid brother lent to the world. And the last name wasn't bad, either — a red-and-blue rainbow over his shoulder blades on the back of his Chicago Cubs jersey, with its thin whisper of cobalt pinstripes. It was almost embarrassingly wholesome, a headline writer's dream. (The worst was behind him: his rookie year. After he throttled Atlanta with a late-inning grand slam, the first of his career, the *Chicago Sun-Times* declared "Columbus Slaughters Braves.")

I believed in the power of names. I believed that CJ would not have been half the player he was had his name been Oswald or Morris. I don't wish to offend people who have those names, but those men are not destined for lives as modern-day ballplayers. They are destined for difficult though probably interesting lives, I think, perhaps involving hostage dramas or studio apartments overrun by cats.

On more than one occasion, I asked my parents where they'd come up with our names. But those discussions, usually part of the meandering family nostalgia that accompanied coffee and dessert after bloated holiday meals, failed to yield satisfying answers. "Your mother liked Charles, your mother liked Joseph," my father would say.

"But did *you* like them?" I would ask.

And he would pause, knowing who was listening from the kitchen. "I liked your mother," he would reply.

I liked my name — I didn't mind the sound of Joe — but I knew that it wasn't remarkable. It didn't come with expectations. But CJ Columbus; oh, the rhythm and whir of it. It brimmed with promise. Say it to yourself if you don't believe me. Say it, as I did, again and again.

You could always count on hearing it at the ballpark. Public address announcers called his name each time he stepped to the plate. Then came the applause, dwindling to a murmur as he dug in, and the jittery silence of the first pitch: would he slap a single, or could he touch them all? Would he tie the game, or win it with just one swing?

I knew who he was when he was four, but my parents must have known much earlier — when he was born, when they looked down at him on those first days home from the hospital and tried out his name, checking to make certain it would fit. And the fit was perfect. He looked up at them from his crib like a CJ, bright blue eyes full of knowing. And so my parents began waiting patiently for the day when he would live up to the obligations of his fan-friendly nickname and show us all what he was capable of.

CJ grew to be six-foot-one, and he weighed one hundred and ninety-five pounds. His blond hair was always cut short. He squinted a little when he smiled, but the grin was familiar, genuine, absolutely perfect. He had what baseball scouts call "the good face" — from an early age, determination and maturity chiseled it a certain way. It was the face of a ballplayer. He was the most popular baseball player in the country at age twenty-three, with that good face, with his blond hair and blue eyes. My hair is black, and my eyes are brown. We looked nothing alike.

It started out as something he did, a game he played, the same way everyone else in the neighborhood played it. There was tee-ball and then Little League, with games three days a week and practices on the days in between. If you liked to play, it was heaven, and if you were good, it was easy to get much better. Owing to the agreeable Southern California climate, the league ran year round. In the late 1970s and early 1980s all the kids in the neighborhood played; baseball was still thriving, not yet immolating itself through labor dispute and arrogance, not yet being eclipsed by suburban soccer leagues or by Michael Jordan and the glamorous surge of professional basketball. All our friends played baseball, and all the parents were friends. It was a closed, inward-looking world. It surrounded us, and we wanted nothing else.

When we started playing, a lot of kids were good; even I was good. That's not saying much. I honestly believe that to be good at any sport when you're a child, you don't have to be talented, you don't even have to be an athlete; you just have to be big. (This is true even in baseball, which is the hardest game of all.) There was one kid, Jeffrey Carder, who was well over four feet when he was ten. He had one eyebrow and no ability whatsoever. But Jeffrey was big, and when he hit the ball, he dented it; his swings were wild and fierce. We knew Jeffrey Carder was picturing the ball as someone's head, and we wondered how long that person had to live. We respected his size as talent, and he scared the shit out of us.

I played first base, largely because of my boyish infatuation with Steve Garvey, the indestructible Dodgers infielder with movie-star looks and Popeye forearms. Growing up, my brother and I were rabid Dodgers fans; South Pasadena was a ten-minute drive from the team's spectacularly beautiful stadium in Chavez Ravine. The stadium had apparently been built by muscling out large numbers of Latino families who lived in the area, though I didn't know that at the time. All I knew was that my father shared three season tickets with two co-workers, we went to many games, and we always stayed until the end and scoffed at those who couldn't tough it out, those who scurried to their cars at the first lick of evening chill or hint of an insurmountable (never!) visitor lead.

My brother and I would fall asleep as the night wore on; in our matching blue hooded sweatshirts, curled against each other, we were like two kittens. Sometimes one of the stadium cameramen would find us, and our pictures would go up on the big screen above left field. The crowd would try to wake us, but we didn't know or care. We only knew the comfort of sleep and of the organist's lullaby; we were in love with it all. This was back when my brother was in the middle years of elementary school and I was finishing up. We were still friends, we did things together, we did things with our parents — shopping at May Company on a Thursday evening, eating burgers and brownie sundaes at Big Boy on a Saturday night — things we wouldn't be caught dead doing with them or with each other in a few years.

Since CJ and I were three years apart, our size was always classified differently, and we never played on the same team. I remember coming home from school one May afternoon — CJ was nine, so I must have been twelve. (As was often the case, I figured out the place in my own life only in relation to the important event happening in his.) I turned the corner and approached our house. CJ was sitting on the steps to our front porch, not the place he usually hung out. Both of us preferred the claustrophobic, air-conditioned chill of the living room. Our street was flat and sleepy, and nothing surprising happened on it.

CJ was still in his uniform from practice, and a large grass stain blotted the left shin of his white pants. There was a little mud mixed in, plus some dried blood where he had dived or slid or just plain fell. His dark green Screaming Eagle jersey was untucked over his right hip.

Back then we were both South Pasadena Screaming Eagles. I never understood why we couldn't just be the Eagles. Apparently it wasn't enough to be named after an Endangered Species; it had to be an Endangered Species that was pissed off about it. My friend Ben Clark's mother had drawn the team logos the previous year; she had some artistic ability but was recently divorced and tended to lose her focus. None of the other parents wanted to indicate that she wasn't good at anything, so they waited and waited for her drawing. Only later did we learn that on all those dewy early mornings we'd seen her around town, sitting on benches with her sketchpad before the heat made everything senseless, she was just staring out at nothing and waiting for life to turn for her.

But she finally did draw the Screaming Eagle, the bird depicted at varying levels of agitation. To me, the assorted eagles looked startled, as if they'd been caught in the middle of some unseemly bird behavior, but the several renditions adorned shirts, caps, and the backs of our green satin jackets. My brother's Screaming Eagle baseball cap was between his feet, and he idly nudged it back and forth.

"Hey," I said.

"Hey."

I noticed that his lips were blue, his tongue as well: Popsicle residue. "Why are you out here?" I asked.

He didn't look at me. He seemed tired, slouched back against the steps. "Mom and Dad are inside talking."

"Mom and Dad?" It was strange for them both to be home so early.

CJ nodded. "They're talking to Mr. Covington."

Mr. Covington was CJ's coach. He owned two Chevrolet dealerships, in Tustin and Monrovia; he was a pleasant man, chubby and grinning. His family consisted of a wife and five daughters, and all those boys on all those teams were the sons he never had. He marveled over every single thing they did, good or bad, with the same expression of startled delight.

"Covington? What did you do?"

"Nothing. What time is it?"

I checked my watch. It was a gold Timex, red liquid electronic digital, a suspiciously heavy source of pride on my scrawny wrist. "Four-fifty," I said.

"Marvosa doubled," CJ said.

"No shit." Nicky Marvosa was a benchwarmer on my brother's team. He didn't want to play, but his parents forced him to. His father came to every game and watched his son's sporadic at-bats while standing apart from the other parents and chain-smoking, grinding the butts into the dirt at his feet. Father and son drove home together in a burgundy van with tinted windows. Nicky was small and spooky; he had a black bowl haircut, and his nose started to bleed when he came up to bat. We were scared of him, too. We understood no one.

"Do you want me to find out what's going on?" I asked. I didn't really care if CJ wanted to know; *I* wanted to know.

CJ burped. "I'm thirsty."

"So go in."

"I can't."

"Are you in trouble?" But I knew he wasn't.

He shrugged.

"What did you do in the game?"

"That's what they're talking about," he said.

He wasn't making sense, and my response sensitively reflected that. "You're being stupid," I said.

"Shut up," he shot back, though his heart wasn't really in it. He burped again.

"You're lazy and stupid. Stop burping." This was the kind of conversation that kids could build a world around, but, sadly, it was the kind of comeback I would still be making to him years later. I always found it difficult to argue with my brother. Even as we grew up and my vocabulary sprawled across a much wider range of evocative adjectives and profanity, I was rarely able to articulate anything other than sputtering rage in the face of his Zen-like impenetrability.

I walked up the steps and past him, my shin hitting his

shoulder, granting me a flicker of perverse pleasure, though I did nothing more than slightly, momentarily buckle him. Between certain brothers, this would have been enough to start a fight, but not between CJ and me. We never threw punches at each other, because our parents would not have tolerated any type of physical confrontation. When we were younger than I can remember, they must have stopped something before it could start. It was a good solution, approached with the intellectual rigor that was typical of the upper-middle-class, book-smart way they had raised us. We would grow up and have to find other ways to be cruel to each other.

As I entered the front door, I saw that everyone was in the kitchen, standing very close to each other. I decided to go about my business as if theirs meant little or nothing to me. I would be mature, without needs, and therefore invisible. My parents would be too enthralled by crisis to notice that every word they said was escaping, declassified, as soon as it left their mouths.

I weaved among them — Mom, Dad, Covington. I was busy and did not need direction. They ignored me, and I listened.

"We'll have to talk about it, Jim," my father said.

"It's out of the question," my mother said.

Covington turned to her. "With all due respect, Gail, I'm not sure you understand what we're dealing with here."

I winced inwardly; Covington really didn't know my mother. All Due Respect was not enough if you were implying that she didn't understand something.

"He's nine years old, Jim," she answered. "How can *you* be sure what we're dealing with here?"

Covington took a moment. When he spoke again, his voice was surprisingly calm and confident. "I've never seen anyone do the things he can do, Gail. Your son isn't running around in circles out there."

"What 'things' exactly?" my mother asked.

Covington thought about it for what seemed a long time. Long enough for me to get the milk, get a glass, and pour it. I glanced at him quickly; he was looking down, rubbing the back of his neck with his hand.

"He understands the game," Covington said. "I don't know how else to explain it."

A silence followed, and I felt myself joining my parents in trying to understand this statement. My mother was staring at Covington, squinting and trying to make sense of him. But my father was looking at me, as if noticing my presence for the first time. He smiled, the kind of smile that said *please leave now.*

I took my Oreos and milk into the living room, put them on the coffee table, and turned on the television. *He understands the game.* The words rocked me — the first external confirmation I'd heard that my brother was different and somehow better. There was awe in Covington's voice, even a tremor. This man had coached hundreds of kids. What could CJ have possibly done, and in only a scrimmage? Was it a sparkling defensive play, or a great at-bat against an overpowering, oversized reliever? I couldn't imagine. It was sometimes a miracle if a pitcher his age could get the ball to the plate or a third baseman could plant and throw to first.

Covington left a half-hour later, and nothing was ever the same. My father adjusted his work schedule so that he could drive my brother thirty miles to play in a different, elite league in Santa Monica. It was called Babe Ruth AA-Select, like some deluxe cardboard carton of eggs. And I was introduced to the game of tennis.

My mother, who to my knowledge had never picked up a racket, insisted that the game was best suited to my physique and intellectual temperament, as if tennis were a bride my parents had chosen after mulling over several applicants. I believed my mother, because I didn't expect her to lie. But what my parents really wanted was for the two of us not to be competing. We were no longer a pair of Screaming Eagles — two brothers who played baseball together on a couple of unambitious neighborhood teams. My parents were not athletes; they deferred to Covington and his accumulated wisdom, and then they made their own, seemingly logical leap. They didn't think I could handle a younger brother who was so much better than me at something we both did. They were probably right.

So I embraced their low expectations. I'd finish the spring baseball season, but would soon become the older brother who played catch for fun. The brother who liked to watch, who could name all the Dodger players — the kind of useless knowledge only nonplayers flaunted. But then I became the brother who hated baseball altogether, who thought it was stupid and slow and boring. This probably didn't bother my parents; I don't think they loved baseball either. And later I became the brother who also hated everyone who played it.

CJ was the ballplayer. He was the one who understood the game; he was the one they came looking for when they came looking. But on that day, with the coach in our kitchen, the finality of it all — those entrenched positions that dictated feelings and defined relationships — was still to come. I walked over to the living room window. CJ, sitting on the porch step, was pulling his Popsicle stick apart, examining the tiny splinters. He had played coy with me, but he damn well knew what they were talking about. He had done *something,* and Covington had seen it, and Covington had asked my brother if he could talk to our parents.

I didn't remember anyone ever corralling my parents on my behalf. I was never told to wait outside. I suppose it was possible that a discussion of my future did take place, in some meaningless moment I overlooked, between breaths, focused elsewhere. And maybe, in one of life's casual symmetries, my brother was around to overhear it, sneaking into the kitchen for a glass of soda, the only witness to a great life-changing debate. Did he tell them what should be done with me, sending me down some road between sips of his drink, sweet fizzy pinpricks that tickled him? He never said.

So I became a tennis player. I was pretty good at it, enjoyed the solitude and the limited number of elements I was required to master, even if I could never hit a topspin lob, or serve and volley without foot-faulting. And I never rose much above mediocre, probably because I practiced against a brick wall up at South Pasadena High, which forced a degree of urgency upon the game and gave me many bad habits in return. The ball would ricochet back to me much faster than it should have — much more like racquetball — and I ended up conditioned to an opposing player who was closer, and a net that was higher, than they actually were. When I returned to the court for a match, my opponent was small and the net was low, the reality fuzzy and disappointing. I wanted my wall back.

And my mother was wrong about my temperament, or she was right and I changed my personality merely to prove her wrong. If a call went against me during a set, or if I made one critical error, I would plummet to earth like flaming wreckage: launching forehands over the fence, double-faulting entire service games away, the whole match over in a matter of minutes. But after the match, I'd quickly forget the loss and go cheerfully about my business. Losing never ruined my entire day, just the part of it when I was actually playing, when the loss might still have been prevented.

In any event, I was too distracted, and there was far too much new noise inside my head. I had discovered a talent for math and science, but, more important, girls were everywhere, in places I'd never noticed them before. They were in front of me at the water fountain, leaning down, hands pulling the straight brown hair back to spare it, revealing the delicate right earlobe with its small silver hoop; or in the front seat of another car at a red light on Fair Oaks Boulevard; or in my stormy subconscious, their faces parading in arcs before me, like pictures of ice cream dishes on a glossy parlor menu. I was moody and constantly feverish, bouncing off all people and objects in my path, or knocking them flat with earnest obliviousness. My parents did their best to act as if everything were normal; the best way to do this was to gather around my brother. CJ was younger, he played baseball, and he did not notice me or anyone else. Thus, he kept everyone focused.

Covington vanished from our lives, fleeing his bold, soapbox-style assertions about my brother's talent, which, in the short term, proved shockingly inaccurate. CJ struggled for the first month in the new league. Early on I watched him play against a towering and tanned team from Newport Beach. It was a beautiful day, and there was a cool breeze from the ocean that blew away any anxiety. But the plays I had seen my brother routinely make were suddenly and puzzlingly beyond him, his instincts dulled, as if he were growing old before my eyes. He couldn't reach a sharply hit ball to his right that I'd seen him swallow many times before. And at the plate he was hesitant and afraid, taking pitches that I knew he could hit, watching them float past for strikes one two and three. "Let the game come to you," they always said, but I got the sense that CJ was letting the game come to him and watching it pass right on by.

Maybe it was the separation, joining a new team mid-season — the Santa Monica Mariners, a group of boys from West LA who had more money than we did and found solidarity in ignoring him. Maybe, more specifically, it was the awkward tenth birthday party held that June, when a few of them grimly piled out of a black Mercedes station wagon and mingled uneasily with us local boys. But no one asked CJ what he wanted, because he didn't have a choice. He had an obligation to his talent. He must have known what had to be done. He understood the game.

After the first sixteen games, he was batting .096. He had nineteen errors. He was a ghost. I listened as my parents considered returning him to the Screaming Eagles. There was talk in the neighborhood that my brother had overstepped, aimed too high; all hype. He was my brother, but he had left me behind as well. So I didn't defend him. I stayed silent and relished it as they smashed him flat.

And although I assumed he was miserable, he never let on. CJ wasn't one to throw his glove and sulk or burst into fits of tears — behavior that characterized many kids his age, even those who didn't play sports. He was still a kid, though it was easy to forget it. He bore the whole thing with grace. It was his first slump; he would get out of it. And he even seemed to sense that there would be others and that he'd manage to rise from them, too.

Still, I couldn't help provoking him. He refused to lean on

me, and at thirteen I saw confrontation and the potential for violence in every rebuffed gesture. I was drawn to the imagined heat of CJ's predicament. Since he didn't need my help, I had no choice but to be cruel, not deviously, behind his back, but brutally, to his face. I would taunt him with unanswerable questions, desperate to get a rise out of him. "What's it like to be the worst player on a team?" I'd ask, shaking my head, intimating genuine curiosity, gleefully unable to make sense of it all. "Don't you think Michael Caruso or Sean McGee should have gotten a chance before you did?"

He wouldn't respond. He'd just toss his glove in the air and catch it, or study the fraying seams of a dirty old baseball that had camped in the mouth of Rusty, the Houstons' limp-legged golden retriever across the street. He'd let me rant for twenty or thirty minutes, sitting there and taking it. "You know, Dad's gonna lose his job because of you. He has to leave work early every day, and he's getting fired next week. Darryl Warner told me." (This was blatantly untrue; my father is part of that generation where all jobs apparently have tenure — he was a seismologist at Cal Tech, and he still worked there years later.) Finally, CJ would leave, and I'd let him, pleased with myself, satisfied for the moment that I had inflicted heavy emotional damage.

After seven weeks of lousy play and evening harassment, CJ and my father returned home one day from a game against Malibu. When the front door opened, I could tell from my father's face that things had not gone well. He murmured something to my mother — later, I found out that a ball had darted between my brother's legs and he had also struck out three times. CJ entered the house behind my father and quickly disappeared down the hall. Our loved one remained in a coma, athletically speaking.

On the other hand, the South Pasadena Intermediate tennis team had obliterated visiting San Marino, and I had won matches in both singles and doubles. It was unusual to play both, but I stepped in when a boy named Jason Wilder cut his foot on a piece of broken glass and had to sit out. I thrilled at the drama of being the Last-Minute Replacement; though completely exhausted, I felt unusually thick-chested that night. I waited until after dinner, when CJ and I were in our room doing homework, to start on him.

Our beds were flush against opposite walls. It was a room that lent itself to symmetry and imaginary dividing lines to protect private space. It was the last year we'd share a bedroom; I would be exiled that fall to the old guest room above the garage, with its mealy gray carpet and odd, crumbling built-in shelving, covered with possibly toxic flaky white paint and housing numerous secret cubbyholes for storing pornography.

CJ was studying for a world geography test, the kind of thing that kept fifth-graders busy. He had flash cards filled with quantifiable, useless facts: the second largest city in Poland, the national anthem of Greece. I should add here that CJ was an above-average student; though he thoroughly outpointed me in athletics, I was not able to declare the clean, cinematic victory in academics that would have granted me consolation and calming projections of inevitable, long-term triumph. (Besides, at that age, I would have gladly chosen dumb jock phenomenon over undersized budding brainiac any day.)

I was staring at my algebra book, bored. I looked over at CJ, shuffling the geography flash cards, mouthing answers to himself, flipping them over for confirmation. He had stacks of these cards, color-coded and organized in rubber-banded stacks on the shelf above his desk. It was my father's idea.

The room was quiet, and I decided that my brother's recent failures were not sufficiently devastating. I had dominated in my chosen sport, a young Borg or McEnroe. He had sucked once again.

"Hey, CJ," I said.

He looked up.

"Let me ask you something." I smiled at him.

I expected him, knowing that I was about to attack, to wilt right away. I always expected that. But he just looked at me.

"Do you think you'll ever be good at baseball again?"

He went back to the flash cards.

"I mean, what's it like to stand out there at third and be hoping the whole time that they don't hit it to you, because you know you'll screw it up if they do? What's it like to be scared every time you go up to the plate?" I imagined it for myself, with delight.

"I'm not scared," he said, his voice low and bored. He kept at the cards.

"You should be. You haven't hit the ball out of the infield in, like, three weeks."

"I will tomorrow."

I laughed. His confidence made my job that much easier. "You say that every day."

"This time I'm right."

"You're sure?"

"Yup."

He sounded so confident that I hesitated. "I don't know. Maybe baseball's got you beat. Maybe you don't have what it takes."

He leaned back in his chair, stretching and unconcerned. "Nah. I figured out what my problem is."

"Right." I laughed again, but his cool tone had begun to irritate me. "Face it. You're terrible, CJ. People are laughing at you. You're making the whole family look bad."

But I'd lost him — my accusation that he had ruined the Columbus name throughout Los Angeles County notwithstanding. He got up and wandered out. I smirked, misjudging everything; I'd thought I could hurt him.

That night, I woke up just after three A.M. I wasn't startled, and I felt myself ease from sleep. The room was dark. I heard the faint whir of a truck shifting, picking up speed, carrying through the still air from some distant street. I was lying on my stomach, tangled in my comforter and constricted by it. My right leg dangled off the edge of the bed as if part of me was itching to go somewhere.

I twisted my neck and looked up. My brother was standing

next to my bed. I rotated onto my back and pulled up the blanket so that both of my feet peeked out. There was little light in the room, and I was in the process of adjusting, but I could tell that it was him — though I couldn't make out his expression, his eyes, or anything other than his unmistakable silhouette.

For the first time, that night, I felt him tower over me. I realized how it would feel not only to look up at him, but to look up and not even be able to see him. Apparently, CJ also felt the poetry of the moment, in those elastic hours before morning. He raised the baseball bat he was carrying, his favorite Easton aluminum, and smashed it down on my exposed lower left leg.

I couldn't see what my brother was doing. There was a slight whiff of movement, a short chopping stroke, then a whistling through the air an instant before the contact. A flashbulb of agony surged through my body, the hollow pop of the bone snapping inside me. CJ dropped the bat. It hit the ground hard and did not roll. He went back to his bed and sat down on the edge, invisible to me.

I screamed. Lights came on, and my parents flooded into the room. Time slowed down, sped up, unrecognizable. I kept screaming. I did not know I could scream so loud. It sounded to my ears as if the scream was coming from someone else, though it definitely wasn't; my brother was sitting there, so I kept screaming to make sure I was doing it louder than this mysterious other person who was filling the room with sound. All the anger and frustration and hurt of my life had been isolated into one forgivable moment where I was allowed to yell as much as I wanted to.

My father carried me out of the house to the station wagon and laid me in the back seat, my good leg bent at the knee, my broken one limp and throbbing, shrouded under an oily beach towel. I closed my eyes, feeling the cool steel of the seatbelt buckle prodding my cheek, which was wet with tears. I felt a sticky dampness below my chin as well, and realized that I had thrown up all over myself.

My father drove me to Huntington Memorial Hospital, where the bone was set and cast, from knee to toe. I was not going to die. It was a clean break. They gave me crutches made of cheap yellow foam and sheeny gray metal, and I took my first awkward steps with them, outside. It was around five in the morning, still cool and quiet, the sky amping slowly toward dawn. We were sent home, and I found out later that while I was being treated, my father had given a statement to a social worker at the hospital, who had been called in because the injury looked suspiciously like child abuse.

When we got home, my mother was waiting for us. She was making French toast, though she had placed a box of Cap'n Crunch on the kitchen table as well. My brother was not around.

My father kissed my mother on the cheek, moved past her, and left the two of us alone.

"You're back," she said. She didn't look up and made no effort to aid me, leaving me to hobble toward the kitchen table and collapse in a chair. She had showered and dressed, and she was beating eggs. Something was sizzling, but I could also smell that something had recently burned.

Her voice was lilting and suspiciously friendly. "Does it hurt?" she asked.

"Yeah," I said. It did. It was aching, and I expected it would throb forever. My lower left leg had seceded from my body and was in the midst of developing its own temperament and behavior patterns. At that moment, it was giving me a big fuck-you.

She came to the table, placed a plate in front of me, and sat down.

"Thank you," I said, halfheartedly. The French toast looked blackened and overcooked. I wondered if she had burned it on purpose to punish me. I didn't have a fork and I was covered in puke. I wasn't hungry.

"Don't eat it if you don't want it," she said.

That made me feel guilty, so I started to tear at it, savagely. The logic of our family was gone. I was a different person, suddenly free to eat without utensils and otherwise behave irrationally. But in the silence, as she watched me, I quickly settled down. "It's great, Mom," I said, feeling some convoluted need to placate her. I kept eating. The bread was crisp and difficult;

I couldn't taste it. I only felt the grit of the charred bread, mixed with the cinnamon sugar, scratching the roof of my mouth. I took smaller and smaller bites, losing energy and interest. Maybe I wanted it to last forever, afraid of what was coming next.

When I glanced up, she was staring at me. My mother was tough and smart. At that time she was a deputy district attorney for the city of Los Angeles. Her black hair was cut stylishly short, and with her pale skin and dark eyes, we looked a lot alike and even seemed to be growing oddly closer in age — she was fighting hers, and I was getting carried away with mine.

"What did you do to him?" she asked.

"Huh?" I was startled by her question.

"To provoke him. What did you do to provoke him?"

"I didn't do anything!" I heard my voice become a whine, all screechy and cracked. My eyes grew large, like an unconvincing gesture of surprise and innocence, right out of a comic book.

"That's impossible. You must have done something." She squinted at me, not suspicious but beyond that. It was the same look she'd given Coach Covington — the look that indicated that she couldn't understand me and I was to blame for it, a gaze that said *I'm on to you.*

I was suddenly infuriated. "So this is all my fault?" I gestured, but I was still clenching the crutch in my left hand. The crutch rose from underneath an empty chair and knocked the chair to the floor.

I ignored the mishap, a self-conscious commitment to the intensity of my innocence. There weren't two sides to this story. Were there? "He hit me with a baseball bat, Mom. He broke my leg."

"You must have done something, Joey."

"So? Does that give him the right? When someone kills someone, they can't just do it because they had a reason to!" I framed the debate in legal terms, learned not from her but from watching too much television. It was my pathetic attempt at common ground.

"Actually, they can. It's called justifiable homicide."

"Well!" I flipped my hand in the air dismissively.

"Tell me what you did."

"Why? Will you break my other leg if I don't?"

She glared at me. I glared back, slowly chewing my mouthful of shitty French toast, swallowing dramatically, and never blinking or looking away. It seemed defiant at the time.

CJ was not punished for what he did. He apologized, one of those mumbly numbers, in a ceremony that made all of us even more uncomfortable. I apologized as well, furious that I was forced to. I took the obvious and irritating reverse tack, enunciating loudly along the lines of: "I'm really sorry, CJ, that I said you were a terrible baseball player and that you would never be good at anything again." Next, I recanted bonus, ad-libbed cruelties — my final, flailing jabs — until my father guided me from the room. It was the only way I could make my apologies palatable.

But that was all for show. I don't think either of us was sorry, and we never spoke of the incident for what it really was: a younger brother's brutal act of retaliation — possibly justified in spirit if not in reality — against an older brother who had persisted in being an asshole.

That afternoon, in a game against Redondo Beach, CJ had a couple of hits. It was nothing overwhelming, nothing other players on other teams hadn't done thousands of times. But the hits *were* in a row — a single to left, followed by a double down the right-field line — and two in a row was almost a bunch, and hits bunched together made all the difference. The coaches and my parents were encouraged; these were the first flickers of life, the fluttering eyelids of a ten-year-old giant rising from dead slumber.

He was also solid defensively — no errors in seven chances. He knocked down a liner slicing into the corner over his head, holding the opposing batter to a single instead of a double. The next batter grounded sharply back to him, and he threw to second to start an inning-ending 5–4–3 double play, a rally killer only possible because his first play had kept it in order.

Santa Monica won two more games that weekend; CJ had three hits in the first, including a home run. The next day he had three more hits, stole two bases, and charged a weak bunt down the line and gunned down the runner at first.

Summer arrived. My cast was sawed open, and I stored it in the closet, shutting the door on the stale signatures of bored boys from the neighborhood who didn't mind crouching over my lower leg. I unzipped the cover to my tennis racket and noted emotionlessly the hole in its middle; the strings had snapped and unraveled. I went to camp for six weeks and worked part-time for a local landscaping company that paid me under the table with a plastic bag of loose change and a deceptively thick stack of one-dollar bills. I saw *Indiana Jones and the Temple of Doom* seven times, and I read a book of short stories by Stephen King, a dog-eared paperback I'd found abandoned at the local pool; its sudden, graphic violence felt forbidden and smutty. I moved into my new bedroom and decorated it badly. And my brother played baseball, every day and every night.

He didn't start to fill out physically for another few years, but the fact that he stayed small, albeit briefly, allowed him to hone other elements of his game. He was never able to fall back on power; his fundamentals, on the other hand, were exquisite. He was quick. He had tremendous vision. He was always perfectly positioned in the field — some of this was coaching; some of it must have been instinct — and he made hard plays look routine. At the plate he could hit the ball to all fields, put the ball in play to advance a runner or play hit-and-run, or bat lead-off and work the count. Somehow, so young, he had managed to grasp all the elements of the game — batting, fielding, running, catching, throwing. He wasn't yet great at all of them, but he knew the way they related and balanced. At times the ebb and flow of the game seemed so natural that it was as if he'd already played the whole game in his head, and was replaying it that day in the field for our entertainment.

He played fall and summer ball with Santa Monica for two more years; springtime was reserved for the brief, less meaningful middle school season. The boys grew up, and the Mariners went to the state championships twice but were shut down each time by a team from Sonoma that featured a genetic anomaly of a pitcher with the unlikely name of Clark Kent. Kent limited them to a handful of hits each year, though CJ had five of them.

CJ immediately joined the varsity team at South Pasadena when he arrived as a freshman. People had started talking about him: the batting average over .500, the remarkable defensive range and perfect mechanics, the composure and comportment beyond his years, maturity that even many pouty pros still lacked. There were always lots of good high school athletes, everyone telling them that they were going to make it, but most of them had already peaked. They were destined to be superstars in only a minor constellation, but they were also so young and blindered and full of confidence that they refused to believe it. CJ was told the same stories, with their same unbelievably happy endings. Were we wrong to think they were real? There were college and professional scouts watching him play; they circled around each other, squinting and chewing gum and calculating, watching my brother — men falling in love with the sun on his great good face.

I was in the twelfth grade when CJ arrived; it was the first time we'd been in the same school together in seven years. We were civil to each other but traveled in different spheres. I gave him a ride to school each morning, but we did not speak of anything important, and after practice or games he found his own way home. We had no friends or interests in common. I had long ago given up tennis, and playing baseball together seemed even more foreign and remote. I was focusing on school, on getting good grades and getting into a good college. This was territory over which I still had some control.

For every story you tell there's one that you don't. Most people thought that CJ played all the time, cultivated his natural gifts, and flourished. But I knew better, even though, in many ways, I never really knew him at all.

When I was seven I moved my brother to third base. The world knew all about that. But all those years, under the radar of inquiring minds, was the second story — of how, when I was twelve, I helped him to succeed there. CJ had told me that he knew what was wrong. He knew why he wasn't playing well. A few hours later, in the middle of the night, he swung and did not miss. He could have caved in my skull, shattered my face and disfigured me, or cracked my knee and made me a cripple. But of course it wasn't about what he was doing to me; he was doing it for himself, the way we all acted out, more often in small and everyday ways, to quiet something inside.

After that, CJ began to surpass expectations instead of slumming beneath them. My broken leg was an anecdote to which I added no drama. There was a neatness to it that I instinctively mistrusted, but not everything that was obvious was also false. I rolled it over in my mind so many times that I had no choice except to embrace it, because even if it was no more than a comforting, delineating lie, I could not outrun it.

Baseball players struggle at the plate; it is a fact of life. They bring their hands together or close their stance, raise their elbows, bend their knees. They watch tapes, study opponents, burrow into themselves. Most of them never figure it out. Baseball is a game of failure; my brother faced it down early. All he needed was contact, the pure and delicious crack of the bat. It was something I helped him to hear and feel. He had looked down on me that night when we were young; he had waited for his confident gaze to open my eyes. Then he found his voice, there was a gorgeous realignment, and the music began.

2

Everyone has a dark period — usually transitional, though occasionally irreversible — and as I made my way through college, and while I was all the way across the country from him, my brother slid into his. CJ's was shorter than most, though one could argue that his also came at a time when he, unlike most sullen teens, had something significant at stake. It featured all the requisite highlights and dubious dramas: he was deliberately and relentlessly contrary, and he wanted to shed my parents like a snake's dead skin. But what was most important — and one might say predictable — was his announcement that he was quitting baseball.

It happened in the fall, as I was beginning my junior year at Georgetown. I'd been home only briefly during the previous twelve months, having spent the summer working in the lab of a middle-aged, recently widowed chemistry professor and renting a crumbling rowhouse with three friends on a slanting alley off M Street, the neighborhood's main thoroughfare.

And I had met Beth that spring. She was from New Jersey (like most of the Georgetown student body, it seemed), fiercely intelligent, and very blond. Physically, she was like a Californian, but there was a sharpness and snap about her that startled me, something I'd never encountered in a woman. It wasn't sarcasm; it was a sort of focus. She wouldn't let me get away with anything. I guess she was like my mother in that way; they say that's who you look for, though I don't allow my thinking to travel far down that road. To be honest, Beth was the first woman I ever thought of as a woman. Before, they'd always been girls.

I wish I could say that our first encounter was romantic or momentous, but it was in the basement of the Sigma Chi fraternity house. I'd been stuck with the tap of the beer keg, and several cheap plastic cups were empty and begging in front of me. One of them was Beth's. She smiled, and, in a moment of rare decisiveness, I filled both our cups, managed to extricate myself from my position of authority by dropping the tap, and followed her.

I had dated a few girls in high school but none of them seriously — I should say that none of them dated *me* seriously. At that point I don't think I knew what I was searching for. Physical appearance mattered to me because it mattered to every guy I knew, but I was suspicious of pure beauty. I wanted a relationship that didn't feel like a relationship — more like a close friendship. I also wanted it to feature sex several times a day. Sex to make up for all the years without sex, and sex to store up in case there stopped being sex in the future. When I was older and wiser, I knew that was sophomoric, but when I met Beth, I was, well, a sophomore. Give me a break.

Beth was understanding, and eventually our relationship eased from semi-torrid to comfortable and sedate. We quickly did everything together. We became the kind of couple that nobody doubted or tried to wedge their way between. I didn't think about it "lasting forever"; I just knew that we were getting along and I was going with it. I thought my roommates and many of the guys in my fraternity wondered how I'd managed to snag Beth, and I wished I could reveal to them that there was some secret, some pickup line or aftershave that had sealed the deal. But I happened to be lucky. During a critical stretch, I acted like myself — intelligent, somewhat funny, generally decent, doubts kept to myself — and for once, mercifully, that was enough.

But Beth wasn't the story here. It was in this Indian summer period of mellow contentment that my brother, the sulking ex–baseball phenomenon, was thrust upon me. The phone rang one October Sunday morning, and it was my mother. I was learning to resist her efforts to manhandle me, often by assuming a distracted, patronizing air during her efforts to engage me in conversation. She'd usually make random suggestions about courses I should be taking or clothes I needed or foods I should avoid. "Is that right?" I'd say, rubbing my temples, nursing a brutal hangover or feeling that I was.

Most often, this infuriated her, and she'd put my father on the phone. But on that Sunday she skipped the needling chit-chat. "Your brother is coming to see you," she announced.

"Really? When?"

"Next Friday." Then silence. She offered no explanation.

"Is that right?" I wondered if she'd gone beyond merely banishing CJ to my care, if maybe she'd kicked him out of the house for an undisclosed, massive fuck-up. The notion pleased me — maybe my mother would be forced to acknowledge that she'd backed the wrong horse.

"Is there a problem?" she asked.

"No," I said. Beth was asleep in bed next to me. I had no real plans for the coming weekend; there would be studying and drinking and more sex. Now my brother was coming to sleep on the floor at my feet.

I met CJ at the airport on a crisp Friday evening. It was Columbus Day weekend, the perfect occasion for a Columbus family reunion. I watched the passengers enter the terminal, keeping my distance from the gate to indicate my dry, ironic affect. My brother appeared, carrying a sky-blue duffel bag and wearing sunglasses, baggy denim shorts, and a black T-shirt. Was that the glint of a diamond stud I saw in his left ear? I nodded at him, trying not to betray my shock; the clean-cut baseball hero had become a scruffy SoCal skate rat. He drifted toward me, one of the last to leave the plane, an adolescent Godzilla that everyone else was running away from.

We shook hands, and I clapped him on the back as I offered

to take his bag. He stiffened and glared at me, as if a friendly pat had, on some previous occasion, been an invitation to a brawl. In any event, he thrust the bag upon me; it was inordinately heavy, as though it were filled with hockey equipment. As I staggered through the terminal, I realized that things must have been pretty awful at home if my parents thought that having CJ visit me was the necessary tonic. They worried about what would happen to my brother if he didn't have his game, and they expected me to set him straight. I planned to begin with a subtle and disarming massage of small talk, ease into an illicit, lubricating complement of alcoholic beverages, and then grab his head with both hands and wrench it hard until he saw the light. You will play baseball again, CJ, and you will like it.

But I didn't think it was going to be easy. We walked out to the subway station. CJ was taller than I was, and he looked hardened and older, his lip curled in a slight snarl. He had muscles on his tanned forearms that were new and imposing; they were like meaty drumsticks, Steve Garvey-esque, hardly human, in my eyes. They didn't look to me like the kind of muscles a guy would cultivate if he was planning to give up the sport that required him to have them.

But for whatever unspoken reasons, life was not giving my brother pleasure. I was secretly thrilled that I'd been called in to rescue him from despair, even though he looked tough. My plan, under the circumstances, was probably a bad one. If I tried to grab him and shake him, he'd probably grab me back — he was certainly quick enough — and there would be that frozen moment, when his eyes would meet mine and chide me for bringing the soft stuff, and then he'd beat the shit out of me.

I found out later that CJ's announcement about retiring from baseball was something he'd happened to mutter one night at dinner — more threat than declaration. My parents were stunned, and the reaction pleased him so much that he went with it. And they took his word for it, since he was barely speaking to them at the time, even though the whole thing didn't make much sense. As he entered his senior year at South Pasadena, he was playing better than ever. He was a high school All-American as a junior and runner-up as California High School Player of the Year. He'd signed a letter of intent to play at UCLA, a perennial College World Series contender. That would keep him close to home and pay his entire tuition. (The free ride was important, because, as my mother ceaselessly reminded me, my Georgetown tuition was sucking us dry.) And many expected him to be chosen early in the amateur draft the following June, though he and my parents had apparently decided that he wouldn't sign.

My mother and father had not made this decision on their own. Bewildered by the thicket of eligibility rules surrounding a vaunted amateur athlete, they'd asked the UCLA coach to help them. Refusing to sign was not as obstinate as it sounded — it was not uncommon for players to go to college and play there, instead of heading directly to the lowest and cruelest rungs of professional rookie ball at age eighteen or nineteen.

I was kept apprised of his progress during those Sunday phone calls, though my father, not my mother, gave me most of the updates. She wasn't able to speak of CJ's accomplishments to me without it sounding as if she was gloating. I guess pride was proper when she was telling other parents about him — the thinly veiled smarminess of the parent who had raised, and thus deserved credit for, a superior child. I guess no one told her that it probably wasn't a good idea to take that same tone with the child's older, less successful but special-in-his-own-way brother. And I decided not to remind my mother that she had little to do with how well he played, other than pointing him in the direction of the nearest baseball field and feeding him when the games were over.

My dad was more straightforward and somehow tolerable; when he spoke about CJ, there was a stunning calm about it all. "Two for two," he'd say, ending on a slight upbeat, or "Real nice catch, Joey, in foul ground." And that was in response to my questions about how CJ was doing; he was still my brother and it was proper to ask, and if you ask about CJ, then you had no choice but to accept box scores and highlight reels in return.

Where my mother's reports took the tone of antagonistic pride, my father never pretended that he had anything to do with CJ's success. He was a fan, and his favorite player happened to be his younger son. In fact, in the spindly branches of the Columbus family tree, you were more likely to be diabetic or bald (or both) than athletically gifted. Before CJ, my great-uncle Archie was the closest we Columbi had come to producing a champion, but his promising upstate New York under-twelve Ping Pong career had been regrettably snuffed out by some oily rags — left on the green-and-white table by his father during the day and inadvertently flung into the furnace by young Archie, who had stealthily descended to the dark basement, late on a cold winter's night, to practice his backhand spin slicer. Archie survived the fire; the house, his eyebrows, and his passion for the game did not.

Sometimes what my brother was doing struck me as preposterous. It would hit home hours after I'd learned of his latest exploits, when I was up late, exhausted from studying, and my mind floated for a moment. But if I examined the truth too closely, it would stop making sense to me — sitting at my desk and rubbing my eyes for other reasons, but still locking in on, imagining, and hardly believing that my brother, in a few years, might be playing professional baseball for a team in the major leagues. Like most people, I'd never known an athlete who made his living at it. I couldn't imagine him in *Sports Illustrated,* or having his name on television, or being available to the public in trading card form, packed in with fifteen other big leaguers and a pink plank of bubble gum. Though all sorts of things could go wrong, the logical signs pointed to this scenario. Nevertheless, even then some mild psychosis fed my denial; I would deal with it when it happened, and even though I knew it would happen, it hadn't happened yet. Until the day I saw him play, I was never able to get my mind around the notion that my brother could become a professional baseball player, success, or superstar.

Of course none of that mattered now, because it was all

over. He'd stopped playing baseball. There were many possible reasons, though none had been offered, by him or my parents. He may have tired of the discipline or the high expectations, or maybe he got bored. It was also possible that he didn't know the reason himself, and I imagined he relished the way my parents, and maybe his high school teammates and coach, puzzled over his moods — sifting through the remnants of his uneaten meals and mulling over his monosyllabic sound bites, like psychics divining at the scene of the crime. You'd call this second-guessing, except that CJ had never offered his own rationale in the first place. It just happened.

On the subway ride from the airport, because I wasn't much good at starting a conversation, I decided to be blunt. "I guess I'm supposed to talk to you about not playing baseball," I said.

He closed his eyes and swayed, letting the train carry him. "There's nothing to talk about."

"So you've pretty much decided, then."

"Yup."

I let it go, knowing I would have three days to pry the truth from him, but I thought it was important up front to let him know that we both knew what this sabbatical was really about. I couldn't believe that CJ had actually given up the game, though part of me hoped that he had; it would have been a thrilling move, so ballsy and unexpected. And it might have made the rest of my life that much easier.

The next morning I headed off to the library, leaving him sleeping on the floor of my room. When I came home, he and Beth were sitting on the couch, watching college football. My roommate Neil, a butcher's son from Brooklyn, was in a chair across from them, a Camel Light between his fingertips. I said hello and asked CJ how long he'd been up.

He didn't answer and didn't look in my direction. The game seemed to captivate him. Beth smiled at me. "I thought he was you."

"What?" I said. I dropped my backpack on the floor and sat down next to her.

She slid over. "I went upstairs and I grabbed him, like this." She grabbed CJ's calf and squeezed it. Again, no reaction.

"I got in your bed," CJ said. "After you left."

Beth laughed. "He was facing the wall. I thought it was you."

"That's so funny," I said, sarcastically. I turned to Neil. "Isn't that funny?"

He raised his eyebrows and exhaled cigarette smoke.

"Shut up," Beth said, swatting my arm.

"CJ, how you doing?" I said.

"I'm good. This is college."

"Yes, it is. I'm sure it's everything you imagined."

He rubbed his temple and gave me a fake, closed-mouth smile. We were off to an excellent start.

We had a party at the house that night. It wasn't in honor of my brother; it had been planned weeks before. I didn't pay attention to his drinking, and as the party swelled I noticed every once in a while that there was a bottle of beer in his hand, but it may have been the same one all night long.

Sometime after midnight I lurched upstairs for a breather. My bedroom was on the second floor, with a rickety back porch extending off it. The party was still going strong, and I wanted to make sure that no one had kicked in my door, rifled through my belongings, or brought a friend to my bed.

The door to the bedroom was open, and CJ was outside on the porch. I could see his legs extended; he was sitting on the floor. I went out and stepped over him into the cold night air, a sharp contrast to the humidity of the house — it was like walking into a freezer. "Hey, man," I said, "you doing all right?"

"Yes, sir." He was drinking a bottle of beer, but he looked awake and alert.

I, on the other hand, was drunk. "I'm gonna sit," I said. It felt like a necessity.

"Right on," he said, gesturing forward with his bottle, a California-style encouragement. I sat in one of the low lawn chairs on the far side of the porch, and CJ got up and climbed into the other one.

"Do you know any of these people?" he asked.

"At the party? Most of them. Maybe half," I said.

"Not the people at the party," he said. "I mean *them*." He waved out to the backyard and beyond, where there were other rowhouses and one low, quiet apartment building.

I thought about it. "Some are students, I guess. Some are just people."

"But do you know them? Are any of them your friends?"

"I don't know, CJ. They're neighbors. They're people."

He shrugged and was silent. I watched him stare out at the buildings, wondering what answer he was looking for. It wasn't small talk, but it wasn't beer-induced existentialism, either — those deep conversations about things that are so meaningful when everyone's young and full of half-ideas and has drunk a lot. I didn't know what it was. Our chairs were angled out toward the clear night, as if we were two old men sinking into the sand of the beach, watching their wives splash in the sea. Someday we might be those creaky old men, older and wiser and physically pained, but at that moment I was feeling no pain. I'd been drinking for several hours. And as I looked across at my brother, his face unlined in the dozy moonlight, I realized that he was better at posing as wise than I was, because he was usually quiet — and when you don't talk, you don't give yourself away.

"You can't quit baseball," I said.

"I know," he said. He knew it. "Beth's really cool," he added.

"She likes you, too."

"What did you tell her about me?"

"Nothing," I said. "I mean, I told her that you were my brother."

"Did you tell her I played baseball?"

"Probably. It's not a secret, CJ."

He didn't answer.

"And it's good you're not quitting," I said.

"Let's not get into it, all right?"

The alcohol was hitting me. My words began to blur, and I wasn't listening to him; our meager dialogue had become a solo rant. I was the foolish boozehound on a mount, or at least a creaking porch. "You can't quit, because you're good. Because you're really good. You're really fucking good. You have what it takes to be . . ."

And I paused, searching for that summarizing clincher, but I tripped on my own simple thought and started over. "You have what it takes to be the best!"

I looked over at him, honestly thinking that I sounded sincere, and not like a guy channeling a junior high pep rally. He glanced at me, then turned away and finished his beer. We sat there in silence.

"I appreciate that," he finally said.

"So do I," I replied, nonsensically. Then I went back in the bedroom, collapsed on my bed, and passed out.

The rest of the weekend passed quickly. The house was quiet until around noon on Sunday, when we cleaned up for a few hours and watched some pro football. Beth came over, and the three of us went out for something cheap to eat.

It was true that Beth and I had discussed my brother. I couldn't remember when exactly, because I didn't think I'd said much more than what I reported to CJ — yes, I had a sibling, a younger brother, and he played baseball. I made no mention of any rivalry, simmering jealousies, or estrangement. Beth had nodded, uninterested; how complicated and riveting could relations between the two of us be? She and I probably discussed it, however briefly, in one of those marathon conversations in the early days of our dating, when everything about each of us was interesting and new to the other. He was a high school jock, feeling his way; I could have told her that he was destined for greatness, the best third baseman in America, but those boasts would have sounded unconvincing, coming from me, and wouldn't have meant a thing.

Beth and my brother got along well enough. She prodded him for incriminating anecdotes from our childhood years, a conniving smile on her face the whole time. I said nothing, thinking that if I tried to stop her, it would look as if there was something to hide, and that would have pushed her further. Beth wasn't a lawyer yet, but one could see it in her future.

CJ smiled but was not forthcoming. Ours was a family

where people held things back, and he was well practiced in avoiding questions he did not want to answer. I noticed that his earring was gone; Mom would be happy about that, though I didn't know whether it had been stolen, misplaced, or pocketed temporarily. I left him in the house that night, watching playoff baseball with my housemates, Marcus and Jeremy, and went off to the library to study.

When I came home after eleven, Marcus was gone, and Jeremy was alone in front of the television, napping on the couch, muttering in his shallow sleep. I trudged upstairs and found CJ, back on the porch, standing with both hands flat on the railing. I had no idea how long he'd been out there. He was facing those other houses and the single apartment building.

"CJ?"

He didn't move. At first I didn't go out to him. The last time we'd talked on the porch, I'd been drunk, filling the air with awkward words of inspiration that, no matter how well intentioned, now seemed stupid. I dropped my bookbag on the desk so that he would know I was there, but he didn't acknowledge me.

I thought he was wearing my navy blue windbreaker, but then I remembered that my mother had bought us both the same indestructible jackets the previous summer. So he must have brought his along. It ruffled around him; there was a breeze now, though the air had felt dead and stagnant as I walked home from the library.

I stopped at the doorway to the porch. "Are you looking at something?" I said. "What are you looking at?"

Still no response. I stepped out and approached him. He was standing absolutely still, and his eyes were closed. He was smiling. "Can you feel it?" he said.

"Feel what?" I asked.

He opened his eyes. "Something incredible is about to happen."

I started to laugh, but it caught deep in my throat and died. He was serious. I wanted to be sarcastic, to deflate the moment and pull the plug on his bold, beatific grin, but my brain had frozen and locked. I wanted to make fun of him for believing in anything at a time when everyone I knew was superior and cynical, but, instead, I felt the puzzling sting of tears in the corners of my eyes. It sounds so foolish after the fact, but I could only look at him, and marvel, and know that we had nothing in common. I felt that nothing I said would have had any effect on him. He indulged me in my efforts to guide him when we were together, but for him I was nothing more than a source of chatter and predictable static. He had decided whether or not he would play baseball. He decided everything. And whatever voice it was that guided him was pitched at a level that no one else could hear. I looked at my brother and knew that games were not games to the people who played them. At that moment I became a believer in fate. I believed that some people were different. And I believed in my own powerlessness and futility and pain.

I wanted to touch him and confirm that he was real, but I was afraid it would break my heart.

My brother kept playing baseball. In early June he won the *USA Today* award as High School Player of the Year, and my parents flew to Washington with him for a ceremony and reception at the paper's headquarters in Arlington, Virginia. And later that month he was drafted, in the ninth round, by the Toronto Blue Jays. As expected, he turned them down for UCLA. I spent my summer teaching biology and math to overachieving seventh-graders and volunteered at a Northeast Washington computer center on weekends — a refurbished, windowless church basement, where the adults learned touch-typing and the kids, wide-eyed and desperate to be off the scorched, dangerous streets, leaned over their parents' shoulders and corrected their spelling.

I had decided that I wanted to be a teacher. I still enjoyed math and science, but I also knew that I didn't have the patience or intellectual dexterity for a life of scientific research. At the same time, I was flush with the power of becoming a responsible young man, wanting to pass along wisdom to others just as fast as I got my hands on it. Teaching seemed the way to go. There wouldn't be a lot of money, but there'd be enough. I would love what I was doing, and that was that.

It was a decision that Beth and my father supported, but it puzzled my mother. Her disappointment, though unspecified, was tangible. "We'll talk about it," she said when I told her, but we never did. Teaching offered neither money nor fame, which was the obvious reason she was against it, but it was possible that nothing I chose would have pleased her. Maybe she thought my career choice showed a lack of engagement on my part, as if I didn't want a job in which competition, no matter how maddening or pointless, was an integral part. I saw the work as noble and sacrificial, the polar opposite of my brother's frivolous, ludicrously well-compensated future occupation. There would be no way for anyone to compare us, which was exactly what I was looking for. I wasn't afraid of competing with the world; I didn't want to compete with him.

As I coasted toward graduation, Beth and I tentatively made plans for our lives together. She wanted to go directly to law school, and I needed a graduate degree in order to teach. We would stay in school, probably move in together, and try to keep things going because they were going so well. I didn't think of it as love; it felt comfortable and inevitable. But I was in love with Beth, and I couldn't imagine my future without her.

My brother started at third base for UCLA as a freshman. He was the only youngster on a veteran, championship-caliber team. He had quite a following by then, having graduated from the "Preps Plus" page of the *Los Angeles Times* Valley supplement to the more august, regular sports section, right next to articles about Kings hockey and the feats of the magical Wayne Gretzky or about the Lakers' sad and distracted swoon in the wake of Magic Johnson's illness and retirement. I read the clippings, which my father sent me in unmarked, brown legal envelopes.

CJ was Freshman of the Year, according to *Baseball America* and *Collegiate Baseball,* publications that I guess know such things. He hit in thirty-seven straight games, which was a PAC–10 and UCLA record. He also set a school record for runs scored in a season, and struck out only six times in 184 at-bats. He was a three-time All-American and the two-time PAC–10 player of the year. At the end of his junior year, on a team that won the College World Series, he won the Dick Howser Award as the nation's top collegiate player.

Three days later, on June 12, Beth and I were married. CJ was my best man, and all of us were walking on rarefied air. He gave the toast, which was eloquent and brief. I don't remember what he said.

Later he pulled me aside to tell me that he was leaving UCLA, a few credits shy of graduation, and was making himself eligible for the June free-agent draft. He said that our parents supported the decision. I had little reaction; it was my wedding day, and besides, my advice had served little purpose in the past. If everyone thought it was the right thing to do, then I assumed that it was. CJ had accomplished everything he could. In the irritating though occasionally accurate parlance of sport, it was time for him to move to the next level.

Beginning in the 1960 season, the Chicago Cubs had a third baseman named Ron Santo. He was great and beloved, a consistent All-Star, five-time Gold Glove winner, and his voice was still heard as the Cubs radio color commentator. (I know all this not because I'm a lifelong Cubs fan, but because it is relevant, and I read it in the team's glossy and fascinating media guide. Did you know, for example, that the only Cub to steal second base, third base, and home plate in the same game was Wilbur Good, who did it on August 18, 1915?) Ron Santo retired in 1973, and apparently the Cubs had failed to acquire a young and steady third baseman ever since, the position having been played by such improbably named, fleeting major leaguers as Joe Kmak and Billy Grabarkewitz (media guide, page 46).

My brother walked in those hallowed, potentially cursed footsteps. He was drafted by the Cubs, the third pick in the first round. None of this was a surprise. Though CJ only told me of his plans at my wedding, the official notification of his availability for Major League Baseball had, according to an NCAA code of law, taken place a few months earlier. CJ knew it would be the Cubs, and despite some initial disappointment that he wasn't drafted by the Dodgers, that had never been a realistic aspiration. The Dodgers were too successful then, and therefore drafting too low, to have a chance at him. In the draft, to the losers go the spoils, and only the desperate need for pitching by the two teams ahead of the Cubs made CJ a three instead of a two or a one.

In July he joined the Orlando Rays, the Cubs AA affiliate. He was called up on September 8, after Juan Valera, the team's current (and immediately expendable) third baseman, was examined that afternoon by team doctors, whose X-ray of his bruised foot, from a foul ball the previous night, revealed a break. CJ arrived at Wrigley Field during the first inning of a game against the Cardinals and made his major league debut as a pinch hitter in the sixth. He singled, then singled again in the ninth and scored the tying run. The Cubs rallied from five runs down to win the game, seven to five, in eleven innings.

He stayed with the team through the end of the season. They were a dismal fifteen games out of first place, and CJ eased effortlessly into the starting lineup. He hit .337 in his first seventeen games, including a base hit in each of his first eight, which was a club record for the longest streak at the start of a major league career. He was the first player from his amateur draft to play in the majors, and he kept the fans coming to the ballpark as September crept toward October and the warm weather packed up and fled, as it did in Chicago, literally overnight. It was the September that I began to teach, and Beth was starting her third and final year at Georgetown Law. We had survived two years together as husband and wife, but we were both still students, so not much had changed. We'd moved into an apartment in Bethesda, a Maryland suburb of Washington. Those were a good couple of years, a carefree and exciting time.

My brother was twenty-one years old. When the major league season ended, he played winter ball in Puerto Rico. And when spring training began, he was still considered a rookie, though he was no longer a secret. The trickle of fawning pieces in LA had, of course, expanded outward, to Chicago, with its two big dailies. Many had seen his September debut, since the Cubs games are shown nationally on cable television, giving the team pockets of devoted and masochistic fans across the country. He was in the starting lineup for opening day; the temperature was in the low fifties, and CJ batted third, coming up for the first time with the bases empty and two outs. He worked the count full and then jerked a home run to left, out of Wrigley altogether and onto Waveland Avenue.

The Cubs managed to lose the game and embraced mediocrity with rare precision that season, never wandering more than seven games above or below .500 the entire year, like a moody patient on steadying yet stultifying medication. It was difficult for such a road show to provide a story line, so CJ dutifully obliged and wove the thread. Every game and every accomplishment was the announcement of his arrival. He broke five different team rookie batting records and one major league rookie record. The stats are listed here merely to quantify his staggering prowess: .361 batting average (second in the National League only to Tony Gwynn), 211 hits, 44 doubles, 27 home runs, 107 runs scored, 101 runs batted in.

Statistics don't mean much if you don't follow baseball, but they can be put in perspective. CJ was doing things much better than almost anyone else, even players who had much more experience. Judging him by his age (now twenty-two) and comparing him with his fellow rookies was unfair. He had what was called a career year, which made his more knowledgeable fans uneasy and his enemies (whoever they might be) smug. It was going to be difficult for him to top his initial work of art.

Imagine doing your job with intimidating efficiency and amazing fucking success every day for one entire year. That's what my brother had done, and I had to admit that though I was busy with my own life, my own challenges and passions, when I stopped to take note of his accomplishment, I realized he had done things beyond what I'd ever imagined. He was a great baseball player — nothing more than that, but it was still something.

I didn't see him play that first year. The closest team to where we lived was the Orioles in Baltimore. Since CJ was playing in the National League, it would have meant a trip to one of the nearest NL cities, probably Philadelphia or New York, or a trip home. I suppose we could have gone to see him play in Chicago — he'd have gladly put us up for the weekend in his newly purchased three-bedroom home in Lincoln Park (courtesy of a $2 million rookie signing bonus).

None of this happened. Of course we were busy, but we weren't *that* busy, at least not that first spring. I was teaching, but Beth was in her final semester of law school, and she'd have the whole summer off before starting work in the fall. Our life did change dramatically then, but even in September, when I was much more alone, I could easily have joined him for a weekend. And when the season ended, I could have invited him to stay with us in Bethesda and speak to my students, reiterating his message against smokeless tobacco, a cause for which he had recently become baseball's youthful and persuasive spokesman. I could have stood with my parents at his side for the mid-November press conference at Wrigley Field, in the howling wind, as he received the National League Rookie of the Year Award.

And yet I did none of those things. We hardly even spoke on the phone, even though my parents had given me the code name that would allow my calls to slip through at hotels on the road. I never knew the right time to call. And what would I have said to him? Great game? Chin up, slugger? His teammates could do it better. Guys fill awkward moments by talking about sports, but my brother *was* sports. He was a public figure who worked in full view, and there was no small talk that could have eased us closer. Without it, I could never figure out a way to get us there. Information created distance. And soon, when there's too much distance, you notice only yourself.

I finally did see him play. It was a year later, during the first month of his second season, in Los Angeles. We had a cluster of seats together, in the narrow mezzanine right above third base, positioned to look down at him like approving elders. Beth was with me, and my parents, along with Uncle Billy (Mom's older brother, a Seattle lawyer), and Spencer Levitt, my brother's agent, who was based in Newport Beach.

I'd met Spencer once before. He had dined at our house during the summer after my freshman year at Georgetown, when CJ was playing in high school. He was in his late thirties and impeccably groomed, with slick black hair and an expensive suit that I imagined was fitted by women who danced around him with tape measures. He wore a gold bracelet, which he saw me staring at and assumed that I coveted. "See?" he'd said, flipping it over. On the other side was a flat gold rectangle, engraved with the timeless creed ALLERGIC TO BEES. "I can get you one," he whispered, as if even his infirmities were marketable.

Spencer, who'd grown up in Beverly Hills, had followed my brother's career since his first tumultuous stint with the Santa Monica Mariners. Or so he said. I thought he reeked of bullshit — so slick and witty, with his pinched rodentlike face, his nostrils flared and craven. Only the born agent would admit tracking the career of an eight-year-old. But Spencer charmed my mother and father that night in our home, and after dinner, when he went down the hall to chat alone with CJ, his magic words successfully lured my brother into his wicked, lifelong sphere.

As Beth and I reached our seats that April evening, we found Spencer already there. He was pacing in a small circle in the largely empty section, banging his knee against the rail in front of him, gesturing forcefully and for the benefit of others. He was *important*, but if you didn't know he was on his cell phone, you might have thought he was a lunatic. He saw me, and as he pulled the phone from his ear, I thought I heard the bark of an angry male on the other end of the line — maybe a client, demanding an immediate trade or a wire of bail money. "Joe. *Joe,*" he said, grabbing my shoulder, not touching it but squeezing it for muscle mass, as if I might be the 10 percent solution to all his problems. He smiled, which made me suspect he was trying to get on my good side in case some dormant gene finally kicked in, transforming me into a killer outfield prospect in need of representation.

I introduced Beth, and he put the phone in his pocket and shook her hand with both of his, as if she were royalty — another ludicrous gesture. "Walk with me," he said. "Let's go see your brother."

We went down to the field, where the Cubs were taking batting practice. My parents were there, and Spencer trailed away to take another phone call. CJ was shagging fly balls in the outfield; it was forty-five minutes before game time. Beth pointed him out to me as he jogged in for batting practice. She had never been to a game before, and I was hoping that I wouldn't have to spend the entire time explaining the intricacies. I wasn't sure I was up to it, and I figured someone else in our group would be more than willing.

My mother's arms were crossed, and she was frowning, irritated that we had come to join her. Her hair was flecked with gray, and her face was overwhelmed by ridiculous large black oval sunglasses. "He waved to us already," she said with a sniff, though even her petty sovereignty didn't bother me. I nodded and smiled, enjoying the lukewarm Southern California night air.

I guess it took seeing him in person to convince me; I could no longer deny what he had become. There he was, on the field, my brother, the starting third baseman for the Chicago Cubs. I watched as he loosened up, grabbing his elbow with the opposite hand and pulling his arm across his body, chatting with his friends on the team, covering his mouth with his gloved hand as he whispered to one and tussled with another.

Everything he did was watched and interpreted. He tossed the glove aside, grabbed a bat, and strode toward the cage around home plate. I saw two young boys in the stands nearby, wearing Cubs jerseys with my last name on them. They were holding baseballs and programs and pens.

The game itself felt lazy and timid. The crowd arrived late, in typical Dodger fashion. It was early in the season, there was nothing at stake, and finding any real drama in the evening required too much imagination. I listened to my wife speak about the game with awkward, endearing expertise. "He's got quite a lead?" Beth said, enunciating carefully, her tone ending on a puzzled uptick, uncertain whether the words would sound right when she'd strung them together. My brother had drawn a third-inning walk and was wandering off first base. "He always does that," my mother reassured her, sounding weary and unimpressed. But her face was filled with a wide smile. She couldn't wait to see what he would do next.

I clapped at the appropriate times, but I sat there vacantly. No one asked how I was feeling. My brother was on the field, and we had come to watch him play; it was a field where we had watched games together many times, but this time he was on it. I should have been delighted, or at least proud, but I felt uneasy and disconnected. It didn't seem real. This wasn't someone related to me by blood; it was someone who belonged to everyone. At one point Beth leaned over and grabbed my arm. "This is so exciting," she said, and I agreed; that was one word for it. My stomach hurt. And yet wherever he was, on the field or on the bench, I could not take my eyes off him.

The Cubs lost meekly, four to one. CJ went two for three — a couple of two-out, bases-empty singles, plus a handful of routine defensive chances. The Cubs were scheduled for a night flight to San Francisco, and he had only a few moments for us in the family waiting room beneath the stadium after the game. First my parents and then Beth and Spencer were on him, peppering him with questions, poking his arm or ruffling his hair, fawning over him. I couldn't get close and had no desire to. He knew I was there, though. His eyes met mine from the bottom of the sea, and his mouth opened as if he were about to speak. Then someone called his name. And he was gone.

There was no sophomore slump. He won the National League batting title with a .380 average. He won his first Gold Glove. He was selected as a reserve for the All-Star game. The Cubs were contenders, finishing only five games behind the Cardinals. Late in the season, in front of packed and passionate Chicago crowds, only a weeklong stretch of ineffective starting pitching kept them from their first division title in over ten years.

And then there was the hitting streak. CJ hit in a remarkable fifty-one straight games from late June into early August, only five games shy of the record of Joe DiMaggio, one of baseball's great untouchables. As CJ closed in on DiMaggio's mark, the public fascination grew. There were human interest stories and front-page charts, usually in the form of a white baseball bat, vertical like a thermometer, with the number fifty-six at the top. With each game, as CJ continued to hit, he filled up that bat. At stadiums across the country, video monitors showed his critical plate appearances to rapt, hushed fans. Sometimes he let them off easy, with a leisurely first-inning single slapped to right. But more than once he went hitless into the eighth or ninth, and twice he kept the streak alive with beautiful ninth-inning drag bunts, beating out the throws at first. On one night he even smacked a tenth-inning opposite-field home run, lunging to make contact with a sure ball four, and breathless crowds everywhere erupted in a triumphant roar.

The streak reached thirty, thirty-five, forty. The pressure must have been tremendous, but CJ seemed to relish it. He grinned at the pack of reporters that crowded him, and he chatted endlessly about how much fun he was having. The streak ended abruptly when the Cubs were no-hit by Pedro Martinez (then an Expo), in nine speedy innings filled with scorching fastballs that popped the catcher's glove like gunfire. It was a disappointing conclusion, but no one felt cheated by the ride CJ had taken them on.

By then my brother was a household name. Some whispered that he had deliberately pulled up short, out of respect for the late great DiMaggio and his contribution to the game. People everywhere were talking about CJ — handsome, talented, and still so young. Every year was going to be a career year. He quickly scaled the ladder of corporate-friendly athletes, but Spencer, to his credit, was selective. CJ signed the big two deals — "the S and S" (shoe and soft drink) — but he refrained from hawking car dealerships or sofa beds. He formed a charitable foundation in Chicago, and signed a three-year, $10 million contract. You didn't have to follow baseball to know who he was. He had transcended that. He had entered the American Pantheon — a hero for playing a game and doing what was expected of him. Whether or not athletes deserved a place there hardly mattered. The decision was made and was never second-guessed; the people had spoken.

It was late January. His third full season was about to begin, filled with the bitter, certain promise of additional triumph and spectacle, and I found myself preoccupied by a recurrent daydream. I pondered neither beautiful women nor tropical islands, subjects you might have thought would entertain me in the dead of winter while my newly minted corporate lawyer wife was working sixteen hours a day. Instead, I was stuck on the perfect bookstore.

This bookstore had everything. It was an actual building, and one could browse and visit, but the shelves stretched off toward an unseen vanishing point. I wandered awhile, but finally I was forced to ask someone to help me find what I was looking for. But when I was ushered there, the section turned out to be a single lonely shelf, a modest and disappointing collection of titles, multiple copies tripping and spilling over one another, failing to fill the space. These were the books written by the brothers of world-famous athletes.

I paged through them. There were chapters on how to sign autographs and how to politely answer questions when the interrogator cares nothing about you. (Pick one story, they suggested, and tell it well.) There was a guide for what to do when you're feeling low and are mired in comparisons — certain that your brother has more wealth, or feels more love, or is just plain *better.* The advice? Surrender to it; corral a passing soul and casually mention that your brother *is* your brother, which will inevitably lead to cheap points of sentiment, all color and smile. Maybe you'll even be asked for an autograph, which, as you recall from the earlier chapters, you already know how to sign.

But in the fantasy, my nagging questions remained, and I left the daydream empty-handed. I had denied my brother's talent, then tacitly accepted it, yet now I had a new question, and I woke to it every day. How could I learn to fight that first reaction, the dread that settled on me whenever I thought of my brother or saw him or heard his name?

There was no answer. I could only remember him standing on my rowhouse porch at a crossroads moment, when I was the only one who could claim to know him. The breeze was ruffling around him, and he loved me enough to ask whether I could feel what he was feeling. I should have grabbed his hand, I should have let him show me, because soon I was lost, left with the dark unraveling that was my heart, and I could not believe that that was what he had in mind.

Part Two

3

It was mid-March, and the Cubs were in spring training in Mesa, Arizona. The previous day they had defeated the Cardinals, nine to two. My brother was one for five — his hit was a bases-loaded triple. It was the end of the quiet time, the time when you had to pay close attention to be aware of him, and I tried not to notice what he was up to. Sort of. There was still the side of me that needed to know, demanded confirmation, a masochistic reassurance that he was out there, achieving and producing and playing the role in my life that I had come to expect — the younger sibling as unqualified success.

But life beyond him went on. Traffic was light as I eased my car, a modest import, through the gentle curves of Heritage Parkway. It was just after seven A.M. I made a left off Heritage onto Driftwood Boulevard, heading toward Selvon Dale Arts Magnet, the high school where I taught. Selvon Dale had been built a few years earlier in an abandoned, rehabilitated swamp on the far northern margins of Montgomery County, Maryland. The swamp had been replaced by miles of gentle man-planned slopes and partitioned housing tracts, properly drained and invitingly zoned, but nothing had come of them. There weren't any houses. It was going to be a planned community, but the developer died in a plane crash the year before.

His company now existed solely for litigation purposes, and only the first half of his dream — a magnet school for the arts, dubbed Selvon Dale through an apparently random selection of syllables from his squabbling grown children's first names — had been realized. It was a magnet school that attracted nothing.

I was more than halfway through my third year of teaching, but as my car climbed and crested Driftwood Boulevard, the school still startled me as it appeared on the horizon, looming like some dreaded vision. I was twenty-seven years old, married and grown, parking my car in the assigned space of the high school where I taught and could conceivably teach for the next forty years. I'd received tenure earlier that year — not as big a deal as it sounded. Tenure was granted much more quickly to public school teachers than to college professors, and with less fanfare, probably because the authorities thought that the sooner they gave you a job for life, the less likely you were to abandon them.

A job for life. It relieved me of having to make certain short-term decisions, but it was also beyond my comprehension. The granting of tenure should be a reflection of your ability to teach — and in my case, it was. But at that point you should also know whether you want to teach, and there I was less sure. I knew I was doing good work in the societal sense — not on the level of, say, an inner-city priest or a person who collects petroleum-drenched birds flopped on foamy North Atlantic rocks and scrubs them clean, but good work nonetheless. But was it enough? Did it satisfy me? The pay wasn't great, and there was a sameness to it. Shouldn't I have been starting my own Internet company? I sensed that possibilities were being squandered. The jury was out.

When I'd started teaching, I was a disciplinarian. Maybe because I wasn't much older than some of my students, I felt it necessary to exert my authority early and often. I frowned on jokes or pretended that I didn't understand them, and I handed out detention to students who scrambled to their seats with good intent as the bell was ringing. Furthermore, I wanted to expand the generational distance between my students and me. I had become a teacher because I was young, but I wanted them to think I was old. I didn't want them to know that we watched the same television programs or listened to some (though probably not much) of the same music. I was their teacher, not their big brother or friend, and they were to believe that we had nothing in common.

On that level, I succeeded, perhaps better than necessary. Few students actively disliked me — I knew that because the real haters, at that age, do their hating to your face — but few students adored me. Most of them would not remember me a few months later. They'd offer up their high school yearbooks to new friends in college on brisk fall evenings, and turn the pages, words rushing from their mouths — high school as exhibit, illustrating cruel joke or romantic history — and they'd flip by my picture, white face gray blur, on their way to somewhere else.

Sitting in my parked car on that cool March morning, watching the lights of cars on Driftwood Boulevard floating closer, full of flickering purpose, like fireflies in a suburban dream, I wanted my students to love me. I wanted them to miss me once they'd gone, and I wanted them to come back and visit, even though, after the first great moment of recognition, we'd have nothing to say to each other. I wanted them to recall our time together with lusty satisfaction. I wanted them to break fingernails and risk paper cuts by hurtling toward my photo (page 163) and then stop, sigh, and point to me — my forehead the size of their restless fingertip — and say: *It was, with him, in there, that my life truly began.*

Jane Pendleton was loved. She had a saggy perm and an uneven smile, and she taught ninth- and tenth-grade English eccentrically, often in Elizabethan costume. Max Muranjian was loved. He was an insane mathematics teacher from Turkey, with the look of an impoverished chess champion and a vague misunderstanding of the nature of American secondary education. I wanted what they were getting — the warm sunbeams of student affection.

But I had placed myself in a situation. It was hard to change one's teaching style overnight. I taught a certain way because of who I was. I was a dork who liked facts, the efficiency and order of the natural world. My assignments often had the students working in groups, and students in groups talk too much and get nothing done, so I was strict. And on top of that, the students who had taken the classes during my first two years — those superstern years — warned the others. Columbus is tough, they said. Several might have added that I was also fair, but most of them didn't care about fairness. At that age, they didn't believe that any older person had their best interests in mind, and a reputation for toughness sets like cement. Though you may secretly hope it will make you more appealing, that the students will endure it and thank you for it and uncover the real you that it hid, it only keeps them from reaching for you.

I was looking for love — from my wife or my brother or a bunch of fifteen-year-olds — but no one was paying attention. Anyone who says they don't care if they're loved is lying. Love is a fragile thing that you cup in your hands. It is life's only valid excuse.

"Hey, Joe."

I turned around and saw Nate Tyler standing in the doorway, holding two coffee mugs. Nate was in his fifties, divorced; he taught music theory. (There were two other science teachers and three math teachers at Selvon Dale; not a large number, but enough for us to protect each other from being shivved by sharpened clarinet reeds or doused with pilfered paint thinner and sparked by a match.)

"Hello, Nate," I said. He'd been a professional musician once, with the Albuquerque Philharmonic, and there were faculty rumors (unconfirmed) of an onstage breakdown.

He held out a mug to me. "Regular or unleaded?" he said. It was Nate's kind of joke — stale, sad, hardly funny — yet I found his awkwardness comforting. It reassured me to know that I wasn't the most socially retarded teacher at Selvon Dale; and this mattered, because I was convinced that someday the students would transcend their drug-induced stupor and suburban circular reasoning and would lead an armed insurrection. And when that happened, Nate's ass would be grass far before mine, his burning corpse tossed over the barricade along with the list of demands: weighted grading, a chopper to Cuba, fresh bong water.

In any event, Nate had coffee. "Thanks," I said, accepting the mug and taking a sip. He brewed it in his office, strong and scalding, as if he'd tapped a spring in earth's caffeinated core.

"Hot," I said, placing the mug on my desk.

"But it's cold in here," he said, looking around my classroom, a sort of bipolar non sequitur that left me groping for a response.

As I surveyed my room that morning, I realized that I'd done nothing to claim it as mine. The desks were arranged in standard fashion, seven across and five deep; no oddball bullshit touchy-feely seating as in some of the other classrooms — the chairs facing each other in romantic pairs, or set in a long snaky strand, single file and baffling. And I hadn't put up any displays, earnest and childish "Science in the News" bulletin boards, for instance. It was lavishly furnished with the clutter of science — long black counters and shiny chrome sinks, potentially and thrillingly explosive methane gas jets, Internet ports, incubators, digital triple-beam balances. Its splendor allowed the county officials to deny the charge that an arts magnet school couldn't turn out well-rounded students, but it looked like a showroom. It *was* cold.

"Maybe there's a draft coming from somewhere," I said.

"Maybe . . ." Nate said, staring into his coffee mug, suddenly shy, as if we were discussing which of our students was the best in bed.

Undaunted, I smiled at Nate as we danced around the void at the center of our conversation. When I started teaching, I'd expected to relish the moments behind the curtain — covert, whispered discussions of how to motivate certain students, expedite the incarceration of others. But it hadn't worked out that way.

Nate was not a sports fan. He didn't have *an angle,* as many

57

of the other teachers did, once word leaked out about who my brother was. When he first visited my room in the mornings, with his thermonuclear coffee and staged cheer, I suspected he was taking his time before hitting me up for tickets or bon mots. So eventually I broached the subject, casually working my baseball-playing sibling into the conversation. "*My brother* was in St. Louis last week," I said, responding to Nate's comment about a recent ballooning accident there that had been in the news.

"Not in a balloon, I hope," he said, in another feeble joke. He made no sports connection, and I laughed with relief, though we did get serious for a moment, agreeing that the odds of two ballooning disasters in one American city were pretty slim, unless the ballooning charter company had a history of accidents, in which case it needed to be shut down immediately. My brother was free to balloon over the Midwest at will, and I made a mental note to be sure to let him know. Nate and I had nothing to say to each other; there was no dodging or pretending, and that was why, in my opinion, we had remained friends.

I checked my watch. "I've got to meet Sully for a conference," I said. Sully — Jack Sullivan — was the principal of Selvon Dale and the man who hired me. He was a burly, take-no-shit Irishman with a booming voice and a head of thick white hair.

"Who is it?" Nate asked.

"Exley," I said. I was putting on my blazer, preparing to head out.

"Who?" Nate wandered behind me as I headed out of my classroom. There was noise in the hallway as the early buses arrived, needlessly ratcheting up my anxiety level.

I coasted down the hall, avoided all eye contact, nodded at Betty in the attendance office, and walked past her into the empty parent-teacher conference room. The room was barely furnished: four orange chairs and a Formica table violently askew, as if something unpleasant had recently gone down there. It was the kind of place you'd see on grainy surveillance tape, time code running along the bottom, money and drugs soundlessly exchanged before the good guys bust in and bring the whole thing to a soothing, white-collar closure. I was early and alone, and recalled that Sully wasn't coming. It was going to be just me and the Exleys. I had a few minutes, so I opened my briefcase and perused Brian's student information folder, better known as his "permanent record." (I loved the horrific idea of the permanent record, the adolescent Book of Life.) It wasn't that I needed to look it over, but I wanted to be doing something teacherly when the parents walked in.

Brian Exley had been playing piano since he was three years old. He had won several national competition titles, including first-place jazz solo at something called the Kellogg Piano Winternationals. This sounded to me like an evening of drag racing or the name of a rejected breakfast cereal, but I didn't ask questions.

Of more immediate concern was that he had been suspended two days earlier and would not be returning to Selvon Dale until he and his parents conferred with all his teachers and came to an understanding of what was expected of him. I knew he had been suspended, but that had nothing to do with me — a dispute with a female violinist had turned physical. Sully, a zero-tolerance man in the age of the gun-toting pissed-off adolescent, decided that Brian should meet with everyone, even those uninvolved in the aforementioned inter-instrumental shoving match, since young Exley was failing two classes and barely passing his two others, including mine.

I watched the ghostly figures of students in the hallway as they floated past the frosted conference room door. This was a largely upper-middle-class community, white-collar suburban NPR–listening professionals and their matched sets of children. I'd met many of the parents; most of them tired and slightly aloof, wondering how they'd ended up with a child who tested highly in third grade on an artistic aptitude test, anecdotally gobbled a jar of paste a few years before that, and now sought a place in the global community of potters. Even though I was a science teacher and could offer the more enterprising parents a way out, there was resignation on their faces. *You look like a nice man,* the faces said, *but you are too late.*

Of course there were also the purebred diehards, well rested and generally alarming, who thought an arts high school was a cause for bleeding-heart celebration. These parents often worked at home, beneficiaries of the booming high-tech suburban corridor. They dressed in the casual clothes they suspected people on the West Coast wore, answered the phone on the first ring, and lived vicariously through the ostensible talents of their children, or rained misery by forcing them to cultivate talents that didn't exist. These were the parents who rallied in support of the developer when he'd first proposed the school and who recently suggested that the fuselage from his downed Gulfstream V be mounted in some kind of crispy courtyard memorial sculpture.

The door to the conference room opened; Brian and his father, Ned, walked in. Brian was tall and lanky, a decent-looking kid, with ice-blue eyes and straight black hair, parted like a slash down the middle. He was wearing a dingy white T-shirt and a pair of wide corduroys an indeterminate shade of brown. I said hello, and I think he nodded back, but the gesture was faint, possibly a nod disguised as a twitch. He slouched into a seat, his hands in his pockets and pulling at his crotch.

Ned was around forty, wearing a worn-out blue ski jacket over a white shirt and cheap gray pants. He was a little thick, and he pumped my hand enthusiastically, an enormous grin on his face. "Joe Columbus," he said, his voice unnecessarily awed and breathy. His black hair was a pair of horseshoes over his ears; the top of his head was shiny, desolate.

I turned to Brian. "Your mother couldn't make it?"

He didn't answer. He sniffled, wiped his nose incongruously with the tip of his index finger as he tilted his head at his father — it was more like a coded signal than a lazy attempt at hygiene.

"Brian's mother passed away three years ago," Ned said, his voice oddly chipper.

"I'm sorry to hear that," I said and sat down. I wondered if that was in Brian's student information folder. It should have been. It should have been flagged. It should have said, in large letters, DEAD MOM. Brian and I made eye contact as I descended to his level. His eyes followed me down, and I suddenly wondered whether the two of them had had something to do with it.

"Joe Columbus," Ned said again, taking a seat and joining us at the table. *That's my name,* I thought. *Don't wear it out!* There were times when the immaturity of my students caught up with me, and I had to remember that I was a teacher, not someone running with the pack. Of course, mine was the comeback of a seven-year-old, but three students in the Hip Hop Club, last fall, had recorded a song whose lyrics were nothing more than the technical specifications of the BMW 5 Series, so I could always chalk my reaction up to the regressive, freewheeling artistic environment in which I found myself.

The discussion about Brian was brief and pointless. I explained that he had not turned in several homework assignments, and that his numerous absences had made it difficult for him to finish the labs, because his lab partner — an openly homosexual aspiring librettist — had been reassigned. Ned and I feebly considered strategies for Brian to make up the work. Brian sat there, drumming his fingertips on the table in a prodigy's private rhythm, as we lobbed his future back and forth over his head.

It was decided that he would come in after school to finish the labs. The conversation moved toward its end, and Ned was still smiling. The smile was large, a sweeping grin. He'd been smiling the entire time I was talking, and I knew exactly where we were heading — the foreplay was over. Ned Exley was undoubtedly a fan.

So I stood up, smiling politely, trying to head him off. "Thanks for coming," I said.

He stood too, grabbing my hand in that monster grip. He was bubbling over, positively psychotic. "*The* Joe Columbus?" he asked.

"The one and only," I said, hopeful that at least my identity had been established. He was trying to get me to open up but was handling it ineptly — like a dumb person who's read somewhere about how to pull his own strings.

"You're CJ's brother," he said.

I nodded, smiled again, and put my hands in my pockets. *I know you are, but what am I?* Brian was below us, still seated, staring off at nothing.

"How's he doing?" Ned asked. He moved closer, smelling of cigarettes; I imagined him and his coworkers, all of them trapped poisonously in some small place, fixing things inadequately, causing accidents.

"He has a groin pull," I said.

"Really?" He sounded shocked.

"Yes." This was a lie, but it came to mind at that moment and I decided to go with it.

"Is he going to need surgery?"

"They don't think so," I said. Did anyone ever need surgery for a groin pull? I had no idea. (And who was "they?")

"Well . . . give him my best," Ned said.

"I'll do that," I said. I hadn't talked to my brother in over three months, but I'd be sure, next time we talked, to let him know that Ned Exley was pulling for his groin. Just like that — in some infinitesimal way, I'd damaged my brother's reputation. It was the first lie I had ever told about him, and it pleased me to think of this guy, this *parent,* blabbing to others about my brother's nonexistent medical condition, spreading a rumor of weakness. You don't recognize the slippery slope, I've learned, until you're flat on your ass and flying down it.

"Are you a fan?" I asked.

"Yeah. Not the Cubs, though. Pirates." He said "Pirates" as if that would tell me everything I needed to know about him, but it didn't even tell me whether he was from Pittsburgh. He eyed me, assessing my reaction. He'd beaten up guys like me — recently, I thought.

At the conference room table, Brian was drawing idly in a cheap spiral notebook — sharp short lines, tallying something mysterious, slashes that, I was certain, betrayed deep psychological problems and a hidden instinct for violence. Either that or he was counting the number of times, in the last month, that his father had made an ass of himself.

Ned took the pad from his son, flipped to a clean sheet, and handed it to me. "For an autograph," he said. His voice was full of confidence, like someone making a toast. *To us.*

"Me?" I laughed heartily, absurdly — going so far as to point to myself, an extreme gesture, accentuating the glorious lie that is modesty. Brian continued drawing, now right on the table.

"Sure, go ahead," Ned said, ignoring my weak resistance, poking the tight wire curls of the notebook into my chest.

"I don't think so, Mr. Exley."

"Come on. It'll be fun," he said.

Fun? "I'm . . . it's not worth anything."

"Do it." His smile faded. I heard in his voice the thrum of menace. Brian looked up, catching the ebb in the conversation, perhaps recognizing his father's to-the-woodshed tone. He bent his head again, snorting a little.

So I signed it. I leaned the notebook against the wall, and halfway through my signature the ballpoint pen ran out of ink. I didn't stop, though, because if I'd stopped, put the pad down, and shaken the pen, one of about ten thousand people I didn't want to see would choose that moment to waltz into the conference room.

"There you go," I said, as if Ned was ten and I carried some weight in the world. I handed him the notebook, smiling like a fool. My brother's autograph was valuable — the ink would begin to dry, and it would be the cause of immediate speculation. He created energy in everything he did. I did not.

"That's great," he said. "Thanks. That's really great." He was studying it.

Brian looked up at his father and smiled. At first I thought that he was happy because his father's mood had lifted. Later, I realized that I had given Brian Exley easy access to one of his teacher's signatures, probably not a good thing.

I decided to leave. I entered the hallway, which was choked

with students, and Brian and Ned stayed behind; they had other teachers to see. Sully was standing in the hall.

"How'd it go?" he asked.

"Fine." I didn't mention the autograph or the groin pull or any of the thoughts running through my head and pulling me down. Brian Exley was back on track. And it was the kids who mattered.

There wasn't much traffic down Interstate 270 back toward Bethesda, and I was home by four-thirty.

Our one-bedroom apartment was on the eleventh floor of a sterile high-rise, and we paid an extra hundred and fifty dollars for a superior view of a Hyatt hotel and several low office buildings with tenants of moderate ambition. Bethesda was fine — there were nice houses, and it was a good place to have children and raise them. The downside: it was expensive as hell (we didn't live in one of the nice houses), and many political pundits lived there. So the apartment was temporary lodging; it was suburbia, sort of, since to both of us suburbia meant a house, and we could never afford one in Bethesda. Beth was making good money, and my teacher paycheck took care of cable, saline solution, and the box of baking powder in the freezer. But we were still trying to whittle down Beth's debt from law school; thus the sterile high-rise.

The past few weeks, Beth hadn't been getting home until after eleven. She was a second-year associate at Cannon, Grossmeyer, a large Washington law firm specializing in international trade. To me, the work sounded stupefying, but to Beth there was only a lot of it. She was enduring that portion of her corporate law career that was a not-so-hidden secret. After the firm plied you for a summer with Kennedy Center tickets and cruises on the Potomac, fattening you up and sucking you in, you were stuck pulling all-nighters, wading through endless stacks of documents, highlighting the name "DeCascio" wherever it appeared, or sitting with a bunch of lawyers in a conference room, where you were known more for what you wore than what you said, which was nothing.

There were many nights when I'd fall asleep, television glow bouncing off me in the dark, and she'd come home literally hours later. I was usually up at five in the morning. Sometimes I jetted up to the top floor of our apartment building to ride a complimentary exercise bike, but lately I'd spent time staring out the apartment window, studying the sports section of the *Post*, or loitering on the Internet, occasionally peering at the Hyatt, spiking my heart rate by imagining an attractive woman behind every drawn curtain fucking her brains out.

Things had certainly changed between Beth and me since the dewy college days. Our schedules were so different and our conversations so monosyllabic that sometimes we were more like roommates than husband and wife. Even our time together on weekends was stolen time, because Beth had begun working most Saturdays and many Sundays. I felt sorry for her and told her so; she hated that. She was at a point in her career where she had to prove something. I understood and tried to be encouraging, though I was fairly certain that my encouragement — pat enthusiasms along the lines of "I'm sure it will all work out" — made no difference to her.

On this night, I heard the key click in the lock and the door swing open. I pictured her doing the things that she did: putting away her coat, flipping through the mail, getting a glass of water. At least ten minutes passed before she came to the bedroom, and the idea of pretending to be asleep entered my mind. My head was pressed against the pillow as if I were a sick child, waiting for her to take my temperature. We had already become a couple without much outward display of affection; it required dramatic flair, which we didn't have. We were too busy, too tired, too familiar.

"Hi," she said, stopping just inside the doorway. She was wearing a navy business suit. Beth consistently dressed better than I did, though, unlike a lot of the teachers at my flake-filled academy, I did wear a tie — one without a pattern of treble clefs, no less.

I scooted up in bed, and she sat down in front of me and leaned back. I lifted her hair and rubbed her neck. "Oooh," she said, indulging me, though we both knew I wasn't very good at it. When we were in college, she told me that I had hands "like a guy with . . . what are those called? *Prosthetics.*"

I kissed her just below the gold clasp of her single strand of pearls, peeking out of the shallow fold of her white silk blouse. She stiffened and got up. "Let me change," she said.

She disappeared into the bathroom and returned a few minutes later, in a sexy silky thing I'd bought her last month, with the help of a saleswoman. I believed that when Beth wore it, its sexiness would indicate her desire to have sex. But she'd worn it four times, and we'd had sex only once — not a batting average to be proud of.

"How was your day?" I asked.

"Lagrima," she said, and that word was enough. It was shorthand for *Lagrima* v. *Grossmeyer,* the firm's in-house sexual harassment lawsuit, which was consuming the time of even the firm's junior associates. The dispute had started several months earlier when, depending on whom you believed, a partner ordered a secretary to hold his calls or his balls. Though it was draining the firm of much local business and putting those lowest on the totem pole (including Beth) in peril of unemployment, it was much more titillating than the other litigation Beth labored on: some monumentally dull bickering over South American sugar tariffs, dragged through windowless hearing rooms in the Department of Commerce. Cannon, Grossmeyer represented the South Americans, who, I assumed for stereotypical reasons, both corporate and ethnic, were the bad guys.

"And you? How was your job?" She tilted her head from side to side to remove her earrings. Beth always diminutively referred to my teaching as *a job,* though we discussed her lawyering in terms of her *career.*

"Uneventful," I said, making it so.

"You're lucky."

"I didn't say it was easy."

"But you said 'uneventful.' Uneventful means nothing happened. If nothing happened, how could it be hard?" She said all this casually, as if explaining to me how my mind worked.

"Forget it," I said, rolling over and burying my face in the pillow.

"What?"

"Forget it." And she let it go. We both wanted to fight, but we didn't want to. I said the words with my head muffled and vibrating. I felt a small drop of spit leaking from my mouth and onto the pillowcase.

"I had dinner with Fomacci tonight," Beth said.

"Fomacci," I repeated, enjoying the sound of my voice in the pillow, so unlinked. I sounded like God, but I was nearing suffocation, so I turned over and sat up. After my showing no interest or energy until that point, the gesture made me look more irritated than I meant it to.

"What was that about?" I asked her.

"He wants some help with a book he's writing."

"Fomacci? I thought you don't like him."

"I don't recall saying that." Such a lawyerly answer.

"I'm pretty sure you did," I said, recalling her several elitist rants against his inexplicable success and inferior Midwestern degree. Henry Fomacci was a senior associate at Cannon, Grossmeyer. I'd never met him, though Beth pointed him out to me across the room at last year's Christmas party so that I could match a face to her periodic diatribes. He had squinty, reptilian eyes and perfectly styled blond hair, and he was laughing heartily at a joke that couldn't have possibly been all that funny. I'd been invited to his thirtieth birthday party in the fall, one of those private-room steakhouse affairs, but I had to chaperone the fall production of *Starlight Express* at Selvon Dale that night.

"Anyway, it's not that kind of book," she said.

"It's not what kind of book? The kind where you have to like him to help him?"

"I don't recall ever saying I didn't like him, Joe." She took a sip of water, whipped her head back to swallow an Advil. "Henry is writing a bestseller."

"Really. I didn't know you just set out to write one of those things."

"Well, you do, apparently. Henry knows a lot about 'those

things.' " Beth had recently begun throwing my words back at me, making them sound small. Maybe this was a legal trick; I wasn't sure.

"What's it about?"

"It's top secret." Top secret? *Please.* "He needs my help with the protagonist."

"A young female lawyer?"

"Mmm-hmm." She removed her gold wristwatch and put it on the low wooden end table, where it rested beneath a massive, inelegant clock-radio with green numbers that glowed toxically, visible from outer space.

I leaned back on my elbow. "He's basing the character on you?"

"Partially. The character is a composite."

"A composite of who?" She didn't answer. "So it's really just you, then."

"Something like that." She climbed into bed next to me, her voice betraying an unspecified regret. This was the kind of thing a happy couple loved to share, in my fantasy of what a happy couple did in their private time. But I could see that my wife wished she hadn't told me.

"That's exciting, honey," I said. It *was* exciting, in its colossal potential for embarrassment and failure. But what it really sounded like was a pathetic ploy that a dumb corporate lawyer, on short notice and with no imagination, would use to get laid. *The plot's top secret,* he would have whispered, *and I need your help.*

But what did I know. I lay down and stared up at the ceiling, feeling her heel brushing my leg and then pulling away. I wondered how it had all come to this so quickly — every exchange between us based on perverse, gleeful hostility, who could say "fuck you" the loudest without uttering the magic words.

Beth adjusted under the covers and pulled the latest issue of *Mirabella* from the nightstand, a proclamation of inaccessibility. It looked as if Joe wouldn't be getting any "color" tonight — a catchword I'd picked up from one of my students. The negligee-equals-sex batting average sank to one for five; poor Joe was in a slump.

"I signed an autograph today," I said.

"Really." She flipped the pages of the magazine, her brow furrowed studiously, as if skimming articles about spring hemlines qualified as superior breeding and behavior. "How did that happen?"

"A man asked me, and I did it."

"Did you know that man?"

"He's a parent."

"You signed something?" She lowered the magazine and peered at me, her voice jumping an octave, as if she'd suddenly realized the gravity of my murderous mistake, an error that somehow placed our entire future in jeopardy.

"Just a piece of paper, Beth."

"*White* paper?"

"Yes."

She considered this for a moment, then dipped back into her magazine.

"Is there something wrong?" I asked. I was confident I had done nothing wrong. I was pretty confident.

"What do you mean?"

"I mean legally. Like you're going to tell me I broke a law, like I'm not supposed to sign things or something?"

She gave a dismissive snort. "You are so paranoid."

"No, I'm not."

She closed the magazine and pulled it away from her face, sliding her body down at the same time. Her eyes were already closed.

"I'm not paranoid, Beth."

She was pretending to be asleep. She'd let me have the last word, but did it really count as a victory when the last word was a feeble, uncontested denial of mental instability?

Her breath was slow and steady, a warm whisper. There was a thin smile on her lips. I wanted more, but I was alone. I wasn't paranoid. My wife had gone somewhere else. She was amused there.

Three hours passed, and I hadn't slept. The apartment building was new and silent. Beth was curled inward, her back to me; I bathed in time's green glow and stared at the ceiling, floored by revelation. Earth was wobbling on its axis, a bauble slipping from God's clumsy fingertips, about to shatter into millions of pieces.

This nonsense sounded dopey even inside the encouraging, humid confines of my own head. I was drawn to the apocalyptic grand gesture, which was probably why I got along at all with my teenage students; for many of them, it was their only form of elegance. But even if it was bullshit, it had come to me so clearly that I had to obsess. Bad things were coming. Lock yourself in.

I got out of bed. In the kitchen was an ancient, sticky bottle of Chivas. I poured what remained into a small crystal tumbler. We were supposed to have eight of those glasses — part of the all-inclusive wedding registration list — but we'd received only six, and I broke one, so we were down to an uneven five. I poured myself more than I could drink, so that when I was unable to finish, I would feel I had defeated the genetic lure of alcoholism, even though I didn't know of any alcoholics in my family.

I took a sip, rolled it around in my mouth, felt it burn, go numb, disappear. I walked out into the sunroom. The spring rain had returned, and I liked to watch it fall in silk threads beneath the streetlights. I couldn't hear it or see it hit the ground. It was action without consequence.

Where was the love? My life had a rhythm and routine, an illusion of movement, and I didn't understand it. I lied to everyone. I told jokes only to amuse myself. I was distant and lacked intensity. I felt strongly about nothing. I dreamed about what it would be like to have no limitations, but I heard my mind denying me, wrapping me tight and holding me back.

I thought of CJ at times like these. When things were going badly, he came to me without calling. I would see him in a week or so at our parents' house in California. It was a good thing, because we had not spoken recently. Our schedules were very different, and we were difficult to reach.

4

I t was spring break, and I was relaxed. I spent the first five days lounging about the apartment, lazily thumbing through my students' lab notebooks, reacquainting myself with their bland spelling mistakes, basic mathematical errors, and dubious conclusions of scientific fact; several of my students had apparently spent more time decorating the lab notebooks with stickers and drawings than on the labs themselves. One afternoon I went downtown and wandered knowingly through a modern art museum, until the crowds of tourist families, in their matching sweatshirts and cheap sunglasses, made me fidgety. Another day I went to a movie matinee, a violent action sequel released just in time for Easter. I was unshaven and wearing a baseball cap pulled low, reveling in my posture of truancy, pretending to be a film critic. I barely remembered the original movie — something involving madmen, a detonator, and day-saving catch phrases — but it didn't matter. Relevant relationships and grudges came back to me, and there were music cues and swooping close-ups to indicate the reappearance of beloved minor characters from the original film: *Oh, yeah, he was That Black Guy.* On a couple of other days, I took naps.

And by the end of the week we were on a United 757, on our way to Los Angeles. It was Holy Thursday, the night of

Christ's Last Supper, and I stared out my scratchy plastic passenger window, wondering whether he — Jesus, I mean — had the chicken mesquite or the vegetarian lasagna. Would Beth enjoy this joke? I decided it wasn't worth waking her. Lawyers don't have spring break, and Beth barely got away with me that weekend. She had been working feverishly on *The People v. Nefarious Sugar Cartel,* and the litigation showed no sign of ending. (*Lagrima,* on the other hand, had moved toward settlement.) She had also been spending two evenings a week with Henry Fomacci, working with him on his bestseller. They brainstormed top secret "plot twists" and honed "character arcs," fictional jargon I didn't understand or, once it was explained, recognize as part of real life.

"It's a good break for me," she'd said about the book, which I tried not to take as the smack that it was. And even though Beth knew that the firm closed at noon on Good Friday, it took an Even Better Tuesday and an Extremely Kick-Ass Wednesday for her to be certain that she'd be free to come along. (The firm would have reimbursed us for her ticket if she hadn't been able to make it.) Her life had become a series of obligations, myself included, and it was unclear whether she was enjoying any of them, other than the time she spent contributing to a crappy novel written by a man who was, until recently, a reviled colleague.

I placed my hand over hers as she slept, and I could feel her clenching the armrest. She had been pale and tired the past few weeks, as if the Cannon, Grossmeyer partners were draining the blood right out of her, but she refused to listen to my suggestions that she slow down, and when I almost pleaded — a good husbandly move, I thought — she got angry. We still weren't getting along. We needed some time and space; a vacation was what we really needed — she more than me, though we needed it together — and this wasn't going to be one. It was more of a fact-finding mission, as if Beth was coming along to study me in my original habitat. I didn't like the sound of that.

* * *

My father picked us up at the airport and whisked us home; it was almost eleven when we got there, but the house was lit up, inside and out, like a construction site. My mother was waiting with a lavish meal: roast chicken and baby potatoes, cinnamon apples, buttery popover rolls. I ate little, having eaten on the plane, and she looked hurt. "I understand," she said, and I immediately felt horrible and served myself a huge plate of food. After I finished, I wiped my oily hands on a paper towel and tossed it in the trash, and there I saw plastic bags folded in on themselves, clearly labeled with the name of a local "home-style" restaurant. My mother had successfully induced guilt with take-out.

My father did not join us for this pseudo-meal; he deposited us in the kitchen and went to sleep. He was only fifty-six, but I found myself concerned about his health — sleeping all the time was the sign of *something*. However, I had no idea how to broach the subject with him, and I dealt with having no idea by deciding that even though he was my parent and I couldn't imagine losing him, it was none of my business.

So it was only my mother sitting with us; she had served weak, presumably homemade cups of coffee, and Beth was telling her about Fomacci's book, which now had a working, hilariously nonfunctional title: *Unnecessary, Absolutely Unnecessary, Justice*. It made no sense on countless levels! My eyeballs rolled back and took a voyage round my skull as Beth riffed enthusiastically on "the hopes and dreams of the characters," which, depending on what character she was talking about, involved bearing children, finding a stolen zip drive, or, in a botched and possibly metaphoric nod to yesterday's headlines, liberating a Serbian mink farm.

I stood up, unable to decide which bothered me most — the stupidity of the project, Beth's passion in describing it, or my mother's wide-eyed interest. I shuffled from the kitchen table and wandered toward the living room — and stopped short in the doorway.

Since our brief visit at Christmas, the room had been redone. Actually, it had been *replaced* — the old off-white couch and worn-out matching chair, the nicked rectangular coffee table, the bookcases, the armoire, the framed black-and-white quartet of Arizona landscape photographs — everything was gone, hocked, chopped into pieces and hurled into a pagan bonfire, for all I knew. Now there was an enormous black leather couch and chair, both bulging and expensive. There was also track lighting, which isolated and created mood, and a sleek wall unit crafted from a rich dark wood that was walnut or mahogany; I didn't have much experience with the finer grains. And inside the wall unit was a television that must have been thirty-five inches diagonally, the biggest and heaviest thing I'd ever seen in a home. It looked like a safe with a glass window, and it dominated the room — a great gray-and-black monolith that was a little scary, in the way that certain sports cars look like predators when their headlights are on.

There was a matching coffee table, completely bare except for a geeky, thumbed copy of *Satellite Programming Monthly* and one enormous remote control, with buttons and levers and, near the bottom, a large threatening dial. This was not a living room I recognized; it belonged in a showroom or on the page of a catalogue. It was a room that you *won,* behind Door Number Three or in the Showcase Showdown. It was a room where you parted the black (black!) curtains, and you weren't in South Pasadena — you were fifty stories up in an urban penthouse, and down below were the cut-glass lights of the city you owned.

"Mom!" I yelled, sounding seven years old. I sat down on the new couch and it did not give; it was flat and noncommittal, like something waiting to be ordered to comfort me.

Beth and my mother arrived in a few moments. They were still chatting about the novel; I heard my mother say, "So *that's* why she travels to Istanbul," and then they were standing in the doorway.

"What happened?" I asked.

"What do you mean?" I noticed that my mother and Beth wore the same irritated expression. Somehow, after we married, Beth and my mother developed an intimate and secretive relationship, an unexpected collusion that I noticed too late to stop. The result of this girlish conspiracy was that my own mother treated me like a son-in-law.

"I mean *this*," I said, sweeping my arm out to encompass the room. She knew what I meant, and I pretty much knew what had happened, but *somebody* had to talk about it.

"We decided we wanted something different," she said, reaching toward the wall and dimming a track light.

"Well, it certainly is different," I said, "and it must have cost a fortune."

"I don't know how much it cost," my mother said. "Your brother paid for it."

"Oh," I said. Beth smiled at me. *You walked right into that one.*

My mother grabbed the remote control with both hands. "Watch this." She pointed it at the wall unit and pressed a button, jerking the whole remote in the process. A cabinet door slid away and revealed several components of a stereo.

"Cool," I said.

Again I couldn't sleep, though I should have been able to. It was after three in the morning, Los Angeles time, which was six A.M. back east. The next day I would be sluggish, grumpy, possibly incoherent. Beth was unconscious next to me, slithered face-down in the guest bed, her right arm raised straight over her head, as if she were in the final frozen pose of a dancer who had just completed a difficult routine. I'd tried to cuddle with her the night before, turned on by being back in my boyhood room with a real girl, but she was stubbornly asleep before I could manage to persuade her. Each night Beth found new bodily contortions that allowed her to rest but filled me with pain, preventing me from getting close enough to touch her. Sometimes I found myself grabbing her hand (as I'd done on the plane) or running my fingertips through her hair as she worked at home or slept — work and sleep both being acts that required her to concentrate — and that way I didn't have to feel the quick sting of shame as, in the guise of movement or gesture, she pulled away from me.

We were in the guest bed in the bedroom that was CJ's, after we each got our own, and was now known as the "guest bed-room," so named by my parents in their reasserted dominion over the home that now existed solely for them, since the mortgage and children were finally gone. My bedroom appeared to have vanished, too; my father, in anticipation of his retirement from Cal Tech, said he planned to do part-time seismic consulting work and was in the process of remodeling it, retrofitting it, and turning the room into an office. What remained of my belongings — stacks of record albums and board games, two framed science fair awards, an intimidating though scallop-heavy seashell collection — had been boxed and stored in the basement, and that final act swept me away and eliminated me from my own family.

I wondered where CJ would sleep when he arrived on Saturday night. Maybe on his fucking leather couch, a sheet tucked on top of it so that the poor baby didn't wake up all sweaty. "Maybe it's time for you to redo the living room," he might have said. Or "Mom, Dad, I'd like to give you a gift that costs thousands of dollars and simultaneously allows you to fulfill all your masturbatory fantasies by watching me play baseball on a giant television." Probably he went with the first option, the latter remaining a mere subtext.

I got up. I had to piss and then I had an urge to wander, and, unlike in our apartment, I had some space to do it. I wanted to see my old bedroom one more time, so I walked into the kitchen to head outside to the garage. I felt the cool tile whispering under my bare feet, a spiky crumb of pretzel salt or honey graham digging in my heel. I stopped at the door leading to the garage, noting next to it an alarm panel, chest-high, with a touch pad and a blinking red light. Had our neighborhood turned sour, or was this the price of peripheral fame? The alarm was new, and I didn't know the code. I fingered the doorknob, brassy gold and a little wobbly, but I could go no farther.

I slept until eleven, exactly eleven. This filled me with foolish pride, oversleeping to the top of the hour; I had the biological alarm clock of a sloth. Beth was already up and gone, though she had thoughtfully opened the curtains so that the California sunlight blinded me. I felt sour and congested, wishing I had slept longer, slept forever, or at least until it was time to go home. My brother would be here in less than thirty-six hours for his twenty-four-hour visit.

I walked downstairs, and my family seemed slightly glad to see me. "I'm on vacation!" I said, a bit too stridently, noting their looks of disapproval at the late hour of my appearance. I grabbed a quick bowl of cereal as my mother and Beth began chopping vegetables, preparing to cook large quantities of food for the party my parents were throwing on Sunday afternoon. It flashed through my mind that I'd never seen Beth chop anything; the only vegetables we ate were in those bags of ready-made salad. It pleased me, in a chauvinistic way, to see her cooking. At the same time, her ease in handling a knife made me a little nervous.

I took a cup of coffee and retreated to the back porch, lugging a recently published book about early American explorers *(I'm on vacation!)*, its narrative and fanfare loosely tied to a public television epic broadcast the previous fall — or so said the circular red sticker on the book's sepia-photograph cover, a sticker that bore tiny marks of struggle at two points where I tried to remove it. Beth also liked to read but no longer had time for it; the last book I bought her — a spoon-fed melodrama about two sisters in Ireland — went directly onto the shelf, spine uncracked. Thus, one more item had been erased from the once-burgeoning blackboard of things we had in common; our marriage was like a restaurant running out of specials.

The weather was perfect, so I sat on the porch, read, and dozed off; the coffee mug cooled. By afternoon my mother and Beth had cooked all the food — marinated mushrooms bobbing in oil, slender strips of sesame chicken, moist trays of brownies lofted like the puffy tops of clouds. The refrigerator was filled with trays covered with foil and crammed with Tupperware containers of different shapes. To celebrate their cooking all this food, we went out to dinner.

We arrived at the restaurant in Old Town Pasadena around

five. Pasadena was technically a town in its own right, not really in Los Angeles but close enough to fall within its effete sphere of influence. To be honest, I was never sure where Los Angeles began or ended. It was more a state of mind — this statement being the kind of bland, meaningless sentimentality that, when stated sincerely, instantly branded one as a Southern Californian. When I was growing up, the Olympics were held here, but that was long ago, the peak of the city's shameless glory and glamour. In the nineties — the decade I spent largely away from it, thank you very much — the city had crumbled and burned, but in typically perfect, tragic Los Angeles fashion. The fires had gone out, and the smog had begun to clear, but the city, to those who lived there and knew it well, still felt heavy and medicated. Yet there were always days when you could wend your way through, hit every traffic light (crucial to happiness), wear your sunglasses, and convince yourself that nothing bad could ever happen here.

The meal was adequate, of the risotto-cilantro-pesto variety, and the conversation, for some reason, settled on the immigration problem. Was it still a problem? To me, it had eased into a cliché. In any event, it was common ground and equally boring to all of us. It bled, however, into an inflamed discussion of affirmative action, with Beth coming out (surprisingly) against it. I waited for her to say something sufficiently racist for me to pounce and act repulsed, but it was all couched in positive rationalization: it's disabling and demeaning, it doesn't help them, etc. I suppose I could have jumped on her use of "them" to describe oppressed minorities, showing that, even though I'd remained silent, I knew what the *real* issues were, but I didn't have the energy for it. My mother claimed she was undecided, and then allowed Beth to convince her, and allowed Beth to think she had convinced her. I looked over at my father, who had made lengthy tunnels out of his uneaten ziti and was trying to roll a fava bean through them. Once an engineer, always an engineer; at least he had smartly ordered a meal he could play with.

As I was leaving the restaurant by myself, I saw a black man, about my age, approach the door. I pulled it open to let him in.

The man was handsome, with a shaved head and goatee, and a black sports jacket over a black shirt. He nodded, smiled at me, and walked by.

I'd seen him before. I searched for a match in the photo database of my mind. Had he been in my honors English class at South Pasadena, a bunkmate at Camp Jericho, a black frat brother at Georgetown? I'd been in too many places to remember everyone, but it dawned on me at that moment that I didn't really have any friends. And I also realized, still unable to place him, that a friend would be a good thing to have. It would be nice to have someone to talk to, about my family or my wife, who wasn't either my family or my wife. This mythical friend's allegiance would be first and foremost to me. He or she (more likely he) would bring me a beer, clap me on the back, and nod while I ranted; then he'd tell me that everything I said was absolutely right.

Maybe it wasn't a friend I wanted; maybe more of a yes man. I regretted having abandoned my college friends; I'd left phone calls unreturned, and naturally the calls stopped. Farewells in front of sedans bulging with belongings had become absolute sendoffs, and that's what my college friends became: friends of a certain era, a time I'd left behind. My friendlessness indicated that I was a man who needed no one but his wife. I was romantically myopic and starting to pay for it.

The sun had set, and I stepped out onto the curb of Colorado Avenue and into the orange twilight. As I waited for my mother and Beth to emerge from the restroom, I watched my father, near the cashier's desk, scraping mints up the side of a bowl into his waiting hand. I turned away and saw a fat man, a few feet from me, take a drag of a cigarette and put it out at the base of a broken parking meter, one with a folded piece of yellow legal paper taped to its top. At that sad, blank moment of revelation, I remembered the black man; I knew how I knew him. He was That Black Guy from the movie, the action sequel I'd just seen; he turned out to be a friend of the madman, and no friend of mine at all.

*   *   *

Saturday was my day to suckle up to the monster television. Once I figured out how to use the remote, I watched auto racing, horse racing, the first half of a college basketball game, and twenty minutes of a documentary about sharks, with a cast of jittery, sexless divers descending to meet their prey in suspiciously dented metal cages. There was also a Cubs preseason game, their last before opening day on Tuesday, but CJ was not playing in it. Nevertheless, my mother wandered in periodically, asking me to put it on.

"He's not playing, Mom," I said.

"But they're his team." She made it sound like our solemn obligation, like always rooting for the American athlete during the Olympics, even if you knew he took drugs or was an asshole. She would watch a pitch or two, excessively using the players' first names while doing so. "Good eye . . . *Julio!*" or "What kind of pitch was that . . . *Terry?*" Then something bad would happen, and she'd storm out, disgusted. They lost 7–1, and she was like the team's naggy mother hen, impossible to satisfy. "Where are you going . . . *Mom?*" I asked, but she ignored me.

By Saturday evening, when the Lakers basketball game began, I'd been watching television for close to seven consecutive hours. My father joined me — Beth and my mother went to the airport to pick up CJ — and we watched the Lakers playing the apparently streaking and rejuvenated Phoenix Suns. Basketball was the game my father loved; he'd played small forward in high school and was on the team of his fraternity at MIT, a source of sweltering embarrassment when I was younger, during that endless period of childhood when it wasn't cool to be smart. My friends were all savvy enough to know that my father's athletic prowess — Hoop King of Nerdland, they called him — was where I was vulnerable. He was still playing competitively when my brother and I were small, in a local adult league over at Pasadena City College. But in one late-night game, he drove to the basket, soared, felt the contact, and fell to the floor in a heap. He'd torn his Achilles' tendon, and he had to hobble on crutches for six weeks, with my mother driving him to work every morning and picking him up each night. Ironically, my father's injury, genuine and debilitating, made him seem more of an athlete to us than when he was playing.

The Lakers were an expensive and generally difficult ticket, even by Los Angeles standards, so my father watched most of their games at home, leaning forward with the body language and running commentary of a former player. "Screen and roll," he'd mutter, unconsciously flattening his hands in front of him. And then, as if he'd called the play himself — clenched right fist, swiveled left index finger and pinkie — it would materialize in front of us. I found out that he was connected to a bizarre network of Lakers aficionados on the Internet, a mailing list of fanatics churning out hundreds of messages a day: lengthy, heated discussions of potential trades or of the advantage of moving back the three-point line a few inches. That's the sort of communication the Internet was designed for, I suppose, but I was fairly certain that the millions of manpower hours squandered on this type of arcana were being wasted on millions of subjects across the globe, and would eventually destroy our civilization.

Basketball, though it lacked the quintessential stature of baseball, was the coolest sport — urban playground culture becoming American culture. In my classes at Selvon Dale, most of the athletically clad students wore puffy NBA Starter jackets and ProLine sweatshirts, and, on their feet, the expensive, complicated sneakers named for their fleeting hardwood heroes. The fact that I was from Los Angeles impressed these students.

At half-time the Lakers were down by twelve, and with the television momentarily muted, I heard my mother's car. My father got up and I followed; we were like a pair of dogs who'd been trapped in the house all day, the change in our pockets jingling like collars, our ears perked by the sound of our returning master. My father went to CJ, Beth, and my mother through the kitchen, but I stayed at the door and watched them walk up the driveway.

They were laughing about something, another joke I wasn't in on, an amusement that would be fleeting and dead by the time I asked about it a moment or two later. Beth turned sharply toward my brother, then walked on. She was an only child, and at that moment I wished she had a sister who was in the United States Senate or was a chess grand master or had scored the winning goal in Women's World Cup Soccer — a superstar sibling I could befriend with ease while Beth fretted and stewed.

I stood at the open door, and Beth and my mother moved past me into the house, followed by my father, leaving CJ and me.

"Hey, man," I said, extending a hand.

He focused on me and wrapped me in a hug. "I have something for you," he said, and before I could even wonder, he placed a bag of airline peanuts in my hand.

"Wow," I said, feeling like a fool for that split second when my hopes were up. "Will you sign them?"

"It'll cost you," he said, and we both laughed. He bent his knees slightly and bounded away, leaving me.

There were lights on in the kitchen, the sound of running water, my mother's voice. Left alone, I looked out across the street. There was a new family with young children in the house where the Dvoraks used to live — two boys around five, maybe twins. They stood motionless, watching me from their driveway, leaning on wobbly banana-seat bikes. I wondered if their parents had told the boys who'd grown up in my house; maybe the parents had been alerted by the real estate agent who, knowing that if the name CJ Columbus had meaning, then it also had value, and the realtor could use this tiny windfall of trickle-down celebrity to jack up the price.

"Catch!" I yelled to the boys, stepping into the driveway and tossing the bag of peanuts toward them. But it landed way short, in the middle of the street — too much air under it, too much arc. The boys whispered to each other, and the bigger one let his bike crash to the ground and went inside. The other one looked at the bag and then at me, clenching his handlebars. He knew he wasn't supposed to leave the yard when it got dark. If his parents were watching and saw him venture off the curb, there would be trouble.

He turned his bike around toward his house. I was disappointed that he wasn't a risk taker, a boy who'd grow up to tempt fate. Or maybe he knew better than to run into the street for a bag of peanuts thrown to him by a stranger. Blessedly, some decisions don't require any more thought or explanation than that.

My father cooked swordfish steaks on the backyard gas grill for a late dinner. Beth and my mother were once again in the kitchen, and I was in the guest room, packing our suitcases, when CJ came in, lugging his duffel bag. At some point it was decided that Beth and I would go to a hotel that night and let CJ take over the guest room, which used to be his room and now belonged to whoever was the latest visitor.

"What the hell happened in here?" he said. *You should see the living room,* I thought, as CJ threw his Nike bag on the bed. During the first quarter of the Lakers game, my father and I had seen CJ's most recent Nike ad, a single slow-motion soft-focus shot of him rounding the bases, with no dialogue or music. ("I don't know what that *means,*" my father had said.) Everything about him was Nike: shirt, sweat pants, baseball cap, sneakers. He was one giant swoosh. "Where's all my stuff?" he asked.

"In the basement with mine, I guess," I said. CJ walked over to the window.

"Do you want to go down and look for it?" I asked. I was suddenly caught up in the sentimental notion of us nursing American beers, rummaging through our belongings, laughing about things that were once painful and unfunny. *Oh, look, CJ, the bat you broke my leg with!*

"Nah," he said. So much for that. I was snapped back to reality. We weren't brothers with secret handshakes and running jokes; we were close when not together only because my obsessive mind brought us there. But cramped in the room we'd shared, for once physically near each other, we had amiably little in common.

"Why didn't you play today?" I asked.

There were ten seconds of silence. "I don't know," he finally said, laughing and sounding genuinely puzzled.

"Is everything all right?" Ned Exley and the groin-pull hoax flitted through my mind.

"Everything's great." He sat on the edge of the bed, queen-size and too big for the room, leaned back, and closed his eyes. He was always able to fall asleep anywhere and at any time, and I wondered whether that meant he was a master of self-control, taking advantage of every one of life's moments, or whether he needed lots of rest to live up to being himself. Maybe both. "This afternoon I sat back, enjoyed the sunshine, the beautiful women in the stands . . ."

"Beautiful women?" I asked foolishly, as if surprised to find that they existed in Arizona.

"They're everywhere, bro," he said, stretching his arms over his head, his voice warped by a yawn. "And I intend to serenade them all."

I laughed, as if I knew what he was talking about. *Serenade?* Was that some sort of slang? I knew slang; I taught high school. "Guess I'm a little out of the loop, is all," I said.

"Oh, you're doing fine." He stared at the ceiling, then shut his eyes again.

"You mean with Beth?"

"No," he said. "I mean with *you.*"

Suddenly he sat up and began rummaging through the narrow end pocket of his duffel. "Look what I got for Mom." He pulled out a dark blue, rectangular case and flipped it open. Inside was an exquisite black pearl necklace.

"Holy shit, CJ. How much did that thing cost?"

"A lot." He snapped the case shut. "Let's go give it to her." He hurried out, and I followed, feeling young again and not wanting to miss the spectacle. It was like Mother's Day at the crack of dawn, and we were hurrying to Mommy's side with homemade cards to curry favor — though this time, I'd forgotten to make one, and my brother's had cost a few thousand dollars. But other than that it was exactly the same.

Where did CJ and I stand? He'd been home for fifteen minutes, and I was already feeling like shit, though it was hard to be jealous of someone who found such boyish, uncomplicated joy in giving. It was hard to envy someone right in front of you who was being indisputably nice to you. The animosity would come later, when I was alone and he couldn't fight back, and I'd been handed enough time to twist everything up in my unreliable mind.

As CJ called my father inside and pulled my mother by the shoulders, away from the kitchen counter, I found myself on the periphery, wandering toward Beth, who looked as if she had no idea why I was there. She was caught up in the moment; like everyone else, she enjoyed herself when good things happened. My brother gave my mother the necklace, and its blackness reminded me of the dark face of the monster television. That was a gift to my father, which meant they'd both received something from CJ, and the next gift would belong to me.

If you don't count the peanuts.

It was only in the past six months or so, since the hitting streak, that my brother achieved a tangible, inescapable level of celebrity — meaning that his name was known outside baseball land, familiar to the general sports fan and beyond, to those who were merely adept at picking up new faces as they skipped across the Zeitgeist. It was hard to pinpoint the moment when he moved from athlete to cultural figure. Was it the self-deprecating ease of his recent appearance on Letterman? The McDonald's commercial with Vince Carter that premiered during the Super Bowl? The lazy denials of a May-December romance with Cher? ("They're just friends," Cher's publicist was quoted as saying, and I wondered how even *that* had happened.)

My brother was not Jesus (though he did have a teammate named Jesus Alvino), but the reception he received at St. Mary's was certainly worthy of him. Everyone swarmed around him on the steps.

"Wow," said my father as the crowd parted and we entered the church. He was saying what we all were thinking — this was *church*, for Christ's sake, and if it was like this in a sanctuary, how crazy must it be out in the real world. We'd been saved a seat in the front pew, as if this were CJ's first communion. Later, he was asked to sign copies of the parish bulletin, and he was careful not to smudge his autographs with fingers still moist from the basin of holy water. And there was Father McNamara's sermon, some piffle about God batting from both sides of the plate at once, then playing center field and taking a home run away from Sin, who apparently played for the Mets. My brother kept a straight face the whole time. I assumed he was reflecting, as I was, on the times he and I had skipped church and the day we got caught hurling rocks at the manger scene out front — toppling the three opaque, electrically lit Wise Men as if it were a midway game.

After church we piled into my father's Audi before the mob of the surging devout could tip it over. At home, Beth, the professed and undisputed agnostic, was waiting for us.

"How was it?" she asked, gamely.

"We won," I replied.

The luncheon with twenty of my parents' closest friends was to begin in less than an hour. After the St. Mary's mania, I considered my attendance optional. I wondered whether CJ would sign autographs in our backyard; maybe my parents would set up a card table. I wondered whether he ever went a whole day without signing anything or posing for a photo with that million-dollar grin.

By five minutes after one, nearly everyone had arrived. I knew most of them; they'd all been friends with my parents for my entire life. They'd been at our wedding, and Beth and I had been invited to their children's weddings. A few were friends from the legal community — two judges (one retired) and a couple of lawyers from the district attorney's office, where my mother used to work. (Four years ago she had become a judge in, of all things, Family Court.) There were also a couple of my father's Cal Tech colleagues with their wives. And the remainder were from the neighborhood: the Silvers, the Houstons, the Hales, all pleasant-sounding clan names, written on welcome mats and mailbox posts. Their children, raised in stable, liberal comfort, had grown up and gone on. These were friends I couldn't conceive of Beth and me having; you needed children and roots; you needed stability and time. You couldn't feel that you were floating.

Pat and Mel Silver tapped on the glass of the kitchen door; my mother let them in. I hadn't seen them since my wedding, almost three years ago. Mel was a youthful and blunt man with curly black hair, the principal of a progressive Westside private school. I'd come in from the backyard to get a few more six packs of beer; Mel asked for one and followed me outside, where the cold ones were buried in the coolers my father had arranged at the foot of the picnic table.

You'd have thought that Mel — Mr. Silver, as I still called him — would have had a lot to talk about with me. I handed him a beer, smiling, expecting a few questions about how school was going, perhaps a primer on the latest avant-garde West Coast educational techniques. But all he said was "Thanks, champ," and he was gone.

"Mr. Van Horn," I said, noticing Jack Van Horn arriving with his wife, Sherry. He shook my hand with a crushing grip, but his eyes, barely visible through his sunglasses, were shamelessly looking beyond me. He worked with my father and had a son my age who was getting a Ph.D. in molecular biology at Stanford. Hey, I knew a little something about science! "Where's the man?" he asked, as he spotted "the man" in the backyard, arms crossed, nodding and smiling as he listened to Phil Houston. Mr. Van Horn brushed past me and headed toward them. Apparently I was *a* man, not *the* man.

So I was left alone, with all sorts of space and time to fill, first loitering near the women, then fleeing from them. I did what I shouldn't have done: I drank. I drank not out of any determined sense of melancholy; quite simply, I drank because there was nothing else to do. It was a warm and sunny afternoon, and I was thirsty. After I drained the first Corona, I had another. After the third, I switched brands, going domestic for beers four and five, tired of cramming the lime wedge into the Corona bottle. From there, it was easy to switch again, from beer to the harder stuff. And then, then! As I started to feel it! A large tumbler of gin and tonic, a preposterously bad addition to what was sloshing around inside me, yet such an economical way to use up those soggy lime wedges that I had cut before.

It hit me all at once. First a tickle, next a severe tug. There was a beer in my hand, but I didn't remember putting it there; it was like the bloody murder weapon from a blacked-out crime. Beth and I usually didn't drink much, and when we did we drank socially — a glass of cheap wine at dinner, chosen by price, not expertise. We certainly didn't drink with the carefree determination of the pickled collegiates we once were, drinking just to get drunk.

But that's exactly what I was doing in my parents' backyard, and, not surprisingly, I felt my mood descend, and the world began to form a series of grim absolutes. No one wanted to talk to me. My parents' friends never liked me. If I left, no one would notice.

And, of course, there was him. Him. Look at him. *Look at him.* Sitting in that lawn chair. He played a game for a living. He hit a ball with a bat and caught a ball with a glove. And he was paid an absurd amount of money to do it. He could get laid five hundred times a day and probably did, yet everybody thought he was so goddamn wholesome. No matter how hard he said he worked, I knew he was lying. He didn't work hard. And it wasn't *work.* It was ridiculous and unfair, and he was too stupid to understand it.

And for the first time, in that reeling state, I recognized the liberating truth. I did not want the things he had. I did not want to be great at baseball. I was not jealous of his life. I was a simpler man than that, more hateful and punitive. What I really wanted was that something, the smallest thing, would be denied him, and the only thing I had the power to revoke was my brotherly love.

"Joe, are you all right?" Beth materialized in my field of vision, arms folded, disapproving and incredulous. "Are you drunk?"

"Fuck you," I said, a little loudly.

"What did you just say?" She grabbed my arm, but it was going to take more than that to snap sense into me.

"I said, 'Fuck you, Beth.' " Louder this time, way too loud. It was one of those moments you hear before you see it, before everything stops, the music and the dancing, and the offender is ushered away. Only in this case, I was the moment. I had created the drama, and as Beth tried to push me toward the house, I had a mad desire to seize the stage.

"You all right, Joe?" It was CJ, grabbing my arm and Beth's hand, stepping between us.

"Look at you," I said as he shoved me into the kitchen. I was laughing like a lunatic, hearing, through the fog, a spark in CJ's voice. It was the voice of the noble man, the man who rescued women. I pushed against him, but he had a strong grip. "Who the fuck are you?"

He let go, and I staggered backward, bouncing off the counter, putting out my right hand to steady myself. My hand sank into something moist and giving. I turned and looked: it was a chocolate sheet cake, mostly covered with white icing. It had said HAPPY BIRTHDAY JOE until I greeted it with my palm, until I ruined it.

"Oh," I said. "Oh, okay." My birthday had been three weeks earlier; in our family we celebrated those things whenever we managed to get everyone together. My shoulders sagged. I was tired. CJ was looking at the floor. There were others in the kitchen — my father, Beth, my mother — and they were crowding in on me, urging me to take it easy. I was a cornered animal, a raving weapon-wielding suspect, and the cops were closing in. *Drop the cake!* I brought my fingers together, squeezing the icing. It felt wonderful. I heard somebody gasp, realizing that I wasn't going to let go of the cake. There was no good way to extricate myself from that moment. They were going to stop staring at me eventually, weren't they? Blinking heavily, I watched CJ. He would know what to do.

I woke up on the floor of my old bedroom. My head was throbbing and my mouth felt full of lint. My hand was like a chocolate paw. I pried my fingers apart and put the index finger in my mouth, mustering some saliva and tasting the sweetness. It was dark outside, so someone must have deposited me there to dry out.

I leaned up on my elbows and saw that my father had not converted my old bedroom into an office. It was filled with memorabilia of my brother's career. Cardboard boxes, overflowing with trophies, award certificates, and team photos, labeled by year, were stacked along the floor. Shoeboxes were filled with pairs of cleats, rising in two towers, from biggest to smallest. There was his Rookie of the Year award and his Gold Glove. Two milk crates were packed with videocassettes; I grabbed one at random and saw my father's tight script on the rectangular sticker: *August 1995.* Nearby were several pictures, framed and leaning against the wall, waiting to be hung — CJ with Ted Williams, Kevin Costner, Al Gore.

I opened the closet; it was a wardrobe of caps and uniforms. All of his jerseys were there, and I ran my hand across them. I felt the cotton and the wide stitching along the team logos — Screaming Eagles and Mariners, Wildcats and Bruins, and Cubs Cubs Cubs. I felt the colored piping and passed my fingers over the back of each one, watching them swivel on the heavy wooden hangers.

They kept his shoes. That's what struck me. Not that they were building a shrine to my brother; not that my father had lied to me about it; not that I had been deposited here, of all places, by someone who wanted me to dry out and wake up in hell. It was that during all those years, my parents had had the foresight to squirrel away his shoes.

I walked downstairs to the garage and back across to the house. My father was in the kitchen, reading the Sunday paper. I heard the television from my parents' bedroom, which meant my mother was upstairs, falling asleep to the noise.

"Feeling better?" my father asked.

"Yeah," I said. Better, but not good. I filled a glass of water, gulped it down, filled another, gulped it down, filled a third and took it to the table and sat across from him. I checked my watch, gradually regaining a sense of function. It was shortly after ten. I'd slept six hours and was going to be up all night.

"Is Beth here?"

"She took CJ to the airport," he said. "His flight was delayed a bit, I think. She's on her way back."

I nodded and glumly rummaged through the newspaper, looking for something with pictures. God only knew what CJ and Beth were talking about. I figured the reckoning from this debacle was going to last a while.

"He can't help who he is, Joe." My father didn't look at me as he said this. "It's too late for all of that."

Who was I to argue? It did feel too late for some things — closeness, possibly friendship. To my parents, those were regrettable but tolerable losses. But that day I'd knocked even civility off the list, and to them that was unacceptable. Certain circumstances existed in my family and my life that I'd not yet learned to deal with. My brother was who he was, and the rest of us were going to have to live around that. Most people enjoyed it, going along for the ride. I found it impossible.

There was nothing I could say to my father. He knew what was going on. We read the paper for a few more minutes, in silence, and then he went to bed.

Beth returned close to midnight. I was still groggy, but I'd taken a shower and cleaned myself up. I was waiting for her in the guest room.

"Hi," I said.

She was wearing a navy Champion sweatshirt and jeans and she looked cute and collegiate. I was almost sick with guilt.

"Hi," she said, coolly.

"He got off all right?"

"Yup." She placed her purse on the dresser. I wondered whether I'd said too much or done too little. I wondered what was irreparable and what was not. If I'd lashed out at my brother, that would have been one thing. But I'd lashed out at her first, and I had no doubt that she'd thought things through in the intervening hours.

"Beth, look. I'm really sorry."

"Are you?" She put her hands on her hips. It wasn't an authoritative stance; she was only steadying herself. Her voice was trembling. "Because I don't know what it means when you act that way to me."

"I wasn't thinking. I was stupid."

"You were drunk." She pulled the sweatshirt up and over her head. "When people are drunk, they say what they really mean." She was wearing a navy T-shirt underneath; it was as if she was getting ready to box with me.

"I was drunk. I was that." I sighed it out. And I was still feeling a woozy flutter, not enough to say the wrong thing but enough to say the right words in the wrong way — the wrong inflection, the wrong tone.

"So did you mean it, Joe? Do you want me to go, or something?"

"No, no . . . *no*." I wanted her back; I desperately wanted her back. "Do you want to go?"

"What I want is for you to get over it." And I realized she had played me perfectly. "Your brother is rich and famous. You seem to have a huge problem with that. Do you agree?"

"Define 'huge.' "

"You think this is funny?"

"I just don't think it's that simple."

"You don't think *what's* that simple?"

"Whatever problems . . . these problems we're having."

That stopped her. She leaned against the dresser, her arms folded.

"Are you having an affair with Henry Fomacci?" I asked. It had entered my mind at that moment, a dim epiphany, and I said it without thinking.

"What do you think?" she said.

"I think . . ." And I stopped short. I was momentarily speechless; she hadn't acted shocked or heatedly denied it. Her face was flushed. She was furious. "I think I have every right to ask, Beth. It's within my rights."

I'd wandered into dangerous legalese again, begging to be

crucified for it. "You do have 'every right,' " she said, "and if the answer is no, will you believe me?"

"Of course," I said, not sure, but asserting it anyway.

She nodded and paused dramatically. "How could you possibly think that?"

And she was right. What was I thinking? I had to believe her. If I didn't believe Beth, I had nothing left.

"You really are an asshole, Joe," she said. "You make everything so fucking complicated."

I stood up, nodded, okay, thanks, I get it. I headed to the door and Beth shut it, hard, behind me. I stood there, not knowing where to go, when I heard the sound of my parents' door closing. Someone had overheard us.

I went down to the living room, sat on the leather couch, and turned on the television. It was happy for the company, I thought.

5

Beth left me three weeks later. I didn't know how those things usually worked; I had expected a fight, me grabbing her by the wrists and her breaking away, tearfully filling a suitcase, hurling insults at me, hitting the accents as she threw her clothes inside — I never want to *see* you again, you never *loved* me, you make me *sick*. She'd pack randomly, blinded by haste: four silk slips, a black cardigan, cold cream. And as I lurked in the background, she'd zip up the bag and hurl it in a waist-high sweep around her, keeping me away (you *animal!*) until she reached the door.

But that's not what happened. I came home from Selvon Dale one afternoon, and she wasn't there. That was normal. I didn't think anything was strange until it was eight o'clock, and she hadn't called. That's when it dawned on me that maybe she was really gone. I went to the bedroom closet and noticed that her garment bag was missing. In the bathroom, I saw that her makeup had been swept away, leaving a small pile of unidentifiable white powder. I knew then that she wouldn't be back that night, though I couldn't tell what she had taken, how long she'd be gone, and why she'd left certain items behind.

The timing was puzzling. After we returned from Los Angeles, things had improved. I had decided we should leave our troubles on the West Coast, and Beth agreed to give it a try. After what had happened, I made an effort to be forthcoming and irreproachably cheery and supportive. I thought that she was working fewer hours, though the job still left her exhausted. We figured that joint activity of some kind would rescue us, so we splurged on mountain bikes and rode them through Rock Creek Park on Saturday mornings and signed up at a nearby gourmet grocery for a wine-tasting course. We bought cookbooks and spent Sunday afternoons, soothed by classical music, preparing dinners for the week. We made love with renewed attentiveness. We were working on fixing things between us, and we'd continue to work until it no longer seemed like work, until we had our rhythm back.

Of course, that was only three weeks, and now she was gone. It was like a graceless teen suicide, without the proper warnings. All sorts of suspicions and dreads ran through my mind: people to accuse and obligatory phone calls I didn't want to make. I wondered about Fomacci. It was Thursday — had they escaped together for a frantic weekend of, shall we say, banging out the first draft? She had friends who might know what had happened and where she'd gone, but I didn't like those friends. They were from law school, mostly, headstrong and greedy, not as smart as they thought they were. They were her friends, not mine.

By ten o'clock all the pondering had left me tired. The suitcase was gone, and I had no reason to expect her back that night. I should have panicked or felt sad, but for some reason I was relieved. The suitcase was key, I decided; it lent the affair a purity that was reassuring. I felt free of blame. She had taken the time to pack, but hadn't found a moment to write a note? How inconsiderate. This was *her* fault.

I woke up at four-thirty in the morning; Beth had not returned. At five, I called the Montgomery County sick-teacher hotline. It was only my second sick day that year. They would find a substitute and I would find my wife.

My first stop was Cannon, Grossmeyer. (I say this as if there were many stops; frankly, I had no idea where I'd go next.) I boarded the subway in Bethesda shortly after seven. The immaculate platform was packed with purposeful men and women, a healthy Great Society mixture of white and black, reading Oprah novels or sections of the *Post*. I assumed that most of them were federal employees, but I honestly had no idea what they did. Teachers, even on the lower rungs, weren't part of the rat race, and the hopes and dreams of the nine-to-fivers were generally beyond me.

We were underground for the entire train ride. In the darkness of the tunnels, I saw my face reflected back at me. As we passed Dupont Circle and my stop was coming up, it dawned on me that I could have called Nina, my wife's competent and unattractive secretary, and casually asked if she knew where Beth was. On second thought, I was glad I hadn't called; it was important for me to take a day off, abandon my career, my *kids,* and be physically involved in the search for my wife. Perhaps I hadn't gone far enough — maybe I needed to be unshaven, babbling incoherently, filled with drastic rage and fear and lust, flapping about in an untied bathrobe and slippers. In any event, a phone call from home certainly wasn't action enough. My wife wasn't gone; she was *missing.* Anything could have happened to her — though it probably hadn't.

I left the train and walked two blocks up Connecticut Avenue, crossed the street, and there it was: 1475, polished and intimidating. The aquamarine windows soared high, though the building was lopped off at about ten stories, like all the other city towers, at the height of the United States Capitol. I walked in and was promptly ignored by a blue-blazered black security guard behind a marble lobby console, so I went to the bank of elevators and waited for one to want me. One finally opened, and I ducked in with an older man and a beautiful young woman, both professionally well dressed. The man, a silver-haired Titan, nodded at me, but the woman ignored me. Was she his associate, his daughter, his lover? Could she even be, in some cruel twilight Title IX reversal, his boss? I watched the numbers go by as we soared in silence, and I knew that, even fully dressed and clean shaven, I didn't belong with these people. They were competitors, slick and confident and full of hidden agendas. They shaped the world, yanking and harassing people like me, the American Worker. I was in their building, and as the elevator door opened and we got out, I felt like their messenger boy.

The Cannon, Grossmeyer reception room was quiet. I'd been to Beth's office only once before; it happened to be Take Our Daughters to Work Day, so I was treated to the sight of two dozen grade school girls re-enacting a defamation suit filed by the beef industry.

A middle-aged black woman was sitting behind a reception desk, with a slender headset curling down from her ear to the front of her mouth. "Can I help you?" she asked.

"I'd like to see Nina Grant, please."

"She's Nina Hitchcock now," she said.

"Oh." The receptionist continued to look at me. Did I have to ask again? "I'd like to see Nina Hitchcock, please." I smiled.

She didn't. "And who may I say is calling?"

"Joseph Columbus." *Joseph?*

"And you are with . . ."

"I'm with Beth Columbus," I said. If she said, "It's Beth Hitchcock now," I would leave.

"Joe, hello." It was Nina, coming into the reception area through a thick oak door I had thought was part of the wall. We shook hands. She looked much better than I remembered; she had lost weight, her black hair was cut short, and her frumpy cat's-eye glasses, trendy for a few months a couple of years ago, had been replaced by small wire frames, silver and sleek.

I followed her into the office, trying, unsuccessfully, not to focus on her curvy ass. Corporate men were different, but so were corporate women. Then I reminded myself that I was married to one.

She asked if I wanted coffee, but I refused. "You look great, Nina."

"Thanks." She led me back toward Beth's office. Two well-dressed men about my age passed the other way and eye-fucked me. I nonchalantly groped at my fly.

"And congratulations on your marriage," I said.

She laughed and half-turned to me, grabbing my elbow and still moving forward. "I just got divorced, actually."

"Oh." The name change was a change *back*. Idiot! "Well, then, congratulations on . . . congratulations." Never mind.

She led me to the door of Beth's office. "Here you go," she said. "I'll be right over there if you need anything." She pointed across the open space to her desk, partitioned by towering file cabinets, sloppy with interrupted work.

"Thanks," I said, reflexively. Nina retreated and closed the door almost all the way, leaving it open a crack. What the hell was going on?

I took a couple of steps into the office and flipped on the light. Nina seemed to know why I was there. I was expected, led right to the office. How could that be? Maybe Beth was dead — bludgeoned with the end of a fire hose by one of the mentally retarded mailroom boys who was nursing a painful and unreciprocated crush, or fed into the famished, screaming jaws of the paper shredder. They were all playing it down because her death was their responsibility, and they wanted to avoid a lawsuit. Then again, she probably wasn't dead.

Her desk was bare to the black leather blotter. The chair was pushed in, and the trash can behind it was empty. I sat down on her burgundy leather couch, tracing my fingers over the brass bullet rivets, cold to the touch. I deduced that this room had been straightened up by a cleaning person during the night and that no one had been in it since.

"Joe?"

Henry Fomacci had opened the door and was standing there.

"Henry, hello." I stood up, but I wasn't as tall as he was. We shook hands. His grip was very strong, and I tried to squeeze back, but the way it probably registered was: *You are strong, and I am a wuss who is crippled by your strength but will pre-*

tend to be strong. I wanted to start the handshake over. "How did you know me?"

"Oh, Beth talks about you all the time," he said, which of course didn't make sense. If Beth talked about me all the time, did she give lengthy descriptions of my physical characteristics and wardrobe? When people asked, "How's your husband?" she must say, "He's fine . . . and frequently dresses in a navy shirt and khaki pants."

But Fomacci was present and accounted for, which was important, because Beth was obviously not here. They were not together, tangled in resort bedsheets, polishing his rough draft, the laser-printed pages stuck to their sweat-slicked, postcoital bodies like hundred-dollar bills. He did look magnificent, dressed in a dark gray suit as if modeling the nightly news, his skin polished like ivory, prissy blue eyes and a girl's long lashes, blond hair grooved and immobile. If I were Beth — and Nazis turned me on — I'd have an affair with him, too.

"So what brings you here?" His tone was a little too studied, vaguely accusatory, but lightly confused, and certainly not interested.

I could have been cagey and lied, or I could have been brutally honest. "I don't think Beth's here," I said, combining the two possible responses into something assertive, yet incomprehensible.

"No, that's right. Beth's in *São Paolo.*" He said the name with a ridiculously thick Spanish accent, the kind he probably used on his housekeeper.

"São Paolo?" As the Ugly American, I refrained from mimicking his inflection. But since I was startled by the news, my inflection sounded even more wrong, as if the next thing I expected to hear were the demands of the kidnappers.

"It's a city in Brazil," Fomacci said, calming me with patronizing basic information. "Four people flew down yesterday morning for emergency meetings in the Malquima case." Malquima, also known as the nefarious sugar cartel. "They'll be back Sunday night. You didn't know?"

"No."

"Huh." He looked honestly baffled. "Beth left a message at your school."

My school. Asshole. "Well, I never got it."

"I was right here when she called you." He didn't even blink. I couldn't remember if that meant a person was telling the truth or was successfully hiding a lie.

"How's the book coming?" I asked.

"It's coming along fine. What does that have to do with anything?"

"Nothing. Just curious. Do you own a tuxedo?"

"Yes, I do," he said, refusing to be humored, his eyelids flattening in a suspicious, Aryan squint. "What does *that* have to do with anything?"

I paused dramatically, keeping him off guard, tracing my finger along the wall like a Bond villain, as if I had now collected enough information to gauge his character and decide which poison I would use to kill him. "I'm thinking about getting one," I said. Which I was, the same way I was thinking about, say, running for Congress or challenging Bill Gates to a high-stakes game of tetherball.

"Well, keep me posted," Fomacci said, confused by the sincerity of my ambitious nonsense. "How's your brother doing?" he asked, steering us back to safer ground.

"CJ's doing well," I said. "His groin has healed."

"Good, good," he said, but he wouldn't bite. I wished I'd picked a different body part to slander, but it was too late.

"They're in Cincinnati this weekend," he added.

"I know. I'm going up there tomorrow."

"Really? That sounds terrific."

I nodded. I wasn't sure if what I'd said was true, because it had just popped into my head. I didn't even know whether the Cubs were playing the Reds. I'd made a concentrated effort not to follow my brother's progress through the season, and the willful blindness was doing wonders for my mental health. I stood there, suffering quality time with Fomacci, his arms folded, ass leaning back on her desk: a junior Titan, aspiring best-seller writer, master of the first impression, predator, moron stocked with relevant information. That settled it. I was going to Cincinnati.

I flew there the next morning, securing a miraculously cheap last-minute ticket on a certain airline. Though the round trip only cost two hundred dollars, I'd been prepared to spend much more. If necessary, I would have arrived at the ticket counter carrying an aluminum briefcase, clicked its silver latches, and revealed banded stacks of twenties. If the only way to get to Cincinnati would have meant hijacking the Concorde, I'd have done it. Or I could have driven my car, since it looked to be only about seven or eight hours from Bethesda. (I figured this out by consulting a map; I'm not an idiot savant who can judge long distances by staring out the window.)

The trip felt like the right thing to do — a choice from the gut that didn't feel wrong even a few hours later. Beth was away for a few days, and the weekend was coming. Everyone would be pleased at my initiative, my personal investment in family harmony and personal growth. For the first time in a while, I would be responsible for a pleasant surprise.

I arrived around noon. For some reason the Cincinnati airport was in Kentucky, though I was pretty sure the city remained in Ohio. I guess there's nothing theoretically wrong with the airport being in another state, though it's probably wise to have it in a state that's adjacent. For instance, it wouldn't be good for the Cincinnati airport to be in Nevada. In any case, I hadn't spent much time in the Midwest, and I approached my visit with the requisite snobbery and sarcasm of a man who has spent his entire life on the East and West Coasts. I expected the Midwest to be different — "slower" and "friendlier" — the only drawback to this landlocked paradise being the traffic jams caused by horse-drawn carriages, though it was entirely possible that I was confusing Midwesterners with the Amish.

No matter. As the shuttle van from Kentucky glided along a bland interstate, past clusters of suburban amenities huddled near the exit ramps for economic warmth, over and into the city itself on an impressive, baby-blue suspension bridge that was surgingly American, my spirits lifted. Beth and I hadn't been on a real vacation since our honeymoon through Europe, but now my wife was in Brazil and I was in Ohio. We were both travelers of the world.

I was going to the Cincinnati Hyatt, the same hotel the team was using. They'd been there since early Friday morning, after losing an extra-inning game in Pittsburgh the night before. They'd played the Reds on Friday night and won, three to two.

Downtown hotels were probably deadening to those whose business cornered them there, but to a novice like me the Hyatt was glittering. I loved the airy atriums and multiple, over-lapping mezzanines, with their tightly patterned carpets and slanting sunroofs welded to walls of windows — pairs of lounge chairs and cocktail tables scooted toward them, for better admiration of their nothing view. Down below was the overpriced convenience store with decaled shot glasses and Boston Baked Beans and canisters of aspirin like shell casings, and, most magnificent of all, those exposed elevator cars, zipping up and down like taffy on string. And there were the weddings and reunions and retirements and retreats, schedules scrolled on recessed blue television screens in the lobby — events at which unimaginative late-night plans were hatched: *eleventh floor . . . by the ice machine.*

I'd called Spencer Levitt in Newport Beach the previous afternoon and secured a single ticket to the Saturday night game. Spencer's voice was foghorn-hollow as he spoke into his speakerphone, and I could picture him, standing with his hands on his hips as we small-talked, ogling his reflection in a framed item of memorabilia until he had dispensed with me. But Spencer took care of me, as good agents were paid to do, and an envelope was waiting for me at the Hyatt front desk. I would be sitting over the Cubs dugout, in a box seat, down the third-base line.

My brother did not know I was in town. I wasn't avoiding him, but I didn't want to bother him. We hadn't spoken since the Easter Sunday Cake Massacre, and I thought it a good idea for me to surprise him at the ballpark, during batting practice. That way he wouldn't be able to make a scene — if he really was furious with me, which I doubted. He'd have the game to worry about. It never entered my mind that I might run into him at the hotel; it wasn't my brother's style to wander around the lobby or peruse postcards in the gift shop. This wasn't a place where he could lose himself, and hotel loitering was an invitation to harassment by people who were more annoying than I was. I suspected that he was up in his room, taking a pregame nap or doing nothing.

I had a few solitary hours before heading to the ballpark, which opened around six. I'd seen it, glaringly white and monumental, when we crossed into town over that suspension bridge. It used to be called Riverfront Stadium, I think, but it's been renamed Cinergy Field, thanks to some company of an unknown, presumably hi-tech commodity — with cash to spare — writing a large check. It was a hulking and charmless mass on the river, within walking distance of downtown, with its feeble, small-town handful of skyscrapers rising optimistically but without any heft. There probably were major corporations headquartered in Cincinnati; I just didn't know what they were.

So with time to kill, I loitered on the Hyatt's second mezzanine and munched barrel-shaped pretzels lifted from a small wooden bowl on the bar. Down in the main lobby, I saw several men and a few women in turquoise polo shirts with a company logo in white on the left breast. Once I noticed them, I found them everywhere — nursing beers at the bar, piling luggage onto bellboy carts, cruising up the see-through elevators like little turquoise blurs, pieces of perfect sky. They were reproducing and taking over the place, like low-level corporate body-snatchers; I figured there was one in my room, the gummy fluid pooling as he emerged from his turquoise pod, rinsing the goo with my complimentary soap and memorizing my personal identification number.

I also noticed a hallway leading off the second mezzanine; above it was an arrow beckoning forward and a red sign labeled SKYWALK. The name seemed to promise adventure, in a United States Space Program kind of way, so I headed in that direction.

I started walking down the alleged Skywalk, and the corridor quickly turned dirty and dim. I saw no one, and I felt like the stooge in a horror movie. I wondered whether the sign would be gone when I got back, as if it had been briefly posted to lure me into a trap, then yanked down by the killer as he followed me in. But I kept walking, avoiding a spilled cup of red punch that someone had left slumped against a wall, and after a few more paces I reached a new sign bolted to the wall: it was a map of downtown with Skywalk superimposed on it.

And there I stood, staring at it, like an idiot. Skywalk was a series of walkways that spanned the entire downtown — all ten blocks of it — and the whole thing was incomprehensible to me. I studied the map, squinting theatrically. (Squinting never helps you understand anything; it only helps other people understand something about *you*.) Skywalk was a jagged and puzzling root system of white lines; there were several dead ends and hexagonal routes and switchbacks, when the straight approach, whether aboveground or on the god-given-damn sidewalk, seemed a much better bet. It all had the air of a mid-seventies flexing of misplaced urban pride, like the Exerwalk trails that some cities built, Day-glo footprints painted on the sidewalk for the amusement of white collar locals, who were supposed to drop everything and plant themselves for deep-knee bends and pull-ups over mulch pits during their lunch breaks.

I hated Skywalk bitterly, with its cheap futuristic promise of gravity-free fun. But I refused to let it beat me. I wandered down, saw it branch off a few times, but there were no intermediate maps to tell me where it was meandering to. I took the third left turn and ended up on the second floor of a different hotel, where crowds of aging white people were huddled over long tables, registering for an insurance convention. I turned back, passing Tower Place Mall, and decided I'd return there, to its certain, rewarding confluence of food court, overpriced music stores, and packs of menacing, unscrubbed youths. But in the process of backtracking I ended up in a walkway on the second-floor mezzanine of some other building, and Skywalk abruptly dead-ended. Thick pieces of wood were spray-painted with warnings and propped over a dusty escalator; they said I could go no farther.

I was ready for that food court, but I heard footsteps. The place was eerily humid and quiet, like a subway station just after the train has left. It dawned on me that this was a place where midwestern crime might occur. I turned, and a young couple dressed in Cubs jerseys and shorts was wandering down toward me. The man had a handlebar mustache and his arm around the woman. She was heavy, wearing glasses, and was much shorter than he; it was as if he were pushing her down, compacting her into something squat and unattractive.

Her sandals clacked and echoed in the empty corridor, and something about that noise made me want to come back to earth, off Skywalk. And so I moved toward a stairwell, at first nonchalantly and then quickly, without heed, down and out into the fanned, genuine heat of the asphalt. I crossed the street back to the Hyatt — I'd traveled only a few blocks, after all that feverish, roundabout Skywalking — and I realized what it was that had unnerved me: the woman had a turquoise handbag slung over her shoulder. It was small but practically glowing, and I thought that the Cubs jerseys were the couple's way to enchant me; his was billowy and had plenty of room for a turquoise polo shirt underneath. The pod people knew my weakness and were planning to make the end come easy for me, in that dead alley of the city.

I knew a guy at Georgetown named Jasper Bervon. He was an absurdly rich Swiss national, and he hung out at our place a lot during our sophomore year. Jasper would wander in with a wrapped meatball sub, say nothing, and sit down on the couch and eat. None of us in the house knew whose friendship had provided him with such a fearless sense of social entitlement, so we spent a lot of time mocking him for being Swiss and for coming from a "pussy country." We'd put on CNN and blame him for everything bad that happened. He thought we were making fun of him because we liked him, but we didn't; he annoyed us, and eventually my housemate Jeremy punched him in the face and called him a Kraut cocksucking bastard, which was wrong for a number of geopolitical reasons, and Jasper never came around again.

But I will always remember Jasper fondly for a single act of spectacular idiocy: he traveled from Washington to Denver, for Presidents' Day weekend, without taking account of the different time zones. It wasn't that he did it on purpose, he explained later — he actually forgot, and he lived his life unaware that he was two hours off the designated pace. Through a quirk that mercifully spanned his entire itinerary, he was never in a situation — dental appointment, matinee movie, dinner date — where he had to show up at a specific time. (And since he was traveling west, he'd have been a couple of hours early.)

So what did this have to do with Cincinnati, land of country music and festering resentment toward the federal government? Jasper's lost moments graced my mind whenever I felt out of place, whenever I wished there was a way for me to slide out of common time and through my own sacred oval of it. As stupid as Jasper may have been, he spent the entire frozen Colorado weekend treading above the ice, oblivious of the thin plane that separated him from the darting, liquid world beneath. And he had a fine time.

I felt it that late afternoon, joining the Saturday crowds moving slowly toward the closed-in open-air stadium, clustering with them at crosswalks. I'd been in Cincinnati long enough to know that these were not my people. I did not want to know them, at home on the riverboat casinos parked on the stagnant, shallow waterway nearby, with their weekend beepers and cheap cell phones and their fruitless air of self-importance, jamming with toe-tapping energy about *that big deal in Kansas City*. These were the people who worked and made more money than I did, but they were doing it in Cincinnati, so I didn't feel threatened. And there were the others, blue-collar and exotically menacing, long-haired men and their chain-smoking girlfriends, picking at the nail polish on their toes, couples strutting with the cockiness of exonerated bombing suspects.

Yesterday it was the East Coast corporate world, and today it was a medium-size city in the Midwest; each day I was finding new parts of society that terrified and excluded me. I was trying to live in my own moment, as Jasper had unwittingly taught me, but my only way out, as it had been all along, was for the game to begin.

About forty minutes before game time, it was already obvious that my plan had been a bad one. CJ was standing near the batting cage, waiting to take his swings. There was no way I could get to him. Prepubescent autograph hounds swamped my front-row seat, T-shirts down below their knees, blue ballpoint ink on their fingers and lips. They yelled at the players, my brother included, but he didn't come over and didn't see me.

As the grounds crew readied the lime-green fake turf field, running a buffer-steamroller over it, I read the photocopied daily insert to the Reds program, with its updated statistics on both teams. The Cubs were fifteen and ten, a first-place start, two games ahead of the Cardinals. The Reds, on the other hand, were seven and nineteen, fluffing their pillow before lying down for a long nap in last place. I looked down their list of players, as if my cursory, sage assessments would enable me to pinpoint the team's weaknesses. Maybe later I'd scribble a note to their manager on a mustard-stained napkin (*trade for a left-handed starter; be more aggressive on the base paths*) and lower the note to the dugout like bait on a fishing line.

A young woman with some vague 4-H credentials sang the national anthem, and the game began. I guess I should have been rooting for the Cubs, but I wasn't a Cubs fan. Everyone liked the Cubs, because they were pretty much endearingly bad, but I thought the key to their fan base was their cute mascot. It was a lesson to other franchises that had sadly gone unlearned. Where were the Pittsburgh Puppies? There could be an entire league of teams named after baby animals. "Kittens edge the Ducklings, three to one." It would have made our world a much nicer place.

My brother batted third, and after the first out he stepped out on deck. He took a few swings, rubbed his bat down with a pine-tarred rag, and looked directly at me. I smiled, trying not to grin like an idiot, but he didn't acknowledge me or smile back. Maybe he didn't see me.

His name was announced, the announcement overlapped by a swelling chorus of boos from the fans as he walked to the plate for the first time. They hadn't booed him in Los Angeles — either those fans knew he was local or they hadn't cared enough — and at first I was morally outraged, though of course the booing made sense. We weren't in Chicago, after all; still, it was strange. Most people don't get booed on their way to work. What had he done to deserve it? Had he made a disparaging remark, bulletin-board fodder about the city's lack of listenable radio stations or the intimidating heft of their homegrown, sunburned women? I supposed it could have been a backhanded sign of respect; they didn't like him because he was good, and that night, against their own team, good meant bad.

There were two outs, and the bases were empty. He was batting a preposterous .434, with seven home runs and twenty-one runs batted in. We were less than a month into the season, so his numbers indicated a hot start but nothing more; his average wasn't even leading the league. CJ fouled the first pitch straight back into the hammocky netting, took the second pitch outside for a ball, fouled off another, then buckled under the impressive swoop of a big breaking ball, called strike three. The crowd roared, relishing it. I hunched forward in my seat, wondering how much he heard or felt. He tossed his batting helmet aside without disgust and walked out to his defensive position at third, removing his batting gloves and chatting with the third-base coach before the coach headed back to the dugout. CJ worked the ball around the horn a couple of times, kicked up a little dirt, did a couple of knee bends, and felt the fake turf. A second baseman named Pokey Reese led off the bottom half of the first. CJ crouched slightly at the first pitch, charged as Reese squared to bunt, but Reese couldn't get on top of the high fastball, and he kicked it foul.

And so it went. It wasn't strange to see my brother out on the field that second time around. And without my mother or Spencer or anyone there to gloat and frown, there was something pleasant about it. The weather was cool but nice, and I was enjoying myself, feeling a certain peace, getting into the leisurely rhythm of the game, the exhorting scoreboard and murmur of the crowd, the call of the beer man, the excitement of a foul ball as it lofted into the seats. I always knew my brother was fortunate to play, but this was the first time in a long time I remembered feeling fortunate just to watch.

The two seats next to me were empty. Beyond that was an older couple, huddling under a Reds blanket, rummaging through a plastic bag of food — popcorn balls, fried chicken drumsticks, seedless red grapes — like a grocer's bottomless pit. The stadium on the whole was, as an optimist would say, half full, capable of generating a pulse but probably not of sustaining it. Some of the cheap sections were full, but if you moved down, into the worst seats of the higher price, there weren't any takers.

Back in my comfy, navy blue–toned elite area were two interesting young women sitting two rows behind me, on the aisle just over my right shoulder. I heard them before I saw them — they were cheering for the Cubs, not loudly but certainly in an unashamed way. In the middle of the third I casually turned around: two attractive blondes wearing jeans jackets and gold jewelry, lots of it. I first thought they were groupies, but they wore the nervous, slightly desperate expressions of women who had already been lucky and were past that; they must have been girlfriends or wives.

I considered revealing myself to them, but what would I say? What did we have in common? We were all getting screwed by baseball players. They sat hunched forward in their seats, unfazed by the crack of the bat, clapping to themselves when the Cubs batters got ahead in the count, but then putting their hands together at their chin, as if in prayer, as if every pitch meant something. One of them could have been CJ's girlfriend. Not that I knew whether my brother had a steady girlfriend. Other than Cher.

CJ batted again in the fourth inning, with the game still scoreless. He lifted a single into left field but was erased on a double play two batters later. The play of both teams was list-less and disengaged; the Cubs managed to strand a runner at third, but through the first five innings the Reds didn't get any-one past second base.

That changed in the bottom of the sixth. The Cubs starter (last name Morton, accent on the second o) suddenly lost con-trol, as if the ball had changed shape on him. He gave up a sin-gle and walked two more, and all of a sudden the bases were loaded, with nobody out. I'm not sure what the Cubs manager (whose name I can't remember) was thinking by leaving El Morton out there — though the manager did take his one al-lotted and fatherly ass-patting trip to the mound. (CJ and the first baseman joined them for the conference.) Maybe it had to do with giving him one more batter, at least, to work his way out of it. Morton had earned something, having pitched so well up to that moment. The other part of the equation — ah, baseball, with all its riveting permutations — was that the Reds were at the bottom of their batting order, so their pitcher would be coming to the plate.

Or would he? The Reds manager, an older man with thick glasses and creaky knees, must have believed it was a pivotal moment. He unceremoniously yanked his starter, a sidearmer named Wilton Durrell, for a pinch hitter with the upbeat-sounding name of Johnny Goldsmith. Young Johnny was a reedy thin white guy, and since I'd never heard of him, I figured he couldn't cause major damage. (Once the Cubs were in dan-ger of falling behind, I began nervously pulling for them.)

As Goldsmith stepped to the plate he looked like a gangly high school pitcher. According to the exhorting electronic scoreboard high above center field — DEE-FENSE, it read, alternating syllables, perhaps an errant download from the Cincinnati Bengals diskette — he wasn't batting a grown man's weight. He lunged at the first pitch and slapped it, a slick ground ball toward my brother at third, and in a split second, with the startled runners getting a late jump and nobody out, you could sense the incredible wanting to happen. CJ took two steps to his left and stepped on third, pivoted, and threw to the shortstop Sanchez covering second, but with the runner bearing down on him, Sanchez leaped and didn't get enough on his throw. Goldsmith was safe at first, a run had been scored, and the Cubs had turned only a double play instead of the mystical triple.

The crowd cheered because the Reds were on top, but when Reese popped out, after all that frantic activity, that one run became one measly run. Good teams do better than that with the bases loaded and nobody out; the Cubs were a good team, and they were probably going to take advantage of their foe's missed opportunity and find a way to win the game.

And that's exactly what happened, with stunning precision, in the top of the seventh. The starting pitcher was gone, an unsteady reliever was in his place, with an early season earned run average in the low nineties. Unfortunately, his fastball was only in the mid-eighties, and he promptly served up a double off the left-field wall and then a turf single in the hole, which brought up my brother with men on the corners. CJ worked the count to three and one, and then smacked a monster bomb, a no-doubt-abouter, into the upper deck in right field. The crowd gasped — you could hear it — and then went back to their disappointed murmuring. They knew the game was over.

CJ rounded the bases in a steady and humble jog, and his teammates, the two he'd brought around, waited to congratulate him at home plate. The ball was long gone, but the home run lingered in the air like the puff of smoke you find yourself following as it trails through the sky, gray on black, after fireworks. The players walked back to the dugout together, and I was bobbing in my seat, grooving on what he had done. One of the girlfriends tapped me on the shoulder and smiled. They'd known all along who I was. Who wouldn't have? And as CJ walked back to the dugout, before taking a few steps down, he pointed at me, and then disappeared. He was, officially, a marvel.

The Cubs added two more runs in the eighth, and by the top of the ninth inning the girlfriends had gone and the ushers had grown less vigilant — a foursome of teenage boys settled into some seats behind me, seats they couldn't possibly have paid for. However well-intentioned, they began regrettably referring to Barry Larkin, one of the Reds' black players and a man who could pound their asses to pavement in about two seconds, as "their boy."

And when my brother came up a final time, they started in on him. *Columbus, you suck!* two of them yelled together, counting "one, two, three" right before so that they would be in sync. "I've heard he's . . ." said one of them, and his voice trailed off, and I could imagine the floppy hand gesture that accompanied it, reassuring the adolescent losers, who weren't getting a tenth of my brother's action. "Hit it with your purse!" said another, as my brother took ball four and trotted to first. CJ was forced at second on a fielder's choice, and though the Reds would bat one more time, I left before the game was over.

He called me in my hotel room a little after eleven. I scrambled for the phone when it rang, grateful that no one was there to see me do it.

"Why didn't you come down?" he asked, meaning to the locker room after the game.

"I didn't think I could," I said, though the thought had never crossed my mind. What business did I have hanging out in the locker room? It didn't matter now.

The team was three floors above me. When I reached his room and knocked, he opened the door, barefoot and dressed in navy shorts, a gray athletic T-shirt, a backward (non-Cubs) baseball cap, and a bulky ice pack taped over his left shoulder.

He looked tired. Most people don't think playing baseball is exhausting, but seeing him there made me realize that it is. It also struck me that you need a brain to play it well, and that even the most dubious major leaguers are still very, very good.

I followed him in. "Joe, this is Justin Holloway." He pointed to the team's fleet-footed left fielder, a well-dressed and smooth-looking black guy. Justin nodded politely and spun away, talking into a cell phone. "One of his bitches," CJ said, sitting down on the bed, and Justin gave him the finger over his shoulder.

"I'm surprised to see you, man," he said.

"Beth's in Brazil until Monday," I said, betraying none of the chaos that surrounded her trip. I leaned against the wall.

"Brazil the country?" CJ said.

I nodded. I wasn't sure what other Brazil CJ may have had in mind, but I let it go.

"How is Beth?" he said.

"Beth's good." The team had been in town only a day, but the room was trashed: crumpled soda cans on top of the television, damp T-shirts on the windowsill, socks over doorknobs, CDs spilling over the nighttable, topped by a sleep mask and an asthma inhaler, not my brother's. Maybe this room was Justin's.

"You're not mad that I came out here, are you?"

"Mad?" He laughed. "I'm just surprised."

"Right." Because it was so unlike me to show any interest in what he did? Or merely because I hadn't called in advance? I tried to view it from his perspective — warming up before a game, glancing at all those meaningless faces in the stands and seeing mine wedged in there. It was hard to imagine.

"This is a *pleasant* surprise, Joe. A good surprise. You know I'm always glad to see you."

He smiled again. Had he forgotten the cake fiasco? Good athletes, I guess, know how to let things go. "What's wrong with your shoulder?"

"It's sore." He lay down. "I'm always sore. Can't get rid of it."

I nodded. Justin, sitting across the room from me at a standard round table, wore brown jeans and a bulky autumn-colored shirt, his feet sheathed in unlaced Timberland boots and propped up on the bed in front of him. He was staring right at us but seemed far away, whispering into the phone, listening, then slumping his shoulders in conspiratorial laughter.

"So. Do you want to go out or something?" I asked.

CJ raised his legs, making an L shape of his body, and lowered them. "Dude. It's *Cincinnati.*"

"We can go downstairs, then." I sounded desperate, but I had come all that way.

"Not tonight, man. Let's get something in the morning." I guess he meant that downstairs he'd have to battle his fans, and he didn't feel like putting on his face that night. Or he was annoyed with me in general and didn't want to spend time with me. Or he had other plans. One of his bitches.

He held his right hand out toward me, the one connected to his un-iced shoulder, and I pulled him up. He put his hand on my shoulder and walked me to the door — a patronizing gesture of sibling rejection.

"I'm just real tired tonight, Joe. I'm sorry."

"But you won," I said.

He smiled and shook his head.

"Did you hit that home run for me?" I asked.

"They're all for you, Joe." He didn't miss a beat.

"Really?" And I was out the door and in the silent hallway.

He yawned and shook his head at the same time. "Good night," he said, looking down at his feet, retreating. The door swept toward me and separated us.

We met downstairs for breakfast the next morning. We'd agreed on nine, but he called and hedged until nine forty-five. The Cubs were to play the final game of the series that afternoon at one-thirty, which meant the team bus would leave for the stadium around eleven. It was the sixth and final game of the road trip, and as soon as the game ended and the players had showered and dressed, they would return to Chicago. Inexplicably, I'd made no effort to get a ticket to the afternoon game and had booked my return flight to Washington for two o'clock, which would be sometime during the second or third inning.

The hotel restaurant, called Bouquets, was crowded, loud with a dish-ringing clamor you'd expect in a roadside diner. There was a lavish brunch beyond a pair of open veranda doors farther in, with overflowing buckets of melon and strawberries and a tall black chef, made even taller by the cylindrical white hat he'd been forced to wear, supervising custom crêpes. I was out front, sipping coffee in the nonlavish and comparatively cheap eggs and bagels section, when I saw my brother greeted by the hostess. He whispered a few words to her, and she pointed him in my general direction.

I felt strongly that I had some unfinished business with my brother that morning. He'd given me the brush-off the night before, which was fine, but I wanted us to have a serious talk, even though I wasn't sure exactly what it would cover. I was tired and grumpy, having sprawled across my bed sleeplessly for much of the night. The bed was sheeted unwrenchably tight, like a tourniquet, and the pillows were spongy rectangles, sharp-edged and unsympathetic. I must have fallen asleep sometime after three, and I woke up a few hours later, clutched with phantom anxiety, lying flat on my stomach, pillows hurled to the floor.

He sat down across from me, clean-shaven, his hair still damp. He was wearing jeans, gleaming Nike sneakers, and a pressed white oxford shirt, though I was pretty sure he wasn't the one who had ironed it. And there was a weighty silver watch slung around his right wrist; he looked like an advertisement for it. Anything around him became something he could sell.

"I like that watch," I said.

He looked at it as if he hadn't known it was there, as if a handler had fused it to his skin while he slept (and I'll bet he *did* sleep, soundly). "You want it?"

Once again he sounded earnest, not as if he was trying to annoy me by showing that he could afford such a watch (or ten) and I could not. My brother's consistent lack of guile was driving me crazy. We were speaking two different languages: his was of the world, sane and normal, while mine was a personal, incomprehensible dialect. "I don't *want* it. I just like it."

The waitress arrived, a poor-complexioned and despairing teen, who looked as if she was forever waiting to hear the harsh rev of her boyfriend's motorcycle pulling up the Hyatt's circular driveway to take her away. We both ordered eggs over easy, sausage links, two slices of toast. CJ asked for a large glass of orange juice, and I continued to mainline caffeine, destroying my insides in a futile, pointless effort to stay alert.

"You guys played well last night," I said, reigning master of ballpark small talk.

"We're doing all right. Hope we can keep it up." I couldn't tell whether he was concerned; the line sounded canned to me.

"They booed you." He laughed a little. "Do you even hear it?"

"You hear it. I mean, you do, but you don't." He shrugged, his orange juice arrived, he gulped it. "It's not like they really hate you or anything."

A throat cleared. Standing next to the table was a woman in her thirties with twin boys, who must have been nine or ten, fair-skinned and wide-eyed redheads. The boys were wearing kiddie Cubs jerseys with my brother's number nine pocket-size on the front.

"Excuse me," the woman said. She was attractive and thin, wearing jeans and a dangerously tight Bulls T-shirt. It was from a championship season several years before, and she must have thought it valuable or been convinced, not altogether wrongly, that she looked good in it. She had one hand on each boy's outside shoulder, her long red fingernails corralling them like talons. No wedding ring.

CJ took a sip of water, swallowed, and turned to them. "Hey, guys."

They murmured something, terrified. "They're big fans of yours," the woman said.

"Let's make a deal," CJ said, ignoring the mother. He was

seated at the boys' level and took advantage of it. "You guys wait outside until my brother and I finish eating, and then I'll tell you how to hit a curveball."

"I can throw a slider," boasted the boy on the left, which had nothing to do with anything but still felt absolutely right.

"I'll bet you can," CJ said. He looked up at the mother. "Okay?"

"Just outside?" she asked, pointing in the general direction of the mezzanine, gliding past his willingness to do it at all, making sure that she'd got the directions right. My brother nodded, and she guided the boys away.

When our food arrived, we ate pretty much in silence. I noticed others around the periphery concentrating on him; my brother ignored them. I was trying to say something — even small talk — but was finding it impossible. It should have been easy for us to talk, so my awkwardness, my inability to hold a natural conversation, depressed me.

"Are you happy?" I asked.

CJ was nudging a sawed triangle of toast into a pool of egg yolk. Though my question had come out of nowhere, he didn't react. "What do you think?"

"I don't know. That's why I am asking."

"And I'm asking you what you think." He looked over my shoulder, nodding at a couple of older men walking past our table, probably trainers or coaches. Then his eyes were back on his plate, intent on his food. I felt I was close to an essential truth about him. "I think you like to play."

"I *love* to play," he said. "Go on."

"You love to play, you love the game. I think you like the attention and the pressure. I think you like having those kids come up to you. I don't think you like being hurt all the time."

For a moment, he didn't answer; he smiled, tracing his fork along his plate. "You're close. You're very good."

"You like being hurt?"

"No, but it doesn't bother me."

"Nothing bothers you?"

He mouthed the word *no*.

"That's bullshit," I said.

He grinned. "It's not allowed. No complaining. Ever."

"I don't believe you. No one's life is that perfect."

"I didn't say it was perfect. There are things."

"What kind of things?"

"I have nothing to be unhappy about. I am incredibly lucky."

"You're lying to yourself." I could hear the hostility in my voice, but I didn't know how to check it.

"You may think that," he said, "but it doesn't matter what you think. It's what I think that matters when the issue is *me*."

He signaled the waitress for the check. This was all idle chatter for him, riveting jerk-off explorations of the jock psyche, but I was growing desperate. I wanted to draw blood, even though he had just indicated — in a response I found surprisingly well articulated, no matter how self-centered — that nothing I said affected him in any way.

"There's something else," he said, now looking straight at me. "I talked to Beth at Easter, when she was taking me to the airport."

"You did?" There was something about his having had a private conversation with my wife that made me uneasy.

"Uh-huh. Right after your meltdown." He smiled as if to let me know it was all right to talk about it, but I felt humiliated. "I told her that I wanted to help pay off some of that debt she has. All that school debt."

"You did?" I repeated. After all, it had worked the first time.

"Of course, at first she said no fucking way." He sighed, as if by then we were both tediously familiar with Beth's dismissive reaction to a hundred thousand dollars dangled in front of her. "But I worked on her a little, and she said she'd talk to you about it and let me know."

I gazed over his left shoulder, shuffling him into the corner of my field of vision. I was getting very angry. "We haven't talked about it."

"She thought you wouldn't like it."

"It's a lot of money."

"Don't worry about that."

"But it's your money."

"Don't worry about that." The check arrived and he signed for it, slid it away. "I have to go."

He stood up, and I stood with him. "Just think about it," he said. "Don't just say no without thinking about it."

"Why would I do that?"

He smiled. "Because I know you."

He put his hand on my back, and I almost physically recoiled. Patronizing fuck. He kept his hand there as I focused and noticed that around forty or fifty people were waiting for him outside the restaurant. Flashbulbs uselessly popped. There were families and older couples, some of the men in turquoise shirts, and even a few young hotel employees, slumming and gawking on company time, while French toast cooled on room service trays and urgent phone messages went undelivered. The woman with the twins was up front, helplessly heading the crowd that surged around her. And him, and me.

"We'll talk," he whispered, and I felt small and young, and all meaning faded as he emerged, smiled, and slid a black felt pen from his pocket to his hand. He was their magician; they moved toward him and swallowed him whole.

Did I hate my brother at that moment? When you say that you hate someone, that's usually not what you mean. An overpaid colleague snorts when he laughs; a convicted politician smugly proclaims his innocence; an elderly driver, his life a growing blind spot, cuts you off. These are vexing and possibly painful moments, but they're momentary annoyances. They fade as time and sanity do their work. None of these common, daily slights, or a million other indignities like them, demand the permanent and muscular devotion that is true, heroic hatred.

Hate is a full-time job that takes no time at all. You call it forth and surrender to its black ease, feeling it press against your eyelids when you wake in the morning, giving them that slight tagging tremor. It may wane during the day — cowering in the sunlight as you're forced to share a laugh or some false or bitter small talk — but then it returns, surging as you sleep, regenerating in night's cool and moist caress. When you hate, it's all you see. It fills your dreams. Your life is two lives. Hate is a destructive form of love, of loving yourself, of turning inward to confront your truest feelings, regardless of consequence or complication, folding into yourself again and again, halving in size each time, until you are packed so tight that hate is the only thing you can be certain of, the only thing that keeps you alive.

6

A week later, on Tuesday, May 5, I received the first of two urgent messages from the Selvon Dale front office. I was teaching my fourth-period honors physics class when a tall, prematurely goateed boy stood in the open doorway and knocked lightly, handing me the pink message slip. The call was from my mother, and the handwritten message said CALL IMMEDIATELY.

I went to the closet-size lounge area, wedged between the two science classrooms at the northern edge of the school, to use the phone. Leaving your class alone wasn't proper teacher behavior, but I took the chance, because my students that period were relatively responsible. More important, my mother would not usually bother me during the day. My fear was that something bad had happened to my father. *I just knew,* people always say, and my mind quickly fanned through a thick deck of worst-case scenarios. Of course people only say *I just knew* when it turns out they were right, discounting all those times in which I'd become a specialist: when you thought you just knew, but you actually knew nothing.

The phone rang, her private line, and she picked it up immediately.

"Mom."

There was a pause, as if she had been exhaling a cigarette

and had failed to calculate the time it would take. "Dennis?" she said.

"*Mom,*" I said.

"Oh. Joe," she said. I was already annoyed. Who was Dennis, and why was he calling this woman Mom? I didn't know anybody named Dennis — perhaps he was my long-lost half-brother, and my mother was about to conference him in.

"I got your message, Mom." I reclined in the gray lounge chair, hoping to relax. I knew if there was a tragedy, most mothers would not notify their children from the office, but, sadly, I also knew my mother would have been an exception. I couldn't rule out her willful acceptance of death's martyr-dom — trooping into work in full Jacqueline Onassis widow regalia, presiding over the morning's burgeoning docket of legalities: placing neglected black babies in foster care and sentencing slump-shouldered fifteen-year-old graffiti kings to the hardening confinement of the California Youth Authority.

"I'm busy, Joe, so I'll get to the point. It's about your brother."

"CJ?" I asked, feeling exposed. I couldn't imagine that my mother was privy to the complications of our sibling relations, since, as far as I could tell, even the other sibling wasn't privy to them. But her tone, all matter-of-fact, made her sound as if she was about to set me straight on something.

"He's been placed on the fifteen-day disabled list."

"Really?" I was surprised. I'd stopped following his daily progress in the papers once again, though over the past couple of weeks my self-imposed news blackout had done little to lighten my mood. I was still sore over my brother's offer to relieve me of a mountain of personal debt (the bastard), and now he was sore, too.

"It's his left shoulder. It's strained. They think it may be serious."

"I'm sure it's nothing, Mom."

"*You don't know that!*" she screamed, and I almost laughed out loud. I let a pondering silence clog the line to allow her time to settle.

"They have good doctors, Mom. Players go on and off the disabled list all the time." I was playing the role of sage baseball-injury analyst, though I was having trouble taking the whole thing seriously.

"Your brother is very upset," she said.

"Is he really?" I said, hoping that read not as delight but as concern, or maybe a general sense of heightened emotion.

"I think you should call him. I think he'd like to hear from you."

I doubted that highly. "Then I'll call him tonight, Mom. Unless you think it might hurt his shoulder more, picking up the phone and all."

A brief pause. "He can use the speakerphone," she replied. The pause, I understood, was my mother seriously weighing the medical merit of my remark.

"Well, thanks for calling." I could hear my students clamoring in the other room, chairs being dragged and drawers slammed. Even the best students, left alone long enough, would find a way to set something on fire. "Now I've got to go."

"What are you doing?" she asked.

"Mom, I'm *teaching*. You called me at school."

Silence as this sank in. "Call your brother," she said again.

I said goodbye, hung up, and returned to class. Nothing was burning, but one oversexed girl was undulating her pierced belly button for a circle of bug-eyed boys. I smiled at all of them — crazy kids — clapped my hands like a fuddy-duddy, and laughed to let them know I was in on the joke. My brother was injured, he was *disabled*, even though it probably wasn't much: a mild separation or a case of tendinitis. Still, it was a promising start.

Four days later I hadn't yet called him. I made excuses to my mother — I said that I kept getting his answering machine, or that I heard a couple of rings, a brief silence, and then a busy signal, as if the local phone company couldn't handle the electrical surge of good will heading his way. I didn't feel bad about these lies, because lying over the phone to my mother was easy; she often thought I was lying when I was telling the truth. And the injury had been diagnosed as a moderate strain — not a real injury, and certainly not a *disabling* one. He couldn't swing very well, and they wanted him to rest the shoulder for ten more days. If I were a Cubs fan, I would have been outraged at my brother's selfish behavior — a two-week vacation for what amounted to little more than a hangnail — and I planned on rousing public opinion against him as soon as somebody gave me the chance.

I'd started reading the sports section again, though. My brother wasn't playing, so his statistics stood, waiting for him to return and poke them around. He was batting .403, dipping a bit but still the best in the majors, and he hovered near the top of the National League in several other offensive categories. He was also leading the NL in the early voting for the All-Star game, a salient fact brought to my attention that very morning by Hunter Kushi, an eleven-year-old freshman and a master of ikebana, the notoriously exacting Japanese art of flower arranging. Hunter was also under suspicion by school officials for selling black-market Asian DVD porn to members of the soccer team.

It was fourth period, with the blundering seniors still languishing on a concave mirror lab that had puzzled them all week, when the same goateed ruffian showed up at my door with the second momentous pink message slip. I opened it: YOUR WIFE IS HERE — SEND HER UP?

She walked into my classroom a couple of minutes later, dressed in a cool cream suit, waving timidly to the students. "This is Mrs. Columbus," I told them, grabbing her hand (which was probably inappropriate) and pulling her toward the lounge. I tried not to look at their faces, but I knew that I was scoring cool points like fat dollar coins spilling from a slot machine. *Damn,* one of them said, not bothering to be polite.

Beth, with a luscious tan, had returned from Brazil the previous Monday, full of apologies about the missed messages from the days before. The Malquima case had come to a satisfying and lucrative closure — fortunately devoid of car bombings or gunplay — details I could better recapitulate had I been listening, instead of nodding and gaping like a sympathetic idiot, clued only by tone, when Beth originally explained them. But it was truly good news; the settlement promised that the coming months would be free of excessive work, and though I planned to teach summer school, we would have plenty of time to relax, finding the way back to those lost days when we liked each other.

Beth was a different person — chatty and funny and uninhibited, attacking me as I crept out of bed in the morning or, stealing daytime moments, kicking closed her office door and leaving salacious, unrepeatable messages on our answering machine to greet me when I arrived home at night. It was clear to me now that Beth's "career" was what had been fucking us over. When she worked like a normal person, and came home at a normal hour, we got along great. We never discussed the debt or my brother's offer. For a brief time we focused on ourselves — not on money or work, the things we had too much of or the things that we lacked. For a brief, wonderful time, we stood still.

"This is a surprise," I said, closing the lounge door behind us, thinking something *could* happen if the two of us were reckless and thrived on the risk, or if we were younger — a despairing reason to rule out anything when you are still in your twenties.

She leaned back against the door, exhaling loudly. "I have some news," she said.

"It couldn't wait?" I said, hopefully, despite a sudden beat of panic.

She shook her head. "I just saw Dr. Steinman," Beth said, referring to Trina Steinman, her gynecologist, a woman I knew nothing about. "I'm pregnant, Joe."

"Pregnant?" I had no time to choose a reaction, and, unfortunately, in such circumstances my instincts were usually bad. At least I knew enough not to say *Are you sure?* or *Is it mine?*

But beyond that, I was in uncharted territory; I had no mental handbook, filled with pages of appropriate facial expressions or vocal tones, to fall back on.

So I walked quickly to her, smiling generously, and embraced her, my mind still awhirl, smothering her with love, since anything more specific surely would have led to trouble. "This is incredible," I whispered, and it certainly was. It was also a blip, a blip with a mouth, unexpected and not necessarily good. "Have you told anyone?"

"Not yet. We're supposed to wait until the end of the first trimester." *Trimester.* One of those pregnancy words, hovering exclusively above the heads of mommies and daddies to be, double-struck in cartoon clouds of print.

"How far along are you?"

"About five weeks."

"Five weeks . . ." It was unavoidable — I quickly started on the math in my head. *Five weeks ago was late March. When the hell did we* . . . but Beth caught me at it, saw my eyes losing focus as I did the calculations.

She grabbed my wrist. "Stop," she said.

I shrugged sheepishly and moved on, avoiding new father panic by nonsensically fixating on ways to work the word *trimester* into the conversation. "Are you happy?" I asked blankly, before I could think better of it.

She stiffened and pushed me away. "Of course I'm happy. What's that supposed to mean?"

"Nothing. It's just that I'm a little surprised."

"You're going to be a father, Joe." She said it without much conviction, as if she would have to say it several hundred times more, in the coming months — aloud, to herself, to Fetus — to make it stick. Was it already a fetus? What did it look like? Wasn't Beth on the pill? How the fuck had it happened? I thought I could scare up some Eisenhower-era filmstrips, once Beth had gone, to refresh my memory.

"I think we're going to have to work a few things out," she said, her arms folded, hugging herself.

"What kinds of things?" I asked, feeling that certain, unspecified privileges were about to be yanked away from me.

"I want this child to be raised in a loving environment. I don't want us fighting."

"Okay."

"Shit." She started to sniffle, dipping her head, rummaging in her pocket for a tissue with her left hand and unconsciously straightening her suit jacket over her stomach with the other.

"We've been getting along great, Beth."

"Four days, Joe! I've been back four days. Do you think it can last?"

I stood there, silent. It was the first time she had admitted that our relationship might be beyond repair, no matter how many mountain bikes or children, God help us, we threw at it. I had thought the same, but I thought of lots of things. It was a shock to hear it so directly from her. It made me remorseful and foolishly determined to make things right.

"I'm sorry," I said.

"Sorry for what?" she asked, the lawyer in her rising up and demanding specificity, not letting me off with a generic, all-inclusive apology. We were at the point where anything I said would be wrong.

"I'm sorry you feel that way. I think things are great. We're going to have a baby. This is great." I looked out the window, grinning madly.

"It is *not* great," she said, full throttle. "And stop smiling like that. You look like a fucking lunatic."

CJ came off the disabled list ten days later. It was printed in the "transactions" area of the sports page, microfine print running low across several columns, like a tiny touch of the classifieds. My brother was being "activated," as if he was a battery-powered dynamo and the switch had been flipped on. The Cubs had lost eight of the nine games he missed, including a three-game sweep by the Dodgers, in which the Cubs managed a total of two runs. The freefall had knocked them from the division lead for the first time since April, and the swoon ably highlighted how the team depended on having my brother in the lineup.

That morning, before leaving for school, I pulled the AP

game preview off my computer. CJ said that he was feeling "one hundred percent" and denied reports that the injury was worse than team officials were letting on. I smirked as I scrolled down and read his quotes. Had he rushed back? "I haven't rushed myself back," he said. "I feel great." Did he think the team couldn't win without him? "We've been on a tough road trip, and we've run into some great pitching. No team relies on one person, and it will take contributions from all of us to make a run at the World Series this year." I could have written those responses.

The late-afternoon game wasn't on television, so I caught the highlights during *Baseball Tonight,* the glossy and exhausting nightly program on ESPN. I didn't want to know but I *had* to know, and I held my breath, waiting for the show to begin, knowing that if the camera picked up his face, it would be because he'd done something good. And of course they showed his face — they led with his face — because he was *back,* baby. Shit. Beth was yelling at me from the bedroom, but I didn't pay any attention. CJ had gone four for four, with three singles and a home run. They showed all of his hits, slap slap boom slap; they showed his teammates crossing the plate in slow motion; they showed him clenching his fist at first base after driving in his fourth and fifth runs of the day. My brother had returned, the Cubs had won, and order was restored to the world.

He called that night, but I wasn't home. I'd gone out to get ice cream for Beth. Not just any ice cream; she demanded the long-lost, outcast blend known as spumoni. I assumed that ice cream craving thing was a myth, but we were in the process of living up to what was expected of us, Beth included. If I thought it was a myth, it was up to my wife to prove me wrong and make it real. I had to admit that spumoni was an impressively unexpected choice and, of course, was impossible to find. I told her this would be the case before I left, and she started crying again — the slightest twinge in life's barometer set her off these days — so I trooped out the door and did as I was told.

At the second gourmet grocery store (fifth stop overall) I

managed to find it, a big untouched and dusty jackpot stack — the box a garish shade of plum, with a perfect tricolored mottled slab of the concoction served up in the foreground, and in the background a dinner party congregating, fuzzy and out of focus, around a living room fireplace. All we needed was a fondue pot and Twister, and we'd be in business.

Instead of checking out and heading home, I lingered, wandering sourly down the fluorescent aisles until the frozen ice cream container, my very reason for being, became drippy in my hands as my hot fingertips melted through the gritty frost that coated the carton. I plopped it down in a basket of green-sheathed fresh corn, as if deciding that those two foodstuffs ought to get to know each other better. I would tell Beth that the store was sold out — victimized by furious, spumoni-hoarding yuppie mobs — and since it was midnight on a Sunday I considered this effort enough.

So it was only when I got home that I learned CJ had called. I was surprised, and Beth surprised me further by saying that, in fact, she had called *him*. She was planning to leave a message, but he had just arrived home from San Diego, so they spoke. She told him about the baby, even though we weren't telling anyone yet. He was happy about the news. I listened to all of this, making a mental note to check the phone bill when it arrived to see how long this conversation had lasted. Beth forgot to ask me about the ice cream, so I returned to the couch.

There, I turned on the television, flipping through the channels. I planned to sleep there that night, my bad mood a thick blanket around me. Beth was up often during the night, and I was granting her space. Two nights before was the last time we'd slept in the same bed; I woke up after two, because she had scratched me across the forehead. I reached out and held her hands in mine, turning them over as she slept, until I found the finger I was looking for, with my incriminating strip of skin, tanned like a potato peel, wedged under the nail. We did not discuss the baby as a good thing or bad thing. The baby was coming, my brother was perfect at the plate, and we were not discussing anything at all.

* * *

Selvon Dale Arts Magnet was wired for television. Each room had a twenty-seven-inch monitor bolted high in the corner, originally used for broadcasting some empowered youth national news program. There were sixty-second reports on celebrated children who flew gliders or apprenticed in four-star restaurants, or longer "investigative" pieces on prepubescent Aussie environmentalists or starving Somalis (around Halloween time, when the orange UNICEF boxes were distributed). These straight-faced tales, full of forced enthusiasm or concern, were generally ignored by Selvon Dale's jaded prodigy populace. They were followed by blocks of demographically correct ads for zit cream or grape bubble gum, which the students found riveting.

All of this was gone, however. The company that beamed the edutainment into our school had vanished just before the descent of angry creditors. One day the picture was electronic snow, and although one teacher thought it was a new form of performance-art programming, eventually the televisions were turned off for good. There was talk of students setting up their own television studio, but no one had solicited my opinion on the topic, so I kept silent. Privately, I thought it was a horrible idea; the last thing Selvon Dale students needed was another outlet for expressing themselves.

On that Tuesday, after all the students had gone, I closed the blinds to ward off the glare and turned on the television to watch my brother play. I had seen Principal Sully in the cafeteria earlier that day, and, deciding it was proper for me to get official go-ahead for any afterschool lounging, I'd mentioned that I might put the game on late in the day. He knew who my brother was and nodded, but his eyes quickly sailed past me, rooting out potential trouble near the pasta bar. I'd figured Sully would be fine with it, and I hoped he'd remember — later that day, as the stacks of administrative matters facing him began to shrink — and maybe stop by.

But I was alone with the televised image of the Cubs, playing an afternoon game at Wrigley against the Giants. The Giants were batting, so I had to wait a pitch for the inning and the score. Finally it appeared in the lower right-hand corner: the count was no balls and two strikes, top of the third, two outs and the Cubs ahead, three to nothing. The gangly Giant at the plate whiffed at a high fastball, and the inning was over. My brother was scheduled to bat second in the next half-inning.

After the first batter grounded out, CJ strode to the plate. Average: .411. Today: one for one. Doubled and scored. I took a few steps back and leaned against a desk in the front row. This was the first time I'd watched a game in the classroom; it had never before occurred to me. But as I was driving to school that morning it seemed crucial and obvious, and I was amazed that I hadn't thought of it before. Afterward, it struck me as stupid. I don't know why I thought that experiencing my personal and professional unhappiness in one location would somehow expose and then remedy both. And yet there was something natural about it, the way I was bringing everything together, giving in, bottoming out. It was my brother and the pitcher on the television screen, framed in the traditional way, but it was really my brother and I. The sound of the television was off. I chewed my lower lip. I was my own form of commentary.

I thought about a report I had read somewhere — in the dentist's waiting room, or, furtively, in my lap during the Irish line-dancing assembly — about machines being susceptible to human touch: if you stroked the photocopier and called it by name, it was less likely to jam on you. The difference was infinitesimal but measurable, and the author went on to relate, with goofy enthusiasm, the global ramifications of the discovery. But what the article never explained was how you knew whether you were calling the copier by the *correct* name; perhaps he wasn't Buddy at all. And what if he was actually a she, who'd once dated a fax machine named Buddy, and all that time you'd been whispering and stroking her spongy blue and green buttons, or fondling her plastic melded frameboards, you were only rubbing it in?

I closed my eyes as CJ readied himself in the batter's box,

bobbing on his knees the way he liked to do. I could see it in the literal dark of my mind. *This* was man against machine, and I wished, for once, for him — whichever he was — to swing and miss.

When I opened my eyes, he was on the ground. I didn't know how he got there. He was on his side, his knees bent up, his forearms covering his face like a battered boxer. A trainer and team doctor were kneeling beside him, clamping a towel to his face. There was blood everywhere, covering everything, spilling on the ground, making pearls of ruddy paste with the ballfield dirt. The catcher staggered back, his mask removed, staring down at him. The pitcher, a wiry Dominican with gold hoops in both ears, stood ten feet away, hands on hips, pacing, clearly distraught. CJ wasn't moving.

I stepped to the television as they showed the replay. CJ was at the plate, batting from the right side against the left-hander. There was the windup, the high leg kick and the pitch — and the ball just took off. It was the high, inside heat: you could see my brother try to escape it, but as he leaned back, the ball tailed up a little more, dogging him, a pitch with all the wrong kinds of late movement. I couldn't see where it hit him — maybe just below the eye, on that hard socket bone. (I caught myself touching mine, feeling the early throb of a phantom ache.) The television producers denied us the tighter, revelatory view that the camera positioned down the first-base line would have provided. Instead, we saw the center-field camera angle two more times, and then we were back in real time, as a stretcher was wheeled toward him and an ambulance appeared from a pair of green barn doors hidden behind the ivy of the right-field wall. We saw the fans in the stands, silent and concerned, trapped witnesses. A boy cried and buried his face against his father; his mother kneaded his small shoulder and absently separated the strands of his fine blond hair before placing a ballcap back on his head. The ambulance slowly made its way around. The doctor held a white towel to my brother's face, his fingers spread apart; he was not applying much pressure. Blood soaked the towel in dime-size spots.

They loaded him into the ambulance, and the game, as if staggering through fog, went on.

I snapped off the television, laughing in nervous disbelief and shaking my head like some shnook in a smoky bar, wondering whether all us working stiffs had seen the same thing. But of course I was alone, in near silence and unobserved, the only sound coming from the closed venetian blinds, clacking against the open windows.

I grabbed my windbreaker and left Selvon Dale. As I drove home, I kept expecting to see that ambulance a few car lengths ahead of me. I listened to the news twice, but it was all traffic, no sports. It was only when I got home, when I heard the messages from Beth and my mother, when I talked to them and let them explain in their halting words, that I knew it was the world's truth as well as my own. What I'd seen in the classroom wasn't a private, fantastical screening. It was fact. It had happened.

He'd broken his nose, and it bled a lot. It looked much worse than it was, and it could have been bad had the ball hit a few inches one way or the other. He could have been abruptly embarking on a permanent, caved-face exile, the dented beginning of a lonely, wayward twilight of extensive self-abuse and might-have-beens. But it was just a broken nose that bled a lot, which would keep him antsy and bench-bound for a couple of weeks, and then he'd be back in the game.

Right after it happened, my mother wanted us to all meet in Chicago. "It's just a broken nose, Mom," I said on the phone.

"It's *very* broken," she said.

"You mean it's a stage two?" I asked. As far as I knew, there was no such thing, but I was staring at a Discovery Channel show about the Apollo program, muted on the living room television, and I felt the desire to fill my speech with rocket vernacular.

"It's a stage *three,*" my mother said.

Was everyone in the world making up shit as they went along? "Trust me, Mom. He'll be fine." And again, as I finished talking to her, I promised to call him.

Late that night I climbed into bed with Beth. She was up late, reading that book about pregnancy, the comprehensive one that everyone read, *What to Expect When You're Expecting*. I'd glanced at the hefty tome when Beth wasn't around. There was a big sympathetic section for fathers, but much larger portions were devoted to cervixes and breast changes that I considered relevant to my life on a purely don't ask, don't tell basis. The front cover claimed NATIONAL BEST-SELLER, and I wondered if Henry Fomacci had been alerted. Even a man of his limited creative reach probably could have come up with a snazzier title — something like *Absolutely Unnecessary Pregnant Justice*.

"You took care of the flowers?" I asked.

"Yes," she said. We'd sent CJ some flowers, the busted honker bouquet or something like that. It struck me as a bad idea. When someone broke his nose, wasn't it cruel to send him a gift he was supposed to smell? But I was overruled.

"What are you learning?" I asked.

There was silence as she reached the end of a paragraph, highlighter in hand, her index finger holding the spot on the page. She was studying the book as if it were a deposition, marking it up and making notes. "About my complexion," she said, "how to take care of it." She peered over at me, through thin reading glasses, and smiled. I'd caught her at a good time.

"Is this about the glow?" I asked. I loved talking about the glow.

"You're a dork," she said.

My brother's injury, and the role I felt I had played in it, was on my mind. "You know I saw CJ get hit today," I said.

"We all saw it, Joe."

"I mean I saw it as it happened." It was a critical distinction. "I was watching the game in my room at school, he came up to the plate, and I closed my eyes. When I opened them, he was on the ground."

She put the book aside. "Why did you close your eyes?"

I leaned back on the pillow and closed them again. "I don't know."

"You cursed him, Joe."

I sat up, but she was smiling at me and shaking her head. "You don't really think that, do you?"

It would have been easier to say nothing, but her tone was patronizing. How dare she doubt my telekinetic ability, or whatever you call it? Why *couldn't* I have cursed my brother?

"I wanted something bad to happen," I said.

"You wanted him to get hit in the face?"

And hearing it spoken by my totally sane pregnant wife, leaning on her elbow and assessing me with total revulsion, I knew how bad it sounded. I began to backtrack.

"I was rooting for the other team," I said.

This seemed to satisfy her. "You need to pick a different sport to follow, Joe. Something less emotional for you." She leaned back and opened her book again. "Without teams," she said, narrowing it down. "Tennis."

I agreed. I was off the hook, but that somehow made it worse. I had lied about my evil thoughts and had got away with it. Lying gave my thoughts a cover; inside my mind I could roam the night at will.

When school ended a few weeks later, my brother had returned to the Cubs lineup in name only. He sat out twelve games after the broken nose, from May 18 to May 31. The Cubs played .300 ball without him, which was acceptable for a single batter but not much of a winning percentage for an entire team. Houston widened their lead to six games, and the Cubs were passed by the Cardinals and slipped into third place.

The day after CJ's nose was smashed, we learned that he'd also suffered a concussion. He could have riskily played with the broken nose if he'd worn a face shield on the basepaths and been willing to switch temporarily to one of the outfield positions (where there was less danger of getting hit again), but the concussion's residual effects would not allow it. He still had occasional dizzy spells and headaches, which kept him off the field and prevented his pinch-hitting. It was only on the first of June that the symptoms finally faded, and he was medically cleared to return.

He came back frustrated and rusty, and some of the beat writers thought he'd become a little wary — standing a few inches farther from the plate, pulling anything that was pitched inside, as if deciding to swat the ball away at the earliest possible moment, as soon as he feared it might be ticketed for him. Of course, this was all speculation; CJ said he felt fine. He said he wouldn't be playing if he wasn't up to it, and after a few days of those generic, write-them-yourself answers, he stopped talking to the media altogether — prima donna behavior very unlike him.

But things didn't get any better. In the next two weeks he slumped like never before in his major league career. In the thirteen games after his return, he had only five hits out of fifty-three at-bats, which worked out to an .094 batting average. He had struck out twenty-six times! His average for the year had dropped almost eighty points. His edge was gone, and I imagined that baseball was all sorts of fun when you were playing it well, but if you were grasping, if the game was leaving you baffled and shaking your head, it must have felt as if it was coming at you, and there was no time to step back, regroup, and recover.

I was watching television when the phone rang. Beth picked it up in the bedroom and I forgot about it, but twenty minutes later, when I went to the bedroom, she was still on the phone, and it was CJ. He had played a day game at Wrigley and gone hitless in four at-bats. The Cubs had lost, seven to one.

"She might like that," Beth said into the phone as I walked in. She had taken to giving him advice on what gifts to buy his current girlfriend.

"Let me talk to him," I said.

"Joe's here," she said, then waited and laughed at his response. I would never know what he had said to my wife that was so damn funny. She handed the phone to me, and I walked away with it.

"Numbah nine," I said, as if I were ordering take-out from a Chinese restaurant.

"Beth sounds good," he said.

"They were talking about your batting stance on ESPN," I said, feeling playful, not caring if he was in the mood.

"Fuck ESPN," he said evenly. I pictured him rubbing his forehead, sad that the part of the conversation he'd enjoyed was over. His mind was probably wandering as he considered alternative, productive things he could be doing with his time, like emptying the dishwasher or making a sandwich.

"How are you feeling?" I asked.

"I'm feeling fine," he said.

"One hundred percent?" I asked.

"I've really got to go."

"You don't want to talk to me, eh?"

"I don't want to be harassed."

"You talked to Beth for a while," I said. "I'm not harassing you."

Silence.

"What do you have to do?"

"Things."

"Just things?"

"Just things. Gotta go, Joe."

I handed the phone back to Beth. She was frowning at me. "You don't have to be an asshole," she said.

"What did I do?" I said.

"You are so obvious," she said, walking away.

Maybe I was. But so was my brother, grounding into his game-ending double plays. By then I was obvious and I didn't care.

It was the beginning of the end at Selvon Dale: two days of academic finals, followed by two days of music and dance recitals, which I was mercifully not required to attend. There would be two mornings of faculty meetings, afternoons of inventories and generalized wrapping-up. In a week I would begin teaching summer school — two straight-up chemistry classes — at a high school farther down county and closer to where I lived.

There wasn't much to do once the exam was handed out.

My eyes were wide and unfixed; the students' faces were fuzzy. I was thinking about my brother. It was the first time he had struggled at baseball since we were kids, and I was obsessing about his slump and how far it would go. I wondered if it was in his head now — if he spent time considering that maybe the beanball had knocked something out of alignment, scattering that critical cluster of cells in his head that played the proper soundtrack. I wondered if he prayed for good luck, or resigned himself to life finally paying him back, evening things out. These were imponderables, since I could never ask him the questions or trust his answers. But they were also the all-day suckers of my life — sourballs tucked in the corner of my mouth, certainly bitter but never losing their undeniably sweet bolt of flavor.

Back on earth there were yearbooks to sign. As my mind wandered, I'd forgotten about them, a black weighty stack on my desk. *Life Is a Cabaret!* read the covers, enunciating the shrill and optimistic theme of the latest edition of *The Pawprint*. (In my opinion, life definitely wasn't a cabaret, and certainly not one with an exclamation point.) I quickly counted *The Pawprints* in front of me: eleven to sign, out of a possible twenty-nine students. I was batting almost .380. My brother should have been so lucky.

Those students who'd paid a modest fee had their names engraved in the lower right-hand corner of the cover. The first yearbook on the stack belonged to Rosemary Puka, a smart girl who tried to fit in by acting dumb, giggled skittishly, got breasts summarily in November, and was derisively referred to by classmates as Spice Vomit. *To Rosemary,* I wrote, and I hurried through my signature to make it look frenzied and important.

The next book on the stack lacked a nameplate, so I opened it to the front few pages of heavier paper, but they were also blank. *This student did not pre-order,* I thought with fussy disgust. He was also way behind in accumulating autographic proof of popularity. I flipped to the back and found two signatures, one in green and one in red, probably done at the same time with one of those fat Bic ballpoints with the four colored wickets you clicked with your thumb. The autographs were dopey and inexpressive. YOU WERE FUNNY IN FIRST PERIOD, asserted one fondly, and the other one brilliantly riffed off the first: TO BRIAN: STAY FUNNY.

Brian. Was I holding the yearbook of the apparently side-splitting Brian Exley? There was one Brianne in my class, but no other Brian (and Brianne wasn't funny at all). I closed the cover, and, sure enough, Brian had put his personal stamp on it. His initials were *carved* into the cover, the loops of the first letter carefully curved and tailored, not the straight lines of someone hacking away. It was as if he had done similar knife-work before. But where? Maybe a girlfriend's initials, laced in perpetuity on the trunk of a tree, or a little late-night stiletto action while sitting Indian-style at the foot of his bed, listening to some Floyd, doodling improv squiggles on the canvas of his forearm.

It was exactly nine educational weeks since I had signed an autograph for Brian's father, and now the son wanted his own. For the first few weeks, at least, young Brian had made a game effort to get his work done and stay afloat. It had been his token act of survival — a month of behaving the way everyone else had behaved all along, demonstrating the capacity buried inside even the most distracted and incapable fuck-up, enough to keep his grade a measly margin above failing. But Brian had disappeared from my class a couple of weeks earlier, and I had no idea how his yearbook ended up on my desk, since I didn't even think he was in the building.

Though I can't say I liked Brian, I had developed a certain respect for him. His confidence, his selfish ability to focus on only what interested him — these were part of it — but, more important, I had been a late witness to his extraordinary artistic talent. Selvon Dale held mandatory recitals every other Friday morning; six students were chosen in strict rotation, performing at various levels of competence and bladder control, in front of the entire school. Brian's number came up in the middle of May, and I didn't know enough about music to judge whether what he played was difficult or whether all the nuances were properly accounted for. I was told that the selection was Chopin, and I sat there, stunned, as Brian played beautifully. Reading about it in his student information folder was not the same as hearing it. He was in control, and focused, and where he belonged. For the first time I had an idea of what my class must have been like for him, how virtually nonsensical when set against this other world, his pure ideal. The performance rubbed off on him, at least in my mind, because from then on, whenever I saw him, I also heard him. Brian had become a student with his own theme, an ironic counterpoint to his honed, knee-jerk indifference.

I signed the other yearbooks until only Brian's remained. I was tempted to incriminate myself with sarcasm: TO A SHITTY STUDENT, I could have written, THANK YOU FOR NOT ALWAYS CHEATING. Or TO A DAMN FINE PIANO PLAYER, HOPE NOTHING BAD HAPPENS TO YOUR HANDS BECAUSE THEN YOU ARE SERIOUSLY FUCKED (AND YOU MIGHT BE FUCKED ANYWAY). Or I could have done something sly, like turning to a random page and using my left hand to scrawl I AM GOING TO KILL YOU. He would have found it months, maybe years, later, wondering who had so passionately and anonymously sought to do him in. But I ended up doing none of those things, and just gave him the standard signature over my shirt and tie. I still hadn't resolved the question of why he even wanted my signature. Though I knew little about him, it seemed most un-Exley-like.

The exam ended, the students fled, and I spotted Brian at the door. He was waiting for all of them to go. Finally it was just the two of us. He had his hands in his pockets as he slouched toward me, the two of us heading for a low-energy showdown, his yearbook the only one on my desk.

"You missed the final, Brian," I said.

"Yeah," he said, imitating regret. "I had this audition, up at Peabody? Couldn't get out of it."

"Really?" I asked. That wasn't a valid excuse, but at least it was interesting.

"No," he said, laughing nervously. He was dressed more nicely than usual: pressed navy pants, a white oxford shirt buttoned up all the way, as if he'd recently loosened and yanked a striped tie from around his neck. Perhaps he had come from some other distasteful obligation he didn't want to tell me about.

"You can take the final tomorrow if you want," I said.

He squinted toward the windows. "I'm not sure that's such a good idea." He made it sound almost like a threat, as if the bomb would go off when he put pencil to paper.

"If you don't take the final, you'll fail, Brian. Don't you want to pass?"

He scratched his head, trying to puzzle a way out of the dilemma that wasn't a dilemma: he needed to take the fucking test.

"You were doing pretty well," I said.

"Nothing lasts," he said.

"Well, it *could* have lasted," I said. He shrugged, quiet and bored. "It's like when you're playing piano —" I said, but stopped short as he cocked an eyebrow.

"Do you want me to help you, Brian?"

"Not really."

I was disappointed, though I shouldn't have been. I was the one who couldn't help myself. And now this unpleasant young man stood before me, stacked with talent, pampered and rotten, unwilling to conform. He probably didn't deserve the chances I was willing to give him.

"You're going to fail this class, Brian," I repeated.

He traced his finger down the wall, along the groove that joined two painted cinder blocks. He stopped short at an intersection, weaved to the right, zigzagged down until his hand was once again at his side.

Then he wandered over and slid the yearbook across my desk toward him until it tipped off the edge and climbed into the crook of his arm. He looked at me, holding the book against his chest like a shield, and backed away.

"Well. Have a good summer, Brian. Keep in touch."

He laughed. "You're funny, man." He shuffled the yearbook low into his left hand, bounced it against his calf, and walked out, slapping the top of the doorway with his fingertips, failing but free.

Nothing lasts. Thus spoke Brian Exley — the sage and brooding Wunderkind. What Brian was saying was that for all elements of life there were statistical norms. In my class he had briefly strayed by doing much better than expected, by acting interested, by having ability. But when he caught himself at it, he used it as a convenient excuse to fall back and eventually fall off. It was only a matter of time before the law of averages caught up with him, he probably figured, so why not get a head start? Because *nothing lasts.* It was pithy, bone-yard wisdom, taken for granted or promptly ignored. Even if you took it seriously, you didn't take it seriously for long; it faded from your mind because nothing lasts, and soon enough you were back where you started, and most likely it was the neighborhood where you'd always belonged.

Brian disappeared from sight that afternoon, and the Cubs kicked off their interleague schedule against the crosstown White Sox. My brother hit for the cycle — a single, double, triple, and home run in one game — and he did it in style. My brother hit for the cycle *in order.* A single in the first, a double in the third, a triple in the sixth, and a home run in the ninth, a three-run exclamation point into the South Side stratosphere. He was the first player to hit for the cycle in sequence in fifteen years.

The Cubs won seventeen of their next nineteen games. My brother had fifty-three hits in eighty-six at-bats (.616), raising his average once again to the top of the majors (.415). It was the highest batting average by a full-time starter at the All-Star break in over fifty years. He arrived at the break with a twenty-game hitting streak, and he would be starting in the All-Star game for the first time, the leading vote-getter among National League players.

None of this should have surprised me, no matter how much

I may have willed him a shower of failure. I had savored a late spring of watching him suffer through a nagging shoulder injury, a career-threatening fastball to the face, and an unprecedented slump. But then summer and my brother both arrived with a vengeance: temperatures in the high nineties for days on end, the air in Maryland aggressively thick, and my brother too good a player, too much the professional, to flare out and give me the happy ending I wanted. There were times when I had believed he'd grow so frustrated that he'd throw up his hands and retire. Once in his life that had already *not* happened, and logic indicated that it was absurd to believe that it ever would, but the deluded man never concerns himself with reality or its particulars. CJ was good, period. He wasn't giving anything up. And I was once again the fool, to think that I had any impact, or to believe it was wise to tie his fortunes to the sweaty rise and fall of my own.

As he continued to surge, there was only obsession. Beth and I celebrated our anniversary and visited her obstetrician. On both occasions I nodded and smiled and asked questions and made comments, latching on to the proper nouns that I remembered hearing a second or two before. But inside my roiling mind I pondered: he was hitting over .400. Where would his average end up? When did he learn to hit the slider? How many doubles had he had this month? What was his fielding percentage last week? How many runs did he drive in last night? I was awash in numbers and statistics, fixated on them, none of them comforting. He had suffered a bad patch and then torn through a good one, but he was not a streaky player. He was reliably great, and the rest of the season was a road that stretched glumly ahead of me, inevitably focused on his accomplishments. There were all the personal accolades — batting .400, winning the triple crown — but there were also his Cubs to deal with. And they clearly were *his,* led by him, unbearably dependent on him. He was the franchise.

As I was driving home from summer school one day in early July, I finally acknowledged that it would never end. I was the last to know but I finally knew it, once and for all. He would play another ten or fifteen years, a shoo-in for the Hall of Fame. And after he stopped playing, after a farewell tour of trotting from the dugout and tipping his cap — under which he'd still have a full head of hair — he'd probably *manage* the Cubs for thirty or forty years. He'd select from the bevy and marry; she would stay home with the kids — a princess to dote on, then three strapping boys, and she would love him unconditionally, indulging his moods and icing his bruises.

I sat at a light on Shady Grove Road, thinking about all of this. I can remember the moment clearly. It was a standard intersection — gas stations, Blockbuster, suburban makeshift fruit and vegetable stand. I heard the sound of my left turn blinker and the huff of the air conditioner on high. As I took this pause, the reality of my life settled in. I felt a strange calm descend on me. I wasn't angry or sad. I accepted it. I could not pinpoint a reason, or a moment, that turned the tide. It was a strange confluence or accumulation, a mountain of accomplishment that had reached a tipping point while I was sitting in traffic, waiting for the light to change. My brother was an amazing baseball player. We weren't close, and I knew that we never would be. But at the very least I would be neutral. Maybe I could learn to watch him without loathing. Maybe I would be able to pull for him. They were small steps, but I was certain that my days of hating, my days of wishing him ill, were over.

That night I was almost drunk with my epiphany; the absence of bad feelings was a feeling in and of itself. I turned on the All-Star Home Run "derby," waiting for my brother to step to the plate. It was a meaningless competition, designed to rouse the fans and fill the stadium for an extra day of "festivities," but, even so, there was something undeniably cool about it — watching the lucky few players who got in a groove and managed to muscle ball after ball out of the yard. That year it was Griffey and Piazza and McGwire who caught the wave, with hitchless and misleadingly fluid swings that looked easy, swings that made you think they were playing the same game you played, made you think you could still tomahawk it, too.

The National League won, but I was puzzled that my brother had never come to the plate. I was sure that, as a marquee player, he'd been penciled in for this affair. I picked up the phone to call my father and find out what had happened, but before I could finish punching the buttons, the ESPN commentator mentioned that CJ was a late scratch for the competition. His previously strained shoulder was acting up, and he wanted to give it an extra day of rest — it made sense at the time. It never entered my mind that it was a lie.

Beth arrived home and I got up to meet her at the door. I had taken to doing that in a pathetic, chivalric attempt at easing her increasingly visible burdens. Work had returned to consume her, as she'd been shuffled from the sugar litigation to an equally intricate and yawn-inducing case involving the pyramid scheme of a Central European dictator, foisted on his grim and ignorant public. Beth insisted that the work was fascinating, but her body language clearly contradicted her. She was sagging, brutalized by the long hours and the insidious summer heat, and I sensed that her supervising partner was trying to wring her completely, since he knew that he would lose her at the end of the year and well into the next.

Thunder rumbled ominously outside the dayroom window, like the sound of furniture being dragged across the floor over our heads, and accompanied by occasional strobes of lightning. The air conditioner hummed, most of the apartment lights remained off, the rain burst in the sky, and we ate in silence, savoring the quiet. Beth took a bath, and shortly after nine she went to sleep.

I stayed up, out in the living room, the television down low. I needed more baseball. That Monday night and Wednesday, the off days that bracketed the All-Star game itself, were the only days of summer without baseball, and I knew there were fans out there who missed it. Every other summer night they came home and turned on one of a handful of games. Some of those fans were devoted, watching their favorite team from start to finish. Others found themselves snared by some unexpected drama, not caring who would win, just wondering how it would all turn out. This idea moved me tremendously, for some reason. I fell asleep with this tiny wisdom humming in my mind, casting off to drift in a sea of sweet, uncomplicated dreams.

The phone woke me, ringing and ringing. Though the volume was constant and the sound persistent, deep sleep made me dull to it. Only after several minutes did it slip from dreamy accompaniment to a sound that required action. I blinked at the clock; it was three-thirty-seven.

I lurched to my feet and fumbled for the phone, spilling a desktop mug of pens and pencils. "Hello?" I said, slumping to the desk chair, looking out at the night. The storm had ended. The sky was clear, with the occasional long and lean residual cloud, the moon chalky and full.

"Joe." The voice was matter-of-fact and deliberate.

"CJ?" I was still half asleep but felt a sudden focus. "It's real late here, CJ."

No answer. There was a surge of energy on the line, like the buzz of a low-flying plane. It was interference from a building with hundreds of people living in it. I leaned back and chased it away, and the line was silent once again.

"Hello?" I said.

"Joe," he said again, his voice trembling and cracking, breaking my name in two.

Part Three

7

The cab ride from Chicago's O'Hare International Airport took Beth and me past Comiskey Park, sterile home of the rival White Sox. I remembered rumors that when the new Comiskey opened, "they" found bullet holes in some of the upper deck seats, as if snipers from the steady rows of high-rise housing projects, skirting the opposite side of the Dan Ryan Expressway, were taking their best welcoming shots. Whether this was true, I had no idea; it sounded to me like the cruel and unnecessary mongering of petty middle-class whites, fishing for reasons to stay away.

Traffic slowed, marred and narrowed by the orange barrels and yellow coin lights of highway construction, until the lanes merged into one, like a stick whittled to nothing. This cab was not air-conditioned, but we didn't notice until we were trapped inside its steamy confines and away from O'Hare. We nudged along, cracking the back windows as far as childproofing allowed, still overwhelmed by the creeping stickiness of the mid-afternoon heat.

We were stuck in a dingy and low-lying industrial area on the southern outskirts of downtown, but as the road bent slightly and opened up, a series of buildings muscled up to the right side of the freeway. And on the side of one was a colossal mural of CJ. The mural must have been five stories high —

there was a dominant close-up of his face, serious and game, charcoal smudged under his eyes. Beneath and to the right was a smaller action sketch: he trailed the bat at his side, his legs scissored and ready to spring from the box, watching the arc of the ball as it popped from his bat. To the left was the big swooshy logo and a single word: FOUND.

The Chicago skyline bore down on us as we passed the billboard, traffic surging to twenty miles an hour and the cab turned inside out and windy, like a giant blow dryer. Beth had never been to Chicago, and she held my hand tight. There was no use talking about anything, because the world was now a different place, coated by one tragic fact, a secret — dug from the grim ground late the night before, when my brother woke me, and a few hours later, when I woke Beth. My parents also knew, and some officials from the league and the team. It would go public officially at five-thirty that night, two hours before the All-Star game, when team physicians would hold a press conference to announce that my brother had acute myeloid leukemia.

In a lifetime of trivial events, petty rivalries, and minor cares, this did not fit in. It was the heavy drama and chance disaster cribbed from someone else's less fortunate story line — inappropriate and unwanted, yet thrust upon us. Setting aside the thumb-twiddling questions of fairness, I found myself wrestling with the plausibility of it all. These things don't happen to us — that's what entitled people always say. But then you stop and realize that the reason they haven't happened is only that they haven't happened. Once they do, it doesn't mean you're unlucky or cursed or have something to be ashamed of. It means that you're alive, like everyone else.

He was to begin chemotherapy immediately. There were no other options, and I supposed that was one of the questions the reporters would ask. The five-year survival rate for acute myeloid leukemia was 25 percent — the word *only* prefacing that lean number, depending on your level of sensitivity. In the first six months, during the first "consolidation" chemotherapy — in which the goal was to induce a remission — 65 percent did go into remission, 25 percent did not go into remission and did not survive, and the remaining 10 percent did not survive as a result, direct or indirect, of the side effects of the chemotherapy.

I was not as wise about this as I sounded. I'd found a lot of information, some of it accurate, on the computer early that morning, after finishing the conversation with my brother and promising to see him at his house the next day. The statistics were there, amidst survivor stories and reviews of clinical protocols — hundreds of pages and links to places I had never wanted to go. Before that I didn't know anything. No one in my family had ever suffered from cancer of any kind.

I had visited Chicago, but I had never seen my brother's house, the one he bought two years before in the posh Lincoln Park area. According to my parents, he had been talking about moving. Though he enjoyed the neighborhood, he had a need for more privacy. The cab wended its way through tight streets, past ferny stores filled with overstuffed furniture, past gourmet groceries where aproned employees probably knew your name and the bread you liked and the train you caught. Attractive mothers in walking shorts and tucked-in T-shirts chatted as their strollered infants poked at each other, and when we moved off the main thoroughfare into the sway- ing shady trees of the street my brother called home, we saw that many of the houses were architectural marvels, slotted squarely and perfectly into tight city spaces.

My brother's house lacked such scale; it was a tidy, decep- tively spacious four-story rowhouse at the end of a quiet block, with a gated triangular side lawn, a one-car garage, and a driveway that dipped down and right up across the sidewalk. The cab let us out, and we buzzed the front gate; it buzzed back and let us in.

My father greeted us at the door, and we followed him into the white-tiled entryway. He seemed all right. I heard my mother's voice upstairs and suspected that the pacing footsteps directly above my head were hers. She was taking charge, demanding answers to questions, formulating plans. This was her immediate way of coping, and whether it was helpful was for my brother to decide.

We shed our bags and trooped upstairs behind my father. We passed the living room, furnished expensively for maximum bachelor comfort, and mouthed hellos to my mother in the second-floor kitchen (she was indeed on the phone), walked up a second, tan-carpeted flight of stairs, past a weight room, guest bedroom, and office. I was glad that we continued to move, because I knew that at the end of all this obligatory motion there would be my brother, and I had no idea what condition he was in. So long as I could keep walking or riding or flying, lulled by passing landmarks big and small, I could avoid any overdramatic assessments and the reason for all this movement in the first place.

We reached the bedroom, and my father peeled away, heading downstairs to my mother. CJ was on the phone, his back to us. I looked for signs to indicate not illness or weakness, but, I guess, an acknowledgment of difference. He was wearing shorts and a T-shirt, holding a pair of navy sweat pants, folding them, with his free hand, into a duffel bag. I'd expected other people to be here — team officials, mysterious drug-dealer type friends, or the parasitic Spencer Levitt, shedding crocodile tears and pawning medical emergency trinkets — but there was no one. Beth said CJ had broken it off with his latest girlfriend a couple of weeks ago, and my brother suffered the isolation of the modern celebrity athlete, never sure whom to trust or rely on. As of that day, we were back to the basics: his family was his only entourage.

He smiled at us and tossed the portable phone on the bed. "Look at you," he said to Beth, marveling at her bulging belly. She walked over and hugged him. I wandered behind; he let go of Beth and gave me a hug.

"How are you feeling?" Beth asked.

"A little fever, but I'm fine," he said, holding out the palms of his hands. "It's like you're tired, but I'm always tired."

"I like the house," I said.

He turned to me. "I thought you'd been here before."

"Nope."

"Oh," he said, and Beth glared at me. It must have sounded like an accusation of rudeness, which I hadn't intended. "Well, if you've made it all the way up here, then you've pretty much seen the whole thing."

"It's nice, CJ," Beth said quietly.

He smiled at her again and then turned toward the bay window, speaking almost to himself. "I do like the view."

I followed his gaze and saw nothing remarkable: the street below, the brick façades of other houses, the hazy distant skyline accompanied by the muffled clamor of a nearby sandy playground. The silence in the bedroom lengthened, leaving each of us alone with our uncomfortable and dishonest thoughts.

"Beth," CJ said, "why don't you get some water."

"Okay," she said, and left the room. It surprised me that she did exactly what he told her. Had I made the same suggestion, she would have withered from dehydration before ceding the point.

CJ crossed past me and pushed the bedroom door so that it was open only a crack. Then he sat down on the end of the bed, checked his watch, and looked up at me.

"Are you going to Wrigley?" I asked.

"For the press conference? No, no," he said, making it sound totally out of the question. I supposed there were events that could take place without him, and now were better off that way. "I just wanted to make sure you know about the bone marrow thing."

"I . . ."

"They're going to want to test you to see if you're a match."

"Okay. Fine." It felt good to be called on, though I didn't understand all it entailed. I lingered on some fuzzy, movie-of-the-week memories, but couldn't remember if the test required the prick of a finger or the presence of your spine (in more ways than one).

"It won't hurt," he said, anticipating my reaction, leaning

back on the bed. He sounded remarkably composed and responsible, making the arrangements and keeping them evenly spaced in his mind. In the same situation, I would have been huddled in the corner, knees to my chin, rocking and muttering unintelligibly.

"What's Mom doing?" I asked.

"Oh, she's talking to the doctors, pondering the great imponderables." He lifted his legs up a few inches, then lowered them. "She wants me to go back to California, but I said no."

"There are good doctors here," I said, noting that I had got into the habit of declaring things that I assumed were true without any way of knowing whether they were.

"That's what I said. Now she's trying to find me a nutritionist."

He raised his hand for me to pull him up, and I did so, though not without a mild fear that I might hurt him, as if some of his considerable musculature had already gone soft and I'd pull his arm out of its socket.

"Are you scared, Joe?" he asked, squinting at me a little.

"A little, yeah," I admitted, with a hiccup of nervous, self-deprecating laughter. (I assumed he meant scared for him, not of him.) "You're not, I take it."

"Yes and no. Yesterday, when they told me . . ." He nodded. "But now, with you standing here . . ."

"I make you not scared?"

"All of you. You're scared *for* me."

I looked into his face, the face of the fighter, the one who had always been one in a million. This was CJ Columbus we were talking about, and there was no reason to be scared. There was no reason to be afraid of anything now.

We were eating dinner in my brother's kitchen — stuffed Chicago pizza, saggy and gut-busting, with the extra top layer of tomatoes and dough — when the first television trucks arrived. We pulled the blinds two floors above the street, where the activity was easy to hover over but harder to ignore. At last my brother, who wasn't eating, anyway, rose from the table and called the police station. He was polite on the phone, alerting "Jerry" of the situation. Jerry was the local officer in charge of whisking away autograph hounds and stalkers. As CJ leaned against the counter, his shirt slid up and I saw the purplish oblong bruise like an oil slick on his left biceps. He'd been plunked by a fastball two weeks before in Houston, and the bruise hadn't gone away; that was the beginning of how they knew.

It was still less than twenty-four hours since my brother had told me he was sick, and the faces at the table, our parents and my wife, the way we chewed our food with small concentrated bites, blankly dabbing at the stray splash of sauce on our lower lips, were evidence that something was wrong. We were supposed to be upbeat, cracking jokes and ignoring what was hovering over us, or dealing bravely with the subject if someone accidentally brought it up — yammering convincingly about beginning "the fight" — but this family failed to follow the conventions. None of us knew what was in store for him or for us. We stared at the table like concubines, timid slaves to fate.

We knew he'd enter Northwestern Memorial that night. There would be blood tests and additional prepping for two days, and the chemotherapy would begin on Friday. Arrangements had been made for us to stay at a downtown hotel within walking distance of the hospital, and as the crowd continued to grow outside my brother's house, we knew, too late, that we should have gone to the hospital before the news was made public. "Next time we'll do it right," my brother said. I smiled grimly, but I was the only one. My brother made the rules as to what was funny, but even he couldn't coax a laugh out of us. There were helicopters above the house, shining spotlights that danced along the windows and plumbed the depths of the kitchen sink. We were under siege, and my brother reached for the phone, this time to chat more insistently with Jerry, exploring the possibilities of an escort.

Fifteen minutes later we heard the squawking of a police car out front. The aforementioned Jerry, burly and mustachioed, doffed his cap at the door. CJ deferred to my father, and the two older men mapped the strategy, with Jerry taking the lead. The rest of us lingered near the door to the garage — our arms crossed, clustering near a pile of suitcases. My mother was even fanning herself for some reason, as if we had broken down by the side of the road. It was like a family vacation gone amuck, and we'd lost our transportation. Blue and red lights were bouncing over us, and there was an incredible amount of noise — a whistle, horns honking, what sounded like a tambourine.

Next, we were loaded into my brother's car, a rust-colored, tanklike Range Rover he'd recently bought. My father took the wheel, and my brother was next to him, a UCLA cap backward on his head. Beth, my mother, and I were in the back. The garage door rumbled open, and we backed out onto the street. As we paused, two police cars floated into formation behind us, along with one car and motorcycle in front, and I was able to see the people that had gathered on hearing the news. They were on both sides of the street, ten deep at spots, held back by a few dozen cops roaming between our car and those low wooden barricades, blue-painted planks mounted on a couple of low A-frames and placed on the thin stretch of grass that the city owned, between the sidewalk and the curb. And there were television vans, with blinding lights that silhouetted the roving reporters who stood in front of them.

We started moving, lurching at first as my father got used to the size of the vehicle. When we reached the next block, I looked back and saw that the police had allowed the crowd to spill into the street behind us. Young people were running to join the others, who froze in place as we reached them and passed.

My brother was facing straight ahead. He leaned back in his seat, rolling a little as the car moved, and since I was sitting directly behind him, I caught myself leaning up and to the right, crushing myself against the window to come around the corner of his face. For some reason, I wanted to see if his eyes were open.

* * *

The bone marrow test did not hurt; it required the pinprick and not the bone saw. (And it wasn't called a bone marrow test; it had a more technical name, but my form of denial was to make no effort to learn the medical terms for anything.) The call had gone out that a bone marrow transplant was CJ's best hope for long-term survival, and since there was no match in the national database, the team had decided to round up players and then, through hastily taped public service announcements, coax devoted fans into testing centers across the country. It was a noble mission with slim odds, because the best chance for a match, and not a particularly good one at that, was me. I was tested the following morning, as were several of my brother's teammates, some of whom came in chuckling but clammed up when they saw me. Did they think the whole thing was my fault, or did my presence make it more serious and real? Justin Holloway was the only one who came over and said hello.

The Lurie Cancer Center was a small part of the enormous Northwestern Memorial Hospital, which sprawled across several city blocks. The dozens of buildings were connected, both under ground and through glass-and-brick walkways at about the third-story level. The bone marrow test was performed in the lobby of an adjacent building. After the test I squeezed off a pint of blood and then, somewhat lightheaded and sucking on an orange, headed back through the tunnel and caught an elevator upstairs to my brother's eighth-floor room. It was empty. I walked over to the nurses' station to query Marge, the middle-aged floor nurse. She told me that CJ had been taken over to radiology for a few tests, and would then go off to "the reproductive center." My parents were with him.

"The reproductive center?" I asked.

"The sperm bank," Marge growled. "Get it?" I hadn't thought that hostile hospital women like Marge, gravel-voiced and intimidating, actually existed.

I nodded and retreated back to my brother's room, which was private and spacious but undistinguished. There were no Picasso loaners from the Chicago Art Institute or trap doors leading to secret bowling lanes or batting cages. Many cancer patients went home after the initial chemotherapy, but because of my brother's celebrity, the doctors decided he should remain in the hospital. In any case, they said that was the reason; I suspected it was the severity of his illness.

Beth was resting back at the hotel, deciding whether to fly back to Washington or do some work, part-time, at Cannon, Grossmeyer's Chicago office, which was relatively close by. If she had to return home, she would commute to Chicago on weekends whenever possible. I had told her that she didn't need to be there. "He needs all of us," she'd replied. Whatever.

I, on the other hand, had completely chucked my summer school teaching responsibilities. I'd called the associate superintendent; he had heard the news and probably would have been disappointed had I decided things any other way. He seemed to know as much about what was happening as I did, and went on to relate an unnecessary and unhappy anecdote about a family friend who had fought the same type of cancer. Only when he finished the story did he realize why it did me no good to hear it.

I had been on the lookout, since we arrived at the hospital, for signs of star treatment. But there had been no fawning, covert autograph-seeking, or other vaguely defined unprofessional behavior. Marge was not a baseball fan — it wasn't clear she was a fan of humanity — and the other nurses were uniformly polite and unimpressed. His two physicians, an olive-skinned young woman named Nita Lozik and a bald, reassuringly expert man named Philip Horner, could not have been more straightforward. It made their cautious optimism believable.

On my walk over from the hotel that morning I had passed dozens of newspaper boxes, and the CJ headlines were in big block letters. I had hurried past and tried not to read them. The television trucks had also followed us to the hospital; I could see them when I looked out my brother's window, but the glass was thick and the floor was quiet. Even though I felt insulated, the world still found the cracks and squeezed through them: a thick stack of telegrams and faxes, curling in on themselves and crisp as fallen leaves, filled two orange Nike shoeboxes next to the bed. The flower arrangements, balloon bouquets, and FedExed boxes of candy, however, were being distributed throughout the hospital, at my brother's request.

Hearing the elevator rumble open, I stepped into the hall. My brother, wearing an olive hospital gown, was being pushed in a wheelchair by one of his teammates. A handful of others were walking alongside, and behind them were my parents. My father looked comfortable, but my mother was frowning, probably worried that they would wear my brother thin, her concern for his health overriding her natural enjoyment of proximate celebrity. What she didn't understand was that the guys didn't take energy from my brother; they gave it to him. When they entered the room, one of them, a squat and cornfed-looking fellow (I was guessing back-up catcher), asked me to take their picture. They huddled above and around CJ and smiled broadly, testaments to the healing power of positive thinking or the unmitigated bliss of total ignorance, grins that I dutifully recorded.

I hung back with my parents as my brother fished a box from under his chair, still yapping with his buds about people and places I didn't know. Inside the box was an electric razor, and I recalled that my brother had announced last night that he was going to shave his head, "like a swimmer," he had said, so that one of the likely side effects of the chemotherapy could be beaten to the punch and told to go fuck itself.

He plugged in the razor and turned it on, filling the room with a high-pitched, oscillating hum, and he took the first swipe himself — a drunken stab that started out straight but bent like a curvy mountain road by the time he reached up and over to the back of his neck. CJ laughed, his mouth open, liberated, and soon everyone was laughing, and the guys were taking turns, evening it out and making low-pitched jokes about other bald players, though the list ran out after two or three. The whole thing was like a fraternity prank, in a brotherhood I hadn't pledged. My brother, despite being stripped virtually naked and deprived of the right to walk from place to place, remained confident and at ease. He was ashamed of nothing and unhumiliated. He remained himself.

Only one blond tuft remained, behind his left ear. "Joe, finish me off," CJ said. It was the kind of statement that made a metaphor of the entire sequence — clanking with symbolism that embarrassed me. I didn't want to do it, but I moved to him, and the players parted to let me get close. And they stopped laughing, which bothered me.

I took the razor in my left hand and palmed his bald head; it was smooth and warm. I didn't enjoy standing there, but I did it. Then I shut off the razor, and the room was suddenly quiet. "All right, guys," my mother said, with a disapproving edge, like the no-fun mom who comes in and snaps off the stereo. She was standing with Dr. Lozik, who looked amused but also waiting for this to be over. I wondered if part of doctor protocol was to keep everything distant and level — avoid being charmed so there'd be no unpleasant emotional connections. That would be difficult with my brother, because he was unusually charming.

The players said goodbye and slouched out. A young male orderly weaved around them, self-consciously touching his own ponytail, which seemed unsanitary in its own right. He started to sweep up my brother's hair, and CJ backed up the wheelchair to give him space.

Lozik told us what would happen next: a dental checkup, the insertion of a chest catheter, another series of blood tests, and a sedative that night to help CJ sleep. He listened and studied his lap, the corners of his mouth raised in acknowledgment, his shiny head lowered and heavy. He rolled a few hairs between his index finger and thumb, and as Lozik continued to lay out the immediate obligations and dangers of his smooth new life, he looked up at me, smiled, and flicked away the last delicate strands.

One of the reporters from the *Tribune,* a guy named Dave Sharkey, suggested to CJ that he set up a Web site for keeping in touch with the fans. CJ liked Sharkey — he liked everyone — and agreed that this was a good idea, the least intrusive way to keep the world aware of his progress. So arrangements were made, and team officials farmed out the design work for the simple page, which was linked to the Cubs site so that my brother could post daily messages and, if sufficiently inspired or amused or up to it, respond to certain well-wishers.

It *was* a good idea, and the site received several thousand visitors over the first few days. On the day my brother began chemotherapy, he spent a few early-bird minutes with his laptop, jotting down his thoughts about the rest of the season and the exercises he planned to do to stay in shape. He closed with a few warm sentences to the fans, thanking them for their support. Beth proofread and signed off, while my mother and father stood around eating doughnuts to replenish their energy after another visit to the blood center. My mother went there several times a day, and I wondered if it would have been better for her just to open a vein and thrust it directly into the tube in my brother's chest.

But over the next six days and nights, the Web site was exposed as an incredibly shitty idea. It was a shitty idea because, once it started, CJ had to keep it going. If the page was the same as the day before, people would think something horrible had happened. And in my opinion, something horrible *had* happened, because in real life, at our end of the signal line, there were no more visiting teammates or wheelchair races in the hallway or clusters of sick boys and girls on the ward learning how to keep their eyes on the ball — IV poles clattering against one another as they knelt at CJ's feet, clutching baseball gloves or stuffed animals or Mom's outstretched hand. There were six mornings and evenings of beer-can-size canisters of toxic chemicals pumped through a tube into a hole in my brother's chest, as we sat and watched, two shows a day, acting as if this were an everyday sight. *The Web site!* someone would say, remembering that we'd forgotten to deal with it, as if we were driving away from home and somebody had left the iron on. And we'd all look at each other and down at my brother — and telling the world about all of that was the last thing we wanted to do.

My brother was physically strong going in, which was good

and bad. It gave him strength, but the chemo was successful only if it thumped you down to nothing. So the stronger he was, the more he had to lose. And it didn't take long for this to happen and for all of us to recognize that the game face for the players, for little Jimmy down the hall, and, of course, for us, was just that. When he was diagnosed, he seemed immune, but by then he was sick, was given medicine that made him sicker, and though we knew the doctors were doing the right thing, it was hard to watch what the drugs did to him and believe that could possibly be true.

The stupid Web site. I was tapped as the keeper, ghostwriter, and conduit to my brother's soul. My brother finished the first round of chemotherapy, and on the seventh day he rested. Some people had few side effects, but he was not one of them, and on top of that was the danger of infection, because of his chemically eviscerated immune system. Late at night I sat with him, surgically masked and scrubbed down. I had the computer on my lap, searching for the words to safely explain him to the world, but all the clichés that used to fill my mind so effortlessly had departed. *I feel pretty good, all things considered!* I wrote. He was lying a few feet away, sticky-mad with fever and groaning as he waited — for another blood transfusion after his gums or nose began to bleed, or for a bag of fresh platelets to stanch the hemorrhage from a melon-size bruise on his thigh from when he stumbled out of the hospital bed and fell to the floor, or for the sores in his mouth to fade, the ones that kept us from understanding his words and what he wanted or needed. Was this for public consumption? Did they need to know how he'd ripped away his gown, covered with vomited baby food fed to him moments before, pureed yams and peas that my mother had decorously poured into serving bowls, removing them from tiny jars before he saw them? *I eat mostly milkshakes and ice cream,* I wrote. *It's heaven.*

So I started writing about baseball. I figured it would be easier, because I could focus on games, the battle, the idea of winning. I considered picking fights, in my brother's name, with players I didn't like, but I settled on watching Cubs games and commenting on the action. But the Cubs weren't much of an inspiration; not surprisingly they had nosedived since CJ abandoned them. They had played eleven games and lost nine of them, including a disastrous, scoreboard-melting nineteen-to-one drubbing by Colorado. It was the kind of game that got called in Little League by the middle innings, when the outfielders on the losing team were sitting down in the field or refusing, teary-eyed and achy, to come to the plate. And my brother's replacement, an aging journeyman named Tim Dooley, was batting a buck and a quarter and had already made four errors, the same number CJ had made all year long.

My brother watched some baseball, but he didn't do it entertainingly. He provided no helpful commentary or rah-rah anecdotes; you didn't feel you were watching the game with someone who played it. His spirits were down, and he had no desire to watch the Cubs, and I couldn't blame him. What they were doing on the field these days wasn't baseball; it was chalking the number nine on your cap and losing your interest in winning with each curve and curl. And then there was the unlucky fan who chose the top of the sixth inning of a midweek matinee as his moment to shine, taking a drunken tumble from the Wrigley bleachers and running around like a ninny on the outfield grass. Usually, when somebody did this, the players stood like statues, hands on hips, waiting for the lumbering crowd-control guys to catch the trespasser, but that day no one was in the mood to wait. When the giddy youngster weaved toward Justin Holloway in center, Justin cut through the bullshit by punching the idiot in the face and knocking him out.

Any time a player got sick, everyone talked about how the illness "put the game in perspective." Winning didn't matter, they said, but what they didn't understand was that in lots of ways, especially to that player, it mattered more than ever. This was one of those little slivers of enlightenment that comes your way only when you're on the other side, making time with the sick player. I could have noted this on the Web site, exhorting the players to get their shit together, but I didn't. None of the players had been around since my brother entered the zero hour, and he didn't want them anyway. The doctors said CJ wouldn't be through "shaking and baking" — their jargon for fever and chills — for another ten days or so, and by that time the Cubs would be on the road, probably another eight or nine notches toward the abyss.

In the meantime, whenever CJ was up to it, we played cards. I'd learned the game of spades, a clubhouse favorite. We also watched movies, popcorn stuff from when we were younger: Mel Brooks, John Belushi, Bill Murray, *Pink Panther, Airplane!* — all still surprisingly funny, though maybe we were so desperate for humor that we would have found anything funny. And we also watched the *Indiana Jones* and *Star Wars* trilogies, complemented by additional spoonfuls of Spielbergian suburbia — *Close Encounters, Poltergeist, Gremlins, Goonies* — full of inconsequential pleasures and upper-middle-class homeowner fears, which reminded us of our California home, which I suppose was the point. It was our own form of treatment, and though CJ often fell asleep, I would keep them running, the way movie theaters would have — a nod to timetables and propriety that seemed increasingly distant from the reeling, clockless world of his hospital room and his illness.

And sometimes we sat in silence, late at night in the moments before my parents and I left him. CJ didn't like it when we did that, when we made things too quiet. He thought we were watching him, and for once he did not want to be on display. He thought we were pondering his fate, and we probably were, though I still did not believe that his life was in danger. He was too strong in every way. He had led a charmed life; he would find a way to turn the whole thing to his advantage, beyond the fact that it had already made him more popular than ever. I expected him to come out of the illness with a fever-bred sixth sense, the ability to hit every single pitch, no matter how fast it was thrown or how deviously it broke. He would be the first player to bat one thousand. He would never end a game or an inning. He would never make an out again.

I rolled the idea over and over, my enthusiasm for it growing. I played the percentages but there was only one: it was perfection, the ultimate statistic. As I watched him thrash with fever or seize with chill, the perfect number strengthened me. One thousand, one thousand, one thousand. Repeating it made me less likely to look away or wince or lose a rare, but nevertheless important, train of thought.

The next Tuesday evening, Dr. Lozik pulled me aside in the hallway. She had been in to see my brother, still battling infections, and she had told my mother that CJ was doing "as well as could be expected." There had been plenty of crises but none of them life-threatening. This was the anxious time, elastic days and nights that stretched and blurred, filled with illness and waiting. Soon he would begin rebuilding himself; happy and healthy new white blood cells would breed in the wake of those torched by the poison. It was corny to visualize them, but I found myself doing it, in reassuring, picture-book fashion. In less than two weeks the doctors would come in and pull out a bit of that fresh marrow, shiny and lavish, like caviar. And if all had gone well, the marrow would be healthy, and CJ would be tentatively cancer-free.

"We've received the results of your HLA test," Lozik said. HLA stood for human leukocyte antigens; the test was to see whether I was a suitable transplant candidate.

"Good?" I asked.

"Not good," she said. I had grown to appreciate Lozik. She wasn't a time-waster, and brutal honesty was refreshing, when it came from someone who wasn't close to you. "We're going to keep looking."

"Okay," I said. I tried to take hope from her statement that they'd keep looking, but unless there was some reclusive Padres fan out there with matching blood, looking was not the same as finding. "The chemotherapy seems to be going well, though, doesn't it?"

Lozik squinted at me. "You have an eyelash," she said, reaching for my cheek and pulling it off. I stood perfectly still, letting her do this, as if she were performing an important medical procedure. "His cancer is very aggressive, Joe. At some point he will need a transplant." Then her beeper went off. She glanced down to her waist to check it, and was gone.

I scrubbed down and suited up, actions once ludicrous and foreign that were now routine. CJ was curled up, asleep, his sheet twisted around him like a vine. There had been concern earlier in the day about bleeding around the entrance to his catheter, but the bleeding had stopped. My father and mother were sitting in chairs. His eyes were closed, the newspaper flapped out on his chest, but my mother was awake and staring at a library book, turning the pages with somber rhythm. She did not acknowledge my presence.

"Mom," I said. She finished the page she was reading, but I could tell she wasn't concentrating, because her eyes were bouncing all over the page. She looked up in response but refused to speak.

"Dr. Lozik got the results of the HLA." I had surrendered to the acronyms and jargon, of BMT and GVHD and ARA-C, which provided a clubby feeling of superiority but no real comfort. It was superiority over people I didn't want to be superior to.

"What were they?" she said, and I realized too late that I had set myself up. I should have told her the results and not phrased it so expectantly. There was no reason for suspense.

"Not good," I said.

She shifted her gaze to the middle distance beyond me, calculating. Both she and my father had remained remarkably calm over the past month, poised and responsive even as the world threatened to collapse and overwhelm them. My father, the supreme logical mind in the family, was as baffled by my brother's adversity as he'd been by his success — both untraceable in our lineage. As for my mother, I'd half-expected her to call on her adversarial training and take my brother's welfare as her only client, complaining constantly to the doctors or berating nurses who moved too slowly or failed to laugh at CJ's jokes. But this hadn't happened, at least not at full volume or in public.

So it surprised me that, as she returned to her book, she muttered, "I guess you're happy now."

I did not think that I'd heard her correctly, so I nodded. But then I processed what she had said. "What?"

She didn't answer; she was paging through her book, some stone-colored five-pound historical fiction doorstop. "What did you say?" I repeated.

But rhetorical ploys don't work with moms. They don't have to repeat a word, no matter how angry you get or certain you are that your ears must have deceived you. They know that you heard them — in their exasperating, offhand tone — whispered cruelties masquerading as throwaways.

I tried to keep my voice level, but I could feel myself clenching up. "That's not fair, Mom."

"Oh, shut up, Joe. You've been jealous of him since you were five years old. Isn't this good for you? You get to walk around while he's in that bed? Aren't you happy now?"

She was breathing hard. I could see the air moving, puffing in and out in a small imperfect circle behind her surgical mask. And it was all I could do — speechless, my heart thumping — not to throttle her and smash her right out the window.

My father had woken up and was looking at the two of us. I didn't know how much he had heard. Grabbing her arm, he said, "Take a walk with me."

He got up, and she stepped around me. They were out the door, and I was staring at the empty chairs, creased where they'd been sitting.

"What happened?" my brother said, his voice cracked and raspy. I moved over to him and picked up a glass of water with a bent straw, which I negotiated between his lips. He took a long sip and coughed some of it back up.

"What happened?" he asked again.

"Nothing," I said.

"Liar," he said. His eyes slid shut again, and as I moved my hand to blot the water that had trickled to his neck, I could feel the heat rising from his skin.

* * *

He was able to return to Lincoln Park eleven days later, and by then he was insisting on it. He wanted to be home. The niggling details of life at the Cancer Center had begun to bother all of us, the sick and the well: the blackened welt of chewing gum on the bank of floor numbers in the elevator, smacked between the 3 and the 4; the "lost" residents and interns who wandered into my brother's room for a quick, verifying peek; the Filipino man with the brain tumor, shuffling from one end of the hall to the other, groaning with public, death-knell agony. No matter how hard the hospital tried — and none of us had any complaints about my brother's treatment — it was a place we wanted to run from.

Doctors Horner and Lozik had handed CJ a provisional clean bill of health, which did not mean that the cancer was gone for good, or that it was gone at all. It meant only that his body was on its way back, and though he certainly wasn't going to be bunting the runners over any time soon, there was no need for him to remain in a disinfected bubble. He was to stay out of the heat, and he had several appointments at the hospital during the next two weeks — in fact, the next day he'd have to come in for the bone marrow aspiration and biopsy, which would determine which kind of new cells were growing inside him. And then after the two weeks, he would start the chemo again, on an outpatient basis if he liked, though considering his physical reaction last time (and barring any treatment adjustments), the doctors thought he would probably be back in his room on the eighth floor.

But that was still two weeks away, and this night he would get to sleep in his own bed. There were warm goodbyes from staff, other patients, and their families. CJ signed a few autographs and kissed that evil nurse Marge, of all people. The reporters were uncooperative but were kept at bay. They wanted a press conference, but the doctors vetoed it, and CJ let them shoulder the blame for his inaccessibility. I volunteered to speak on his behalf, claiming authority based on my ghost-writing the Web site. Everyone laughed at this except my mother.

Beth flew in that morning, and I met her at O'Hare, surprising her at the gate. As I was searching for her, I calculated that these three weeks were the longest I had ever gone without seeing her. "You look different," she said, sizing me up after I kissed her. I *felt* different — older, fortified, smirking at less of the world — I guess I had undergone treatment of my own. And of course she looked different too: wary of being jostled, walking with a slight sideward movement, holding herself carefully. I was going to be a father in a few months, in case I had forgotten — another splash of reality in a life suddenly drowning in it.

We took a cab to Lincoln Park, and everyone was there, including Spencer Levitt. He had flown in the night before to dine with another client — a disgruntled Bull, I was told — and had decided to surprise CJ when he arrived home. Frankly, I thought it reprehensible of Spencer not to have shown up earlier. When pressed, I suspected, he would plead that "keeping his distance" was his way of helping my brother get well, that CJ didn't need any "business" distractions. But we all knew that he cringed at what was going on, with its appalling lack of upside — a decade of green money dreams suddenly shredded, like paper torn into tiny pieces and flung from a skyscraper window. Spencer had no excuse, and I detested him for his absence, but at the same time I was grateful for it. Having him around all that time might have been the scariest part of the whole thing.

Spencer had commandeered the living room, his briefcase clicked open at a right angle on the couch. He was sitting on the edge of the coffee table, his creasy black loafers kicked off, and was kneading his bare feet as he talked on his cellular. I was disgusted, and he sensed it, but oddly his first action was to snap the briefcase shut. When he stopped talking, he came over to hug me, which disgusted me more. "He looks great, just great," Spencer said, and I wondered which of his other clients he pictured as he said this: someone still burly and winning, with an image and stat sheet that allowed him to lie convincingly.

"We're going upstairs," I said. "You can get back to what you were doing."

Was that rude or cold? That was the best thing about Spencer: you could never hurt him. Not because he was invincible, like CJ, but because he was too stupid and self-involved to realize that you were trying to hurt him. As Beth and I headed up, I thought about inviting him to join us, but when I turned back, he had already taken me up on my first offer — he was yakking into the phone, the call he'd probably not cut off, and for a split second I wondered if that "he looks great" had even been directed at me in the first place.

My brother was thrilled to see Beth; they were two people with bodies gone haywire. He got out of bed to hug her, and for the first time I noticed the changes in him. He had lost over twenty pounds, down from the one-nineties to around one-seventy. His hair was gone, and he had sores and scabs and other indelible chemo signatures — the loss of hearing in his left ear, the occasional loss of balance, sensitivity to light. His body would sputter for a while.

We had been spending a lot of time together, my brother and I, but I took no pleasure in it. It wasn't the type of family time I'd ever had in mind, and I had seen him undergo things in the past few weeks that I could have lived without. But we had no choice; it was a time without alternatives, and there was no room for wavering. Beyond the obviously physical, he was the same as always. The voice was the same, as were the bearing and the charm. His interior dominated, and I found him more impressive and threatening than ever.

Spencer loitered for a while, but my brother's sleep schedule was still erratic — he nodded off around six-thirty, just as we were getting ready for dinner, and three hours later he was still sleeping, so we left him undisturbed. Because the Cubs weren't playing that night, we powered up the big-screen television and lifted a West Coast game off the satellite dish: Texas at Seattle. My father and Spencer and I watched, while upstairs the women caught up at the kitchen table, my mother nursing a glass of red wine, smoking her mint-death menthols, and blowing the silvery, backlit smoke away from Beth and our unborn child and out a cranked-open crack of the window. The house seemed full, small pockets of activity all over the place, and the low-level *wallah* from the television, the sound of a baseball crowd, provided a pleasant undercurrent, a murmurous layer around our feet. It felt like a holiday.

My father and I had no interest in the game whatsoever, but Spencer watched it, hunched forward in his seat, as if he were at the ballpark. "Strike *three!*" he growled, all low and bassy, like every fan who dreams of making the umpire's call. And Spencer was *there,* man, mingling among the slack-jawed masses without getting stomped. Later, he complained about not "enjoying" the game anymore, once he'd seen it from "the other side."

"When did you see it from the regular side?" I said, daring to challenge him, feeling my third or fourth beer.

"Huh?" he said.

"You said 'the other side.' But you never played, did you? So you never saw it from the regular side." I wished Beth were there; she would have been proud of my quibbling over semantics.

I was looking straight at him, but he didn't answer. The silence made me aware that conversation for Spencer did not involve conversing; it was a routine, and I'd lifted the needle from the record player right in the middle of it.

"The world of athletics has many sides, Joe," he said.

"Oh," I said. And that was that. Then Spencer resumed namedropping — the jocks he knew, the famous places they'd been, the life lessons he had gleaned from them — highlighted by a meandering, quasi-mystical anecdote about a whitewater rafting trip with the Roger Staubachs. An hour later, Spencer fell asleep on the couch with a half-filled beer bottle in his hand; some time after that, his grip tightened on the beaded bottle just enough for it to pop from his fingers. It spilled down his white shirt and onto his gray suit pants. By the time we noticed it, having called a cab to slingshot his ass away from us, the beer bottle was virtually empty. My father pulled it from his hand, turned it upside down, and emptied the final drops right on him.

CJ and my parents headed back to Lurie the next morning for the bone marrow aspiration, biopsy, and some additional tests. Beth and I stayed at the house, and though we'd talked on the phone every day, it was still a good chance for us to spend some unhurried time together. I was anxious about my brother's test results, so I was glad to have her with me.

"I'd love a house like this," she said, sipping a cup of decaf, standing with one foot up on a stool in some back-salvaging maneuver, gazing out the crosshatched window over the kitchen sink.

"We could do that," I said, chomping through a bowl of cereal. I talked as if I held the key to the house of our (her) dreams. As long as Beth worked, she would make more money than I did, and though we made joint decisions about our pooled resources, I'd long felt that she had the upper hand and was waiting for the opportunity to flaunt it. I had resigned myself to this once her paychecks started rolling in, consoled by the idea that my profession was praised and hers was reviled, although, as usual, nothing turned out to be that simple.

"I hate the job, Joe," she said, turning to face me. "I want to have the baby, and then I don't want to go back."

"You don't want to work at all?" I asked.

"No. I don't know. I hate the firm. And I don't think I'm doing good work there anymore."

I kept eating, studying the narrow, data-heavy side of the corn flakes box. How much riboflavin did a man really need? I didn't like the idea of Beth being a full-time mother. It seemed so frumpy and diminishing, though deep down I knew this prejudice was preposterous. "Maybe you'll feel different in a few months."

"In a few months the baby will be born," she said, her voice suddenly dreamy and thin. "No, I don't think so." This last part was more to herself, as if she were taking a stand, willing herself not to return to work. "You don't want me to keep working there. You hate it, too."

Maybe I did hate it, but I didn't like the idea of her being so determined to be aimless, and I didn't like her telling me how I felt. The only clear opinion I had about Cannon, Grossmeyer had to do with the diabolical Henry Fomacci. "I just want you to be happy," I said.

She dumped the rest of her coffee, slapped on the faucet, and rinsed it down. "Don't say that, Joe. It's demeaning."

"How is it demeaning?" I stood up and crowded behind her, still assuming this was a conversation and not a fight, putting my cereal bowl in the sink and opening the high cabinet to find a coffee cup.

"Because it's vague. It's something you say to someone you don't really know." She turned to me, turned on me. "You're always vague, you know that? If you're going to be encouraging, I'd like your encouragement to be a little more specific. It would at least show that you're listening."

"Maybe I'm vague because I don't know what you want."

"Who cares what I want. Say something *real*."

She wiped her hands on a towel and handed it to me, indicating that this was all an abstract exercise to her, but her tone flipped a switch in me, and the words just spilled out.

"Okay. I think you went to law school because when you were still in college, you didn't know what you really wanted to do. And then you were good at it, and you sort of liked it, and you got a good job. A well-paying job with a bunch of assholes who, you convinced yourself, weren't assholes. And you needed that job because you had a lot of debt, and now you don't have that debt anymore because of my brother, and you're married to *me,* and you're twenty-seven years old. You're twenty-seven, and you're having a kid and you have no idea what the fuck has happened and you're scared that your life is already over."

There. It had pauses, and sentences, but it was all one long rant. She smiled at me, a wounded smile, the lying and mechanical grin of someone trying to deny that she'd been pegged. It didn't feel as good as I thought it would while it was going on.

Her eyes clicked off to the right and then back. She brushed a stray hair from her forehead. "My life is *not* over," she said.

And she waddled out, laying it on a little thick, in my opinion, up the stairs and out of reach. She was going to use my brother's treadmill and work on some work, and would do all of this on a different level of the house so that I wouldn't be able to see or hear any of it. This *would* be a good house for us, I thought.

I turned on the big television and watched talk shows for a couple of hours, carrying the cordless phone with me, waiting for it to ring. Every twenty minutes or so I pressed the orange TALK button just to hear the dial tone, to make sure there wasn't an extension off the hook somewhere, making it impossible for my parents to get through. By lunchtime, when they still hadn't called, I considered driving to the hospital, but I didn't have a car.

Finally, I had eaten a cup of soup and some crackers, and was taking a catnap, when the phone startled me awake. I located the cordless and brought it to my ear, but before I could say hello, Beth had already answered. It was my mother. They sounded so much alike, their voices crowding against each other, that it was hard for me to tell which of them was crying.

My brother's body had taken a brief break, but the new white blood cells were as useless as the old ones. He had two options, according to Dr. Horner, neither of them promising. He could enter a clinical trial of chemotherapy with different drugs, which might be more effective but probably wouldn't be, since the high-dose chemo he'd started with had been chosen over the trial drugs, a month before, as more likely to induce a remission. Or he could be given an autogenic bone marrow transplant, which involved taking some of my brother's bone marrow, purging the cancer, and then sticking it back in — a transplant given to himself. This treatment worked best for patients who had reached a first remission,

but it was rarely successful on my brother's aggressive and re-
sistant level. Dr. Horner was strongly against the procedure,
claiming that it was far too risky; the odds were too great, and
my brother would in all likelihood not survive it.

And then my brother had asked the one big question, the
topic that had not yet been broached, the question that only he
could ask. Dr. Horner told him that he had up to six months,
that it was time to make some decisions and plans. That was
when my mother left the room and called us and recounted it
all to Beth.

My parents and CJ came home in the early evening. The car
rumbled into the garage, but no one entered the house, stretching on for several minutes. Finally the car doors opened as
Beth and I stood awkwardly in the foyer — and there they
were, still going about the business of living, all the obligations
that keep you sane in the face of devastation. Then there were
sputtering tears and rage at the world as we sat around the
kitchen table, dazed and hollow, making more plans, Beth
writing everything down. My brother had decided on the
chemotherapy, and at the same time he told us that he wanted
no one else to know of his deteriorating state of health. I
doubted we could keep such a thing a secret. Certainly work-
ers at the hospital would whisper the scandalous, valuable
truth to friends or loved ones. But it was what my brother
wanted, so we agreed to it, and, as with everything from then
on, we did what we could to make it happen.

The following Sunday there was a break in the weather, the
temperature dipping pleasantly into the high seventies, and my
brother made a hastily arranged visit to Wrigley Field, where
the Cubs, losers of twenty-seven of their last thirty-two games,
were facing the Phillies. My parents went with him, but Beth
and I stayed in the townhouse. She wasn't feeling well and
needed to rest. She lay on the couch, her head in my lap, and
we watched the brief pregame ceremony on television.

Most of the events at Wrigley weren't for public consumption — it was not a tribute, and there were no freebies, other
than my brother's appearance, for the fans. CJ wanted to see

his teammates. He wanted to give them a pep talk and get them out of the rut, which, he had confessed to me on more than one occasion, he felt responsible for. And he wanted to sit down in front of his locker, run his feet back and forth on the clubhouse carpet, let the beat reporters crowd around him like in the good old days, their cue-card-size notepads at the ready, while CJ made convincing statements about when he'd put on the uniform once again.

As game time neared, he was introduced by the public address announcer — a surprise special guest — though word was out, and everyone knew he was there. CJ walked out to the field, my parents on either side of him. A full house rose to their feet for several minutes of applause. A microphone stand had been placed at third base, and there were brief comments by the team's manager and by Justin Holloway, speaking on behalf of the players.

Justin's voice shook as he tried to keep it together, reading from a sheet of paper that flapped away from him in the field's breeze, and I felt for him. CJ bailed Justin out, giving him a hug as he finished, whispering something that made them both laugh.

Then my brother moved into the spotlight. He was wearing jeans and a long-sleeved white T-shirt, his old baseball cap on his head. He pulled my parents toward the microphone with him. The crowd was absolutely silent. He looked out at them, took a deep breath, and smiled with pure delight. "I am so proud to be a Chicago Cub today," he said, and they applauded deliriously. He told them how much their support had meant, how he had followed the team from the hospital and home, how he couldn't wait to get back on the field next season. And he slipped in the public service message, urging everyone to get screened for the bone marrow transplant donor program.

The crowd quieted again; the medical talk had brought everyone back to reality. CJ sized them up a final time, squinting into the sunlight, scratching his cheek with the tip of his index finger. "I'll see you again," he said. "You make me very happy."

And for a moment, with the camera tight on his face and my heart beating hard, I thought that he really was out there — on the field, owning the corner, ready for anything that was hit his way. And he said thank you, and the camera pulled back, and he waved to every side of the diamond. They clapped and cheered until it hurt. He had not let them down. He had touched them all.

Four days later, he returned to the hospital. It was only a few days before the date he had been originally scheduled for his second round of high-dose chemo. Many of those he had previously charmed — orderlies, nurses, other patients — didn't suspect a thing. I drew wheelchair duty from the elevator to his old room, so I was right in the center of the slow parade that greeted him. CJ signed napkins, gloves, a broken arm, a silvery get-well balloon temporarily smothered in his lap. He remembered names, faces, relevant details. He asked about a young boy and was told by a nurse that he "was gone." Everyone acted as if they knew CJ, and I suppose that they *did* know him. He was genuine, and that was why they loved him.

The tests began again, with the same bantering medical visitors and their weary, canned lines. It was the second performance of a play that none of us wanted to star in. But some things were different. We had all lost the power of long-term concentration; reading books was out of the question. We ended up passing around dog-eared, dated copies of *People* and *Time,* commenting to each other on articles that meant nothing to any of us. My mother even bought a Technicolor book of dimwit word finds, which to her must have been like buying pornography. And we watched more movies, though we found ourselves grasping for themes. Somehow, it was harder to build a festive atmosphere around Kurt Russell night. We locked in on regular television mini-dramas: cop-show reruns or wild-animal documentaries, the animals lolling about and suddenly mauling and fucking each other. These were programs that in ordinary life would hardly have registered, but in our underfed, brooding collective consciousness we latched on to them, staring vacantly up at the television, as though the outcome had meaning and mattered.

And on the following Monday, as the new chemotherapy began, the ability to keep my spirits presentably high slipped away from me. I found myself unable to stay in his room for more than a few minutes without my pulse racing, thumps that I felt all over my body, my palms tingling with a mad case of anxiety. I kept this strange psychosomatic malady to myself and began loitering like a vampire at the blood bank, flirting with a pretty Korean nurse named Jenny. And I took mind-clearing walks outside, despite the stifling August heat — around the hospital and occasionally wading away from the muffled cone of silence that seemed to cover all the nearby streets, streets below buildings filled with people who were trying to get better.

Later that week, my father joined me on my walks. I could tell he was pleased to be out of the hospital, but he would never have walked with me unless I'd asked him. We wandered for a few minutes among the hospital buildings. I pointed out the maternity ward, the veterans' hospital, and an enormous expansion and redevelopment project that dwarfed the existing buildings, including the one my brother was in. I spoke knowingly about those things to my father, as if I were a wealthy trustee in a hardhat, though all I knew was what I had read on the massive, bulleted detail board that was part of the barrier wall blocking the construction zone. It told who was footing the bill, how many new parking spaces there would be. It flaunted the improvements in treatment that patients could look forward to — those lucky enough to get sick after the renovation was finished.

My father squinted up at the construction, hand over his eyes. "Have you been to Niketown?" he asked.

Niketown was a three-story shrine to product, located on Michigan Avenue. Three blocks away but a world apart. "No. Have you?"

"Oh, yeah," he said, almost dreamily, as if he'd fallen in love with someone who worked there. "Let's go."

So we hiked up to Niketown, a five-minute walk inland and away from the lake. There were long multicolored flags flapping against the building; it was as if we had wandered into a parade. We worked our way inside, through gabby and shameless crowds, dizzied in the revolving doors and then hit with a blast of arctic air. There was tight spotlighting, glass cases filled with stylishly presented memorabilia, and conveyors running in see-through plastic tubes along the walls, descending from the ceiling, slowly shuttling the footwear from storage to customer.

My father hurried on, past first-floor alcoves of extreme sports, tennis, and volleyball. We climbed the escalator and passed billboard-size wall hangings of athletes exerting and winning (never just looking at you) — Moss, Sampras, Woods — modern gods under contract, divine and monumental, dressed for success.

"Where are we going?" I asked, but my father didn't hear me. We were surrounded by noise. There must have been hundreds of employees in shiny blue warm-up suits, restocking a wall of cubbyholes filled with T-shirts, helping a no-chance fat kid into a pair of soccer cleats, guiding a man my age to the dressing room, a half-dozen golf pants and polo shirts clenched in his arms. It was like a giant party, a slick and manufactured celebration of *something* — difficult to finger, that evasive hipness that Nike had wrestled away from everyone else by monopolizing and commodifying athletic cool.

And the third floor was the top of the temple: baseball and basketball. As the escalator rose, straight in front of me was something called Michael Jordan's Practice Court, glassed-in and empty. It seemed like the last place he'd ever come to shoot hoops. I skipped off the escalator as the steps glided flat beneath my feet, and that was when I noticed my brother hanging in midair above my head. It was a full-size plaster sculpture of him, lifelike and in no way artistic, as if it had been cast from a mold. His body was like buffed white plaster, with eyes nose and mouth but no color to any of them — his face perfectly sculpted but bland and bare. Over this form he was wearing his Cubs uniform, as if it was the focal point of the display. The uniform wore the athlete (any athlete, even *you*), and not the other way around.

The fake CJ hung perilously, from invisible strings, over the atrium. The ends of his uniform sleeves were flapped open and down, from gravity. A group of Japanese men snapped pictures of it; two black boys mimicked the frozen action pose.

"Isn't it great?" my father said. I had joined him out of the flow of traffic, leaning against a pillar with a fire alarm, and staring up at it.

"Yeah," I said, lying. My brother hanging there, the two of us watching him, the whole place — I didn't like any of it. But I stayed. I watched my father, his mouth slightly open, gazing up, up. We stood there for almost an hour without saying a word. No one recognized us or bothered us. I wondered how many times my father had been here, his chapel, his inexplicable fount of calm.

Eventually I decided that we should return to the hospital. "Let's go, Dad," I said, and grabbed his trembling hand.

The chemotherapy abruptly ended two days later, when my brother went into cardiac arrest. He was stabilized quickly, but it was the terrifying climax of forty-eight hours of horrible side effects. There had been projectile vomiting from the first moment — he threw up in the car even before we got to the hospital, as if his body knew what was coming and wanted to lodge a complaint in advance. He blew his blood vessels in both eyes; they were red flowers, giving him a ghoulish appearance even when he was wide awake. And there was the bleeding, from his nose and gums as before, but this time also from his rear, which seemed the ultimate unnecessary humiliation.

That was it for induction chemotherapy; it induced nothing. It was the end of his treatment. It would be another month before his system stabilized to the point that it could be determined whether the autogenic bone marrow transplant was even a remote possibility, and a month seemed very far away.

He was on a heart monitor and a feel-good IV drip, which for some reason concerned Beth. She became obsessed by the fear that CJ would become addicted to painkillers. Finally, after much prodding from her, I cornered Dr. Horner and asked whether my brother needed so much of it. Horner grabbed my shoulder with a fatherly shake. "There's pain you can't see, Joe," he whispered.

"Okay," I replied, taking his statement at face value and assigning no deeper, literary meaning, though, like so much else, it begged for it. He walked away from me to the nurses' station.

On Friday afternoon, August 28, my brother was lucid enough to sit up and watch the Cubs lose their fourth in a row at home to the Marlins. Beth and I watched with him, and he didn't say much during the game, even as a Cub rally in the late innings flared and then fell short. My parents had gone back to the hotel; CJ had taken a slightly stricter stand with them, especially my mother — making sure that she spent some time away from his room, marshaling the energy to raise his voice and tell her to go shopping or to a museum, though it was obvious, even before she relented, that those activities would no longer give pleasure to her.

As we watched the game together, my brother lying in his bed, behind me to my left, Horner's words about unseen pain feathered through my mind. I knew that a sad corner had been turned. Was I the first or the last to grasp it? I turned to look at CJ as I asked a question while Florida changed pitchers in the eighth, and I quickly assessed the collage of evidence that was before me — the way his shoulders bowed and his mouth sagged, the way his breaths were long and deep, sounding like work. And his eyes blinked and closed, but the close was long, too long, long enough to unnerve me and probably put a stupid look of relief on my face when they opened again.

Justin came to visit him that night, on the heels of the loss, before the team trooped to New York for the weekend. We left them alone — my parents, Beth, and I — retreating to the common lounge at the end of the hall, where we made small talk with a young couple who had recently arrived with a very sick baby daughter. The newcomers were frazzled and bewildered; things were just beginning to come undone. My mother continued to look extraordinarily pained, but she and my father said all the right things: where to eat their lunch and park their car. I mentioned that the better gift shop was in the nearby neuroscience building. The couple nodded, grateful but grim, processing none of it. We recognized them as us; we were the worldly upperclassmen, welcoming the eighteen-year-olds to the dorm.

Justin walked out of my brother's room about a half-hour later. He started toward the elevator at the other end of the hall but stopped after a few steps and turned back toward us. It was too far to make out his face, but he seemed to be waiting for something. "Go," my father said, so I got up and trotted over to him.

"Justin, hey," I said, and we shook hands, a slender gold bracelet sliding down his wrist and gracing my fingertips. He was wearing a blue track suit, a backward baseball cap, and sunglasses, even though it was dark and we were indoors.

He started slowly walking toward the elevator, and I followed him into it. Down in the lobby, when he still hadn't said anything, I knew that he didn't want me and had nothing to say.

"You all right?" I asked.

"Yeah, you know," he said. Then he shook his head. "Shit."

"Shit tears you up, man," I said, and felt like an asshole for saying it. I was talking to Justin not only as if I was his friend, but as if I was his black friend, like two cancer ward b-boys who used to run track together. A young autograph-seeker approached, but Justin went right past the boy, and quickly we were through the automatic doors and outside, where the air was still muggy and thick, moths dancing in the halogens overhead.

"Well," I said, but before I could extend my hand Justin wrapped me in a hug. He was a big guy and I was not a hugger, but this was for him, I thought, and he squeezed me for a long time. When he pulled away, his sunglasses were askew, his watery eyes peeking out from behind them. He had joined the tortured ranks, broken down inside like all of us.

"You're a cool guy, Justin," I said, leaning back from him, hopping a step. It was all I could think to say.

"I'm pretty cool," he said, looking at his feet.

"Go," I said. He nodded, still looking down, puffing out his cheeks and exhaling, his mouth widening in a quick wince. And he walked off, alone on the sidewalk, waiting for a silent ambulance to pass before he angled across the street and disappeared into the night.

Dr. Horner gathered us the next morning outside my brother's room and told us we should stay close to the hospital. He held my mother's hand as he spoke, but when he was finished he did not stay.

CJ slept most of the time. The nurses visited every once in a while, treading softly in their white-soled shoes, but the traffic in and out had slowed. We still saw two alternating Catholic priests and the grandmotherly coordinator of a cancer support group, but overall it felt as if we had been removed from the tour.

During a break from mooning over my plaster brother at Niketown, my father had gone on a bizarre board-game shopping spree at F.A.O. Schwarz, so we played Monopoly and Sorry! and Yahtzee. We had several games going on at once, boards opened all over the room, pieces and cards and dice stuck between moves. My brother chipped in with trash talk and even played when he was up to it. We always left the blue pieces aside, if the game had them, in case he woke up or indicated that he wanted to join in. We even played bridge, which my father had taught Beth and me, and, in need of a fourth, he even lured my mother into playing, a cheery flashback to the early days of their marriage — before my brother and I were born, a time that must have been quiet and wonderful and empty all at once.

The game-playing was undoubtedly the mini-competitive activity of a group of people in massive, final denial. There was shaking dice, picking cards, and moving pieces, complimenting your opponent on winning but secretly fuming, forcing the anger, desperate for ways to keep one's mind occupied in the face of reality. We knew what was coming but we didn't know when, and my heart caught as I wondered whether I was supposed to isolate a moment to say goodbye, to know what to say and be able to say it — or was that his job, to know, did he really know, and would he ever let on?

On Sunday night, I fell asleep in his room; there were beds for us by then, but I nodded off in my chair before I could make my way down the hall to them. I woke with a start, my mouth pasty, my legs cramped. The world spun for a moment and settled as my blood started churning again. The room was dark. A squeaky-wheeled cart was rolled down the hall. A woman's voice echoed from an uncertain distance, and on the street below a garbage truck hissed to a stop, beeped, and backed up. I wasn't sure how much time had passed.

And my brother was looking at me. The sheet was pulled up to his neck, so at first I thought he was shivering, but as I peered closer and my eyes adjusted, I saw that he was breathing regularly, his head turned in my direction, tilted up on a couple of pillows.

I stretched my arms and yawned audibly. "Hey," I whispered, and he kept looking at me, a shimmering triangle of light reflecting from somewhere, adding depth to the edge of his nose and the corner of his mouth, and a glassy sheen to his right blue eye. Suddenly my stomach tightened, my face fell, and I froze with my arms extended over my head.

"Not yet," he said, and I knew that he knew what I was thinking. In some ways he had always known. He smiled and made a noise that I thought was a laugh, and he traced his palm over the sheet, bouncing it against his leg. I exhaled deeply, shaking my head and laughing myself, though I wasn't sure that the noise that came out of me sounded much like a laugh, either.

I was wide awake by then. "Do you need anything?" I asked, but he shook his head.

"How are you?" I asked.

"Tired. Bad," he said. "Do you remember Cincinnati, when you came to see me?"

"Yeah," I said, my voice not sentimental but wary, trying to recall whether I'd said something wrong, whether the visit had ended badly, or whether I'd kept things to myself.

"I was thinking about that," he said.

"For any particular reason?" I put my socked feet up on the edge of his bed and kicked my chair back perilously, like a fidgety kid at the dinner table. Then I had a vision of the chair whipsawing out from under me, so I came crashing back down.

"No," he said, his voice trailing off, eyes fixed out at nothing.

"You had a great game that night," I said. That big bop to right center.

"I had a lot of great games, didn't I?"

I wondered whether this was the first time he was putting it all together. "They'll remember, CJ," I said. "You've done things."

"Yeah," he said. I wasn't sure what exactly I meant, but it pleased him, and that pleased me.

He frowned suddenly, turning his whole body to one side, reaching his hand below and behind him. He fished underneath the sheet and then held out two of the blue plastic pieces from Sorry! And he laughed as he held them up to the light.

"Here," he said, dropping them gently into my palm as if they were bullet fragments just removed. They were worth something, like everything he touched. We were silent for a few minutes as I rolled them back and forth between my fingers.

"Don't name your son after me," he said, out of nowhere.

He was looking at me again. "How do you know it's a boy?"

"I get tips," he said, smiling, and I understood belatedly that this was our moment, and that he was in charge, and that I had to let him take me wherever he wanted us to go.

"I know you don't like me," he said.

I kicked back the chair again, against my better judgment, and made a *sheesh* noise; it seemed better than a flat denial, which would have been trembly and unconvincing. I found it hard to lie effectively in response to a statement that, whether or not completely true, had certainly crossed my mind. And that night, of all nights, I could not lie.

"You love me but you don't like me, you know?" he said.

"No, I don't," I said.

"Yes, you do. I'm too much for you, in certain ways. You think you always wanted what I have, but if you ever got it, Joe, you wouldn't want it."

I didn't answer.

"You always act as if you don't understand things or don't think about things, but I know that you think a lot. Probably too much."

"Maybe," I said, a croaking statement of admission as I felt my face grow hot.

"And yet. If you could only see yourself. You're a lot more than you think you are. I never thought I'd need to say it to you, you know?"

"None of us are really good at saying things."

"That's not it." He sounded gentle and wise. "I just always thought you knew. Now. Do you know?"

"Yes," I said.

"Come here," he said. I looked at his extended hand and scooted up close to the bed, leaning my face down to his. He pulled me in, a warm hand on the back of my head, a whisper in my ear. "You are fucking amazing."

"I'm not."

"You are," he said.

"I thought bad thoughts."

"It doesn't matter."

"It does."

"It doesn't," he said. "I am not your fault. I am not your fault." He said it over and over, wrapping me up in his words as I kept my head down, forehead foundering against his feverish shoulder.

"Oh, fuck," I said, pushing myself up and away from the bed, wiping at my eyes. "Okay. Okay."

"Go to sleep," he said.

"Okay." I took a deep breath and staggered out the door, wiping my nose with the back of my hand. I did not look back. I did not cry. I had promised myself that I would not cry.

He was much weaker the next morning. We met in his room after breakfast, the games cleared away. We sat on both edges of his bed. He looked into our faces. We took turns holding his hands.

A few minutes after eleven he looked up and over my mother's shoulder, toward the window. "Go there," he said. His voice was very faint.

My mother smiled. "Yes," she said, thinking she understood, but she did not.

"Tell me what you see," he said.

"What?" she asked.

"See. Regular," he said.

"He wants us to go to the window," I said, standing up. I knew this. I was so glad that I knew this.

"But . . ." my mother said.

I walked to the window. "The view. He wants us to tell him about the view."

She turned back to him. CJ smiled with his closed parched lips. "Go," he said to her.

"Come on," I said.

My father helped Beth to her feet. They walked past the bed and joined me.

"I see the lake, CJ," I said, looking straight ahead at it, my voice nice and strong. For a moment no one said anything. "There's lots of light on it," I added.

"A couple of boats out there, too," Beth said. "A yacht. A speedboat." I grabbed her hand and held it tight.

"Dad?" I said.

"The highway. Lake Shore Drive. North is slow but the south . . . it's moving. Moving pretty good."

"Mom?" I said. But there was nothing except the sound of her sobbing. "Mom. What do you —"

"Oh, God, I see a mailbox. A tow truck. Birds."

"Birds?" Beth asked. "Where?"

"There," my father said, pointing down.

"I don't . . . oh, yeah," I said. Two of them. City birds. We stood there together, watching them fly. They made it look so easy. Regular.

8

The funeral was three days later, back in Southern California. It was an off day for the team, so they were all there. They filled the first three rows of St. Mary's, big bodies in expensive, broad-shouldered suits. The church was overflowing and stuffy in the strong late-morning sunlight. I recognized few of the people, though everyone acted as if they belonged. I felt I was inside another stadium, filled with faces of anonymous, entitled fans. I studied the crowd only briefly before we slipped into our seats in the front pew, but I felt their eyes on our backs.

The public reaction, fanned by the media, had been overwhelming. My brother was the only story during that languid week of apparent nonevents — no international conflicts or IPOs could trump him. Retrospectives ran in newspapers and magazines; television shows of all stripes wallowed in fond remembrances of his finest moments. It was everywhere you looked if you looked, but you could shut it all out, keep the television off and the paper slapped face down. You could live without the news when the news was you. The public was not so easily pacified, though, so loudspeakers were set up on the St. Mary's lawn for the uninvited hundreds who had chosen to gather on that sunny Thursday — he had been theirs, too, and everyone agreed that they should be accommodated.

My parents had done their best to arrange everything, in the brutal, detail-heavy three days since my brother's death. We were still astonished, but there was no time to be sapped. Though my parents kept things moving, it seemed to me that we were led from place to place by an invisible hand. Airline tickets were stuffed into our shirt pockets by someone, gone before we could thank him. A man met us at the Los Angeles airport, holding a sign that said COLUMBUS, and he led us to a limo. Then we were home, where friends smothered us with platters of deviled eggs and casseroles to be frozen and forgotten. These friends were worried about us. They touched us when they talked, a quick tap on the forearm or a full hand on the shoulder, pulling us in. They kept going just as we kept going, whether the "love" or words of comfort they offered, cold as stones rattling around inside us, were wanted or not.

By Sunday — day seven of the reconfigured world — the parade dwindled down, and Beth and I made our plans to return to Washington; I had already missed the first week of the new school year. That Sunday, as we silently picked at a final lunch together, my father told me that the Cubs were planning to honor CJ at a ceremony on Sunday, September 19, which was the team's last home game of the year. The Cubs organization wanted our family to participate in the planning. "Your mother and I would like you to be in charge," my father said, and I agreed without hesitation. They were both worn out; it was my opportunity to help them. I was the only one around to do it.

So Beth and I returned to Washington that night, and the next afternoon I called Kelly Maxwell, the director of special projects for the team. She sounded perky at first, until she realized that a surviving Columbus was on the other end of the line. And it was quickly obvious that Kelly didn't want my suggestions, that she had her own vision of what the day should be. But she spent a few moments politely "running things by me" in case I had a serious problem with any of them. And I didn't; the plan sounded restrained, more celebratory than mournful, which was the type of event we needed at that time.

After her description, there was a long silence, and I knew there was something she was avoiding.

"I received a call this morning from Cher's office," Kelly said. She went on to explain that Cher was a big fan of the Cubs and of my brother, and was interested in participating.

"Uh, I'd rather we not do that," I said, cutting Kelly off before she got too far along and took my silence to mean acceptance. Why did Cher have an "office"?

"Okay," Kelly said, sounding patient, like a therapist who had only begun to explore a significant problem. "May I ask why?"

It was a good question. "Our family doesn't like Cher," I said, which may or may not have been true. I didn't recall us sitting down and discussing her.

"Um, I'm pretty sure that your brother liked her very much," Kelly said, and even though this was an allusion to a tabloid rumor, I became certain at that moment that my brother had slept with Kelly Maxwell. I didn't know how I knew, but I pictured Kelly buying my brother some Cher CD afterward, thinking they'd find "their song" on it. "He mentioned Cher specifically," she said.

"Really?" I said. "He told me he thought she was a whore."

"A what?"

"A whore," I said. "We discussed it the day before he died. He said Cher was nothing but a whore. So there you have it." I made it sound as if my brother had spent his final hours expressing his opinions about a list of celebrities, being pithy and judgmental, and frowning at them all. I hated to do that to Kelly (or Cher, for that matter). But I refused to admit that he liked Cher "very much" or had confessed this affection to Kelly Maxwell. In my narrow and nettled mind, where spark plugs of logic were firing only intermittently, it had suddenly become a crucially important point.

Kelly said she would look for someone else, a performer whom we could agree on. (*Someone not so loose*, I should have added, but that was probably understood.) I thanked her and hung up, convinced that the conversation had gone well. I was fulfilling my obligations; it was all thought-provoking and pointless.

For the next two weeks I wandered through life. I was counting the days until we returned to Chicago, where I assumed the answers were waiting — maybe a shaft of light would strike me, or a shudder of revelation would course through me — and the world would logically reconnect and make sense once again. It was, in retrospect, a foolish dream.

I spent most of my time at Selvon Dale, and for once it was a haven. I suppose any full-time job would have been. My fellow teachers offered brief condolences; one was having her music composition students work on a requiem mass. They were there if I needed them, my colleagues told me, but even if I had needed them, I did not want them. I did not *know* them, and this was hardly the time for me to camp out in their classrooms or gather with them in the lounge, letting them nod sympathetically as I filled the air with backstop memories or halting, inarticulate gasps of emotion. These were scenes I could hardly imagine taking place.

The students were beautifully studentlike, spirited and oblivious and obsessed by the momentary, overreacting to small things and playing down the big ones. There were rumors, I was sure, about where I really had been during that first week of school — country club prison, upstate psych ward, Tinseltown rehab — and that may have fortuitously been good for my reputation. It was a touch of intrigue, like a drop of dark food coloring plunked into a glass of clear cold water. Occasionally, I caught a cluster of three or four, gossiping furtively and gauging me as they waited for the bell to ring, hoping for signs of a crack-up to punctuate their day. But nothing verifiable filtered back to me, and that was probably because it was Sully, of all people, who had taught the first week of class in my absence. He must have roared at them about minding their manners.

Beth also returned to work, though her supervising partner had been placed on indefinite leave of absence. The sexual harassment lawsuit had returned and was threatening, Watergate-like, to bring the whole place down. So Beth was shuffled under the wing of the only female partner at Cannon, Grossmeyer, a kind but tough woman in her late fifties named Darla Bracken. She immediately sympathized with all the elements of Beth's plight and even let her work at home a few mornings and afternoons. Darla had two grown children about our age. One was in medical school at Duke, and the other, having graduated from Columbia Law School, was working in the Seattle district attorney's office. Darla behaved with a civility and compassion that made us both feel guilty with gratitude; it allowed Beth to envision her own morally acceptable long-term future at the firm, something she had not been able to do for some time. Darla, on the few occasions when I met her, did not size me up the way the male partners at Cannon, Grossmeyer did — shaking the ice cubes at the bottom of their drinks when Beth introduced me at holiday parties, wondering whether I was the kind of guy who threw a punch when a cad made a move.

And speaking of boorish legal foot soldiers, Fomacci had, surprisingly, decided to move on. He called Beth while we were in Chicago, but she'd forgotten to tell me about it, an omission I had no opinion about. The first draft of his bestseller (mercifully retitled *Lethal Objection*) had received an enthusiastic response from book agents in Los Angeles, and he had decided to leave the firm, move to the West Coast, like so many other gritty dreamers, and commit himself to writing (mostly screenplays) full time. He was excited, Beth said, about having the freedom to devote himself to his craft, and he planned to make a list of all the great books he hadn't read. There was no indication, however, that he intended to read them.

I was happy to be rid of Fomacci and wondered about the conversation between him and Beth — whether there had been a hint of swallowed, half-aired longing on his part and assorted, gracious no-thank-yous from my loyal, pregnant wife. By the time the Fomacci coda got back to me, Beth had the chance to deliver it right — slick and concise without whatever mad, unspoken desires and awkward silences had choked the line. When I reviewed the story in my unreliable mind, I realized that I had never had a single indication that Fomacci had illicit feelings for Beth. I also didn't care. It was easy to say after the fact, but it was true.

With both of our careers secure, we could consider our future as a family unit. On that front I made no guarantees. I didn't know whether we were still in love. I wondered whether we had ever been in love, or if we'd been glued into something comfortable and were too lazy or weak to get out of it. We got married too quickly; that was true. If we hadn't gotten married, and had simply lived together in sin, we could have gone our separate ways, sadly but without regret. I knew that we had once been happy, and I held on to that. But I believed that Beth had expected more of me; she wanted a husband who challenged life and was himself a challenge. She wanted someone, on all levels, who would fight, and she made me doubt myself for not always wanting to do so. For the first time since I met her, I could imagine life without her, which was a horrible thing to think about the woman who was carrying your child.

Henry Fomacci may not have loved Beth, but I think my brother did. I don't know that I'll ever understand the relationship that developed between my wife and CJ. I'd like to think it was a way for one or the other to get closer to me, but that interpretation seems egotistical and wrong. They had me in common, but I'm not sure whether either of them was all that interested in me — when they were talking on the phone or doing whatever they did in their moments together. I've tried to recount their interactions exactly as I saw them, sticking to the facts. Was it friendship, or was there more? My wife conceived around Easter, when we were out in Los Angeles. She had driven my brother to the airport and was gone for several hours. Beyond that I can only wonder, and I know that some may be appalled that I even suggest such a connection. Maybe the answers will emerge over time, tuned in like the colors of a Polaroid. I will have a son; I believe that. But in a few years, when he's old enough for sports, maybe baseball will come naturally to him. Maybe he will radiate a mysterious calm. Maybe he will grow up and get very, very sick.

That was the shallow extent of my devotion to my wife. In fact, there were times in those two weeks after my brother's death when I forgot she was there. The tether had snapped, and I was floating away. I found myself forgetting elemental information about myself. I went to the eye doctor, and as we waltzed through the preliminaries and he asked me my age, I could not remember. "Twenty . . . six. No, seven," I said, and he made some joke and I laughed along; inside, I was trembling. It was puzzling and alarming, the way that large chunks of stability were slipping away from me. I was losing the tender things at the center of my personal space, the names and numbers and faces that traveled through my blood and separated me from the stringy-haired sign-holders who begged for change at intersections while touting the apocalypse. On the day I went to the eye doctor, a construction crane tipped over on East West Highway and crushed a man in his car as he drove beneath it. He was forty-four, with a wife and two kids, and when I heard the news I knew I would always remember it. Forty-four. Would I live that long? I mourned the survivors; I did not know how old I really was.

Wrigley Field was not just old-fashioned; it was old. There were no video screens or garish accompaniments. There was a valiant organist and a hand-cranked scoreboard high above a lush field of hunter green, with the elevated trains rumbling on tracks beyond right center. And there was the crowd, the fans a tolerant mix of upscale Lincoln Park and third-generation Teamster, shirtless and beer crazy. Even a brute cynic was likely to get caught up in it, that comfy sense that when the game was about to begin, when you had taken all of this in and everyone came together, you had somehow found the essence of the city.

The Cubs would finish the season on the road and then disperse to parts unknown. The playoffs and World Series were dreams flubbed away weeks ago. The team had lost thirty more than it had won since the All-Star break, when CJ left them. The Cubs without my brother had devolved into the Cubs of old. They were charming and unfortunate and completely embraceable. They tried.

Fall had come to Chicago when we returned there that Sunday in September. The temperature was in the middle sixties, with a persistent breeze that reddened cheeks and nagged at the back of the neck. But it was bright and sunny, and there were no clouds in the sky, just a beautiful dome of blue. Many people told me how perfect it was for baseball, how CJ would have wanted it that way. That was a debatable point — he would have wanted it *what* way, exactly? — but I let it go, just as I ignored those who said that CJ was "watching us." I wasn't high on such earnest mysticism at the time, angry at God for all of the obvious bitter reasons, though more certain than ever of his existence.

I was met at the airport — Beth had stayed in Washington — and driven to Wrigley by a chunky young man named Dusty or Rusty. Since I didn't expect to see him again, I made no effort to clarify. He worked in the Cubs front office, in some fervent low-level capacity, and filled the ride to Wrigley with bright chatter about when the stadium had been built, who had hit the first home run there, the largest crowd ever to see a game. I commented politely and looked out the window. As we approached the stadium, crawling in tight city traffic, I believed that an explosion of knowledge would soon be upon me, and I began to brace myself for that epiphany.

But it didn't happen. The tribute before the game was short, over in a matter of minutes. There were statements by the baseball commissioner and the mayor of Chicago. The Cubs had even flown in CJ's college coach from UCLA, as well as a Santa Monica Mariner teammate from the Westside who had grown into a successful television actor. Each spoke briefly, in the thirty-second range, sound bites of fond memory, and I stood on the field, wondering who the tribute was for.

My mother was the last to speak. She murmured a few phrases of thanks, holding my father's hand tight, her eyes fixed on the index card in her hand. The experience had crippled her. I was unable to help; none of us could. She would suffer no explanations or condolences. She was furious, virtually homicidal, and looking back, I think it should have been my father who spoke for the family. He seemed relatively sane, bearing his grief privately, as was his way, sifting through it in his mind until it came out calculated, assessed, and neutralized. He even looked the same, unlike my mother, who had weakened and leapfrogged two age brackets overnight — her hair completely white, her hands gripping banisters with a desperate ferocity as she slowly made her way up and down the stairs. She looked dangerously thin in clothes she'd worn for years. She had made no overtures toward me since our falling-out in the hospital. We were strangers.

At one point the crowd began to applaud her, pleased by something she had said, and she stood there, almost irritated, waiting them out, still looking at the card as the grass around her feet shivered in the wind, the slight heave of her shoulders the only hint that she was alive. And then a flag was raised behind home plate and above the press boxes — white with the number nine centered in blue, flapping mightily for all time. The fans turned toward it; they cheered and remembered. There was no singing.

We went back through the dugout and the concourse and up to the owner's box, where we watched the game as honored guests. The next two hours were completely forgettable. I stared at the field intently, as if the rhythms of the game were my only balm, though I drew only slight amusement from it. The Cubs scored a half-dozen runs in the first two innings, and after that, no facet of the game engaged me, not even the delight of the right-field bleacher bums, tackling each other in a mad scrum for the home run ball off Justin Holloway's eighth-inning bat. I lingered near the back of the luxury box, smiling enough so that no one thought I was in agony and felt obliged to seek me out, but I was uncomfortable and sensed that my parents were, too. Our one entree to this fantasy land was gone. Only the number nine flag over our heads remained, and I knew we would never return.

When it was over at last, my parents and I went to O'Hare. They were eager to leave for California, and told me of their plans to come to Washington for Thanksgiving. They hoped to coordinate that trip with my mother's testifying on Capitol Hill, as she had recently been asked to do, on funding for leukemia research. I kissed them both goodbye with genuine affection. In my opinion the summer had not brought us closer or ripped us apart. It had merely obliterated us all.

I glided from sleep in those days, ungrateful to be roused, fighting it all the way. Those first few moments of the morning, my feet planted firmly in both worlds, were a milky cross-fade. When I woke up, he was still alive, I was the brother of one of the world's greatest athletes, but then — that ache, that hole, that missing thing. My brother's absence, the daily permanence of it, returned. It was a blind lowered as quick as a blink. No more highlights, no more having him out there, hovering and unreachable but nevertheless the entire world that I lowered my shoulder against. He would always be around because of what he did, but he was history — the inescapable kind. CJ was written and done.

It had been one month, and there were extremes that needed my attention. I knew it was wrong, posthumously, to sentimentalize our relationship. We were not as close as we could have been, and we did not crowd each other with our secret hopes and fears. I was in awe of him because he did things I could never do, but the world shared this awe — they couldn't do those things, either — so my articulated or awkward respect was no way for me to have pulled him in. I had decided to be suspicious of him, and claim that I didn't understand him, and ultimately assert that I hated him — but was it ever really hate? It never went that far. It was bleak passion of a different sort, much nearer to lust in that unlit neighborhood. I craved his acknowledgment and dependence, but nothing real is ever that simple. It was all bounced around and wrapped up inside a hundred other conflicts careening through my desperate, overheated head.

I consoled myself with this revised narrative, this sanitized truth, because the alternative, the idea I had locked out of my mind once he got sick, was unendurable. Could I have caused my brother's death, with a one-in-a-million wish to do him harm? How else to explain his swiftly poetic and medically inexplicable demise? I survived because I clung to the belief that my brother was perfect and therefore immune to any of my curses or charms. He was a victim of his own unsustainable magnificence. It was not a new story; it may have been an instance of the unhealthy, deluded way we remember anyone we lose far too soon. But in this case it was true. He *was* perfect; there was no one else like him. And no matter how nobly he tried to exonerate me at the end, he did not deserve me as a brother. And certainly I did not deserve him.

But who really knows? I was slinking through a world without answers; I bled from the inside out. It was early evening, and the sun was starting to set, the last sighs of summer in the first week of October. The baseball play-offs had begun, eight teams chasing glory and riches and that transcendent moment, that surge of winning feeling, with its high-flying rocket of a heartbeat. We could applaud it or loathe it, but I would never understand it. I would not be watching, because I had the knowledge that ruined. I knew that even those lucky enough to be kissed by good fortune would one day feel nothing, because nothing lasted, and nobody ever won.

I had been looking around for a baseball field. In ten days of driving around the windy backroads of the county, I had inspected many, in the dusky hours after school, but it was only on that day that I had happened upon what I truly wanted — in a town called Poolesville, when I parked my car in front of a closed elementary school, built on the edge of endless farms whose lands lay fallow.

It was just after five, that twilight time, the magic hour. I was free to rummage and plunder and wander. I got out of the car in front of the school and walked around the single rectangular building, through thick grass that needed mowing. I kept my hands in my pockets, feeling the cool air dancing around me. The voices met me before I rounded the corner — high-pitched and young, exuberant with petty conflicts and enthusiasms that faded in the wake of anything new. I crossed a cracked basketball blacktop with two netless rims, and after another ten feet of pebbly dirt, I was there. I perched on a modest ridge, flanked by gentle hills still richly green and alive, with only an orange hint of changing leaves. And below me, four boys played baseball on a battered fishbowl of a field.

They were ten or eleven and alone in the world. Only a solitary maroon-shingled farmhouse was visible in the middle distance, paired with a dull silver silo that bounced a pinkish band of setting sun. It was a flat field without a backstop or outfield walls, but it had good light, and the grass grew strong. It was a stretch of land that had become a place to play, with base paths indicating heavy foot traffic and the weighty, certain presence of athletic heroes. One boy was at the plate while the other three opposed him: one on the mound, another between second and first, and the last a few steps into left center. I watched them. They were only practicing, rotating around, barking at each other, reveling in capability, but they played well. They were arranged in a proper constellation. They understood the game.

It was getting dark. Color was draining from the sky; the chilly air was settling in; the breeze was picking up. My jacket was in the car, and I was cold. But the game enthralled me. The boys below, I could see them. I would always be able to see them. The batter swatted a fly ball over the lone outfielder's head, and I gave them nicknames. The pitcher tossed his glove in the air, switched places with the second baseman, and I fed them dreams.

I could feel it. It was baseball to me — stripped-down and dusty, hopelessly ragged, gloriously literal. It was the only thing that made sense.

I missed my brother terribly. I sat and watched the game, drowning in a life of fading light, permanently haunted, crying uncontrollably, until the shadows covered us all.

Acknowledgments

My thanks to John Gregory Brown, Elizabeth Carroll, James Diener, Diane Doherty, Dr. Ross Donehower, M.D., Craig Freeman, David and Dianne Friedman, Shannon Gaulding, Chris Gemmiti, Jeffrey Hammonds, Matthew Johnson, Pam Jones, Ethan Kline, Dan Kois, David Ladd, Shawn Levy, Sunil Nayar, Marty and Kathy Patt, Pam Ruff, Raphael Sagalyn, Chad Snopek, Cathy Spencer, Danielle Sterling, June Streckfus, John Tomko, and Laith Zawawi. A special thanks to my parents, Morton and Ann Friedman.

For an excellent nonfiction account of a young man battling disease, I recommend *Time on Fire*, by Evan Handler.